Praise for *The Ringer*

"Adroitly fusing what he learned from Philip Roth with what he learned from Don Rickles with what he wrote for David Letterman, Scheft has succeeded where more celebrated cutups have failed. He has written a book that is actually funny. . . . Scheft keeps the material coming at machine-gun pace. The jokes are plentiful and very high in quality."

—*New York Times Book Review* (featured)

"A moving story about love between wounded souls that will linger in the mind far longer than the laughs."

—Bruce McCall, author of *Zany Afternoons* and *The Last Dream-O-Rama*

"A winning debut. Scheft blends crackling banter, pithy prose, and empathy for his characters in a punchy Raymond Chandler-meets-Bruce Jay Friedman style. . . . A sparkling discovery."

—*Entertainment Weekly* (Editor's Choice)

"Bill Scheft's *The Ringer* is the most interesting book I have read since Dave Eggers's *Heartbreaking Work of Staggering Genius*. It's funny, energetic, intelligent, touching, and funny. If you don't enjoy this book, there is something wrong with you."

—David Letterman

"Delightful. . . . Full of likable eccentrics, unlikely situations, and clever comic riffs. *The Ringer* is a funny, bighearted book."

—Tom Perrotta, author of *Election* and *Joe College*

"Scheft infuses his book with compassion as well as laughs. . . . A touching story about family, responsibility, and a thirty-five-year-old deciding it might be time to grov [illegible]" —*Boston Globe*

"Bill Scheft's novel produces the kin[illegible] create an unsanitary condition."

"Amazing debut. A no-miss read. . . . A tightly crafted, fast-moving book, frequently funny and thought provoking."

—*Rocky Mountain News*

"Damn funny, and ultimately moving. Four stars." —*Maxim*

"Funny, insightful, and profound. . . . I'm outraged."

—Larry David, cocreator of *Seinfeld* and creator of *Curb Your Enthusiasm*

"Several hilarious but touching characters in what looks to be the summer's funniest novel. . . . A wonderful and swift-moving piece of fiction." —*Trenton Times*

"Well conceived." —*Publishers Weekly*

"Bill Scheft has written a first novel that is much, much better than it has any right to be for someone already so successful."

—Peter Sagal, host of NPR's *Wait Wait . . . Don't Tell Me!*

"The illegitimate child of Elmore Leonard and Christopher Buckley. Witty, satiric dialogue and quirky but believable characters. . . . Even when [Scheft's] being serious, he's still funny. He's one of the rare authors who captures the way people actually talk."

—CurledUpwithaGoodBook.com (four and a half stars)

* Recommended Summer Reading, *USA Today*

* BEST BET, *New York* magazine

* *New York Daily News* Book Club

About the Author

BILL SCHEFT is a columnist for *Sports Illustrated* and has spent the last eleven years as a monologue writer for David Letterman. *The Ringer* is his first novel. He lives in New York.

a novel by

BILL SCHEFT

Perennial
An Imprint of HarperCollins*Publishers*

For Adrianne

This is a work of fiction. The characters, incidents, and dialogues are products of the author's imagination and are not to be construed as real. Any resemblance to actual persons, living or dead, is entirely coincidental.

A hardcover edition of this book was published in 2002 by HarperCollins Publishers.

HarperCollins books may be purchased for educational, business, or sales promotional use. For information please write: Special Markets Department, HarperCollins Publishers Inc., 10 East 53rd Street, New York, NY 10022.

First Perennial edition published 2003.

Designed by Nancy B. Field

The Library of Congress has catalogued the hardcover edition as follows:

Scheft, Bill.
The ringer : a novel / by Bill Scheft.—1st ed.
p. cm.
ISBN 0-06-009052-9
1. Softball players—Fiction. 2. Nephews—Fiction. Uncles—Fiction.
I. Title.
PS36'9.C345 R56 2002
813'.6—dc21 2001059378

ISBN 0-06-051258-X (pbk.)

03 04 05 06 07 ❖/RRD 10 9 8 7 6 5 4 3 2

Quare habe tibi quidquid hoc libelli
Qualecumque, quod, o patrona virgo,
Plus uno maneat perenne saeclo.

CATULLUS I, 8–10

Beethoven was so deaf, he thought he was painting.

RIP TAYLOR

"Well, what about it, Jim? Are you ready to cut out the yelling and play ball?"

JOE CRONIN,
from the movie *Fear Strikes Out*

Part One

1

Don't flush too early. He always had to remind himself. At least make it seem like you're taking a piss.

As scores went, this was pretty good. Fifteen yellows, ten light blues. Enough to extend his stash at home for a couple of weeks, until the next time he and his uncle would meet for dinner. How could he do this to his uncle, a man he so clearly admired? A family member whose company he actually enjoyed? A man who lived a life to which he could only aspire?

Simple. Volume.

Don't flush too early.

He turned off the water and dawdled a bit, as he always did, to read the label on each decidedly non-child-proof-capped bottle. The Tower Chemists Gazette.

5/14/91
M.M. Spell
CONTROLLED SUBSTANCE.
TAKE THREE (3) AT NIGHT BEFORE
BED AS DIRECTED.
60 Valium 10 mg.
DR. Levitz Refills: 4

• • •

4/10/91
M.M. Spell
CONTROLLED SUBSTANCE.
TAKE UP TO SIX (6) AT NIGHT BEFORE
BED AS NEEDED.
120 Valium 5 mg.
DR. Levitz Refills: 3

"Now there," he thought as he always thought. "There's a guy with a problem."

He flushed. He reran the water. Then he jostled a hand towel.

"Nice going, College Boy."

The neck was still a little cranky from the Riis Park doubleheader, which had ended three hours ago. He considered banging back a five-milligram yellow now and getting a head start with the healing process, then decided against it. The second bourbon with the uncle would do just as well. Then the yellow for dessert.

"Okay, ready to go."

"Let me hop in there, doctor." His uncle sidestepped into the bathroom and made a move for the medicine cabinet before becoming distracted by the mirror. *Phew.* He adjusted the brim on his cap. Herringbone. Brown. Wool. Heavy, heavy wool. It almost went with the gray herringbone sportcoat. Wool. Slightly less heavy wool. A week to go until Memorial Day. The end of the heavy wool season for those who observed such things. Other people.

He walked out toward the door and stopped to pat the shoulders of his nephew's blazer with both hands.

"Nice padding, kid. Looks like you have enough in there for Arafat's winter headquarters." How long had his uncle been doing the "padding" line on him? At least twenty-five years. The tenants had changed as history dictated—Nasser, Batista, Le Duc Tho, Bani-Sadr—but there was always someone in the shoulders of his jacket, and it was always their "winter headquarters."

And he always laughed, even though he hadn't been a kid for almost twenty years. "Good one, Mort." It was the least he could do for a single, childless, seventy-five-year-old man whose idea of the family dynamic was not asking for help with the dinner check. Come to think of it, it was his idea, too. "Hey, where are we going, Ruc?"

"I think they're expecting us at P. J.'s."

He couldn't mean P. J. Moriarty's, the great chop hangout once three blocks away. The site of ninety percent of their dinners his first four years in New York until it had closed in 1982, three years before his first Valium heist. His uncle couldn't mean *that* P. J. Moriarty's.

"Do you mean P. J. Clarke's?"

"Christ no. I might bump into Gifford, and I'm all out of compliments. No, Moriarty's."

Do something. "Mort, aren't they closed? Some renovation?"

"Renovation, my ass," his uncle confided with the back of his hand to the side of his mouth, "I bet that haircut Lindsay rented the back room to look at cufflinks."

"Mayor Lindsay?"

"Ah, yes, quite. We should talk about him at dinner. I thought we'd go to Ruc. That seems to work out damn well for us."

"Fine." Whatever that had been was over. Seventy-five years old. It happens. "Ready to go?"

"What time do you have?"

"Seven twenty-five."

"Let's watch Vanna come out."

"Mort, it's Sunday."

"You're right on it tonight, kid, aren't you? How's the performing, acting, whatever it is that keeps you these days?"

"Well, you know."

"I think I do."

Now the door. Forty years at 301 East Sixty-fifth Street, and the apartment door and its locks still proved positively Gordian for his uncle. And he knew better than to offer his help. He did, however, move the large suitcase that was blocking Mort's angle of disarmament.

"You going away, Mort?"

"No."

"That's right, you are. This week. To get that award in L. A."

"The Dottie Sussman Breach of Confidentiality Ribbon. Don't rub it in."

"You don't like this fuss, do you?"

His uncle grabbed the knob for traction and the front door popped open.

"Well, that was too easy."

"Mort, I gotta go to the john again. Sorry."

He broke all his rules. He didn't run the water. He popped a yellow on an empty stomach and before a few drinks. He did not save it for dessert after the Prague Roast at Ruc.

And he flushed way, way too early.

"Let's go, doctor. Vanna is waiting."

And it didn't matter.

2

Man, these guys worked fast. Ten minutes from the time she had called, they were here at the apartment. Five minutes to revive the old man and get him on the gurney, or whatever that collapsible tea cart with straps was called. Now things had slowed to on-hold time, as the taller one, Jeff, was on the bedroom phone, waiting to hear where they were supposed to take the old man now that the ER at Lenox Hill was stacked up like Newark.

"We should be hearing soon," said the shorter one, Mark or Matt. "Mount Sinai probably."

"Great. So, you're sure he's okay until then?"

"He's getting fluids and we got his pressure back to where he can travel." He patted the gurney. These guys all look like firemen. "It's a little, ah, messy, there where we picked him up off the floor."

She glanced over and saw blood, shit, piss, and what looked like a crushed pep-o-mint Life Saver. "Don't worry. It's nothing I haven't dealt with before."

Sheila, forever in check, finally gave her insides permission to calm down. She unfastened the belt on her white linen trenchcoat and thought about heading into the bathroom to change into her work clothes and, if the lighting and ambience was just right, throw up. She hung her great red head and briefly cracked herself up with some old cartoon she had remembered. A couple picnicking next to a dead guy covered in a checkered tablecloth as paramedics rushed in. *How many times do I have to tell you? I said ambience! Ambience! Not ambulance!*

Mark or Matt caught the outside corner of her quick smile to herself and the sniff of what might be construed as brave worry. He couldn't miss it. He was staring. Nothing new for Sheila, the staring. First time, though, it had ever come from an EMT in the middle of a gig.

She straightened up and tossed the coat onto the wing chair. She had on the short, black cocktail dress. Which meant one thing and one thing only. It was Laundry Day. The old man had seen her a couple of times in the black dress and become uncharacteristically lunge-ful. She'd thought it was safe to wear today because she hadn't been expecting to find him back from California on Thursday. Which meant she hadn't expected him lying facedown on the living room rug. But he hadn't seen the dress. What a break.

"Hey, nice dress. What is that, cotton?"

"Ah, yeah." Not with this guy, she thought. Not now.

Sheila had discovered Mort sprawled on the rug only after she had pulled the vacuum out of the front closet. Seventeen minutes ago. At first, he was just in her way. Then she realized that had not been his intent.

"Too bad about your . . . uh . . . father?"

"No."

"Uncle?"

"Ah, no."

"Grandfather, right?"

"Jesus."

"What?"

"I told you. I told you both when you got here. I'm Mr. Spell's cleaning woman. That's how I found him. Today's my day. To fucking clean."

"You don't look like any cleaning woman that I've seen."

"Hey, what can I tell you? I'm not in my working clothes."

"What you've got on is working for me."

She yanked open the door. "Get the fuck out of here, asshole. And you better take care of him. Take him the fuck out into the hall and wait for your buddy."

Mark or Matt gave her a weak smile as he pushed the old man hallward. He coughed. "Sorry."

"You couldn't afford me, pal. As a cleaning woman." Sheila saw he wasn't lingering over her odd syntax. And so, she softened. "I'll be up to see you, Mr. Spell. Mort," she said to the disappearing blankness behind the oxygen cone.

The taller one, Jeff, emerged from the bedroom.

"It's Sinai."

"Good," she said.

"Where's Marty?"

"Out in the hall."

"Was he bothering you, miss? Because"—Jeff braced his left hand against the door jamb, as if creating a hypothetical booth for himself and Sheila—"if he's a problem, I'll take care of it. Because I can do that."

"I appreciate it."

"Because I wouldn't do it for everyone."

"You boys don't take the 'emergency' part of your title very seriously."

"Oh, I'm serious."

"Mark?"

"Jeff."

"Jeff, take Mr. Spell to fucking Sinai before my next 911 call is for you."

There is a thing some women can do to men using only their eyes. Something—almost—like chemical castration. Well, Sheila Manning was one of those women.

"Marty, Sinai. Stat!"

These guys worked fast.

3

"Help me out here. What golf course is this again?"

The nurse answered the question as politely as she had the first ten times. *"Mount Sinai Hospital, Mr. Spell."*

"Thank you for coming up with that so quickly. And what fairway is that out there? The 16th?"

"Fifth Avenue."

"Right, the 5th. Is everyone here as knowledgeable as you?"

Morton Martin Spell, as his byline read, was delirious. Being delirious was not in Mort's plans. But this was Day Three and he was still quite good at it. If Mort Spell had been talking to himself, which he wasn't, thank God, he would have said, "You're really quite good at being delirious." No, that's wrong. He would have said that if he had been another person. Mort Spell only had a limitless supply of flattery for everyone else. Especially a woman who kept sweetly telling him where he was and where he wasn't.

"You're looking awfully well today."

"Thank you, Mr. Spell."

"Is the pro coming by this afternoon?"

"You mean the doctor? Yes."

"Good! I have to thank him. I really think these straps are going to help my swing."

Compliments and accolades only worked in one direction. Away from Morton Martin Spell. Five days ago, he had flown to Los Angeles to finally receive an award in person. Six thousand miles, two falls, and a full catheter later, here he was, overlooking the 16th fairway. No, the 5th.

The Bertram Hargan Cup was presented every four years to that athlete, coach, executive, broadcaster, or writer who "embodies the essence and ideals of American sport which Bertram Hargan so cherished." Very prestigious. The last four winners had been Olympic decathlon champion Rafer Johnson (1975), Pittsburgh Steelers owner Art Rooney (1979), Howard Cosell (1983), and the late Bertram Hargan (1987). "I guess they ran out of dead people" was Mort Spell's explanation. Everybody, including his nephew, the actor, said he should open his acceptance speech with that line. But Mort would never say such a thing. He'd be more comfortable turning to a portrait of the late Bertram Hargan and saying, "You're looking awfully well today."

The Crosby piece. That's why they were giving it to him. Sure, the Hargan Cup people had mumbled something on paper about his body of work, but when you're seventy-five years old and some cocktail jockey uses the phrase "body of work," you know what you're dealing with. You're dealing with a guy who knows your work only as a signpost in a table of contents. The piece he has to riffle through on the way to his real destination—some snap, crackle, pap about Keith Hernandez correcting a flaw in his stance after dinner with Marsha Mason. This guy, Brent or Connor or Theron, something like that, who, when he finally meets you at the award dinner, will say something like—no exactly like—"Every month, when the *New Yorker* comes out, I look for your articles." And you can't say, "I don't write for the *New Yorker* anymore. And it's a weekly, you putz." Which is why Morton Martin Spell didn't accept awards in person.

He hadn't contributed to the *New Yorker* since 1982, shortly before Reagan had deregulated the ten-thousand-word magazine piece. He had moved across the street to the fledgling biweekly *Civilized Man* as its "Sports Historian in Residence." That's what the masthead and everyone else started calling him. Sports Historian Morton Martin Spell. That's when the awards started coming. That's when he started not showing up.

"What does someone like Wayne Gretzky say when you introduce yourself?" his nephew had asked not too long ago.

"He says, 'get me that guy from *Newsweek*.'"

Sports Historian. There weren't even the letters to make the word "writer." Was there any phrase more odious to Mort Spell? You know, other than "body of work?"

But he was seventy-five years old and it was for the Crosby piece and Bing would be pissed off if he didn't show. And, if you count Bertram Hargan, that would be two dead guys angry with him.

"Would it be possible not to have that large black woman visit me again today?"

"Mr. Spell, no one has been in here all day."

"There was a large black woman in here talking to me an hour ago. Around four o'clock."

"Was it Oprah Winfrey?"

"Yes. Is she a friend of yours?"

"No."

"Good. You're well rid of her."

He had originally written "Bing Crosby: Sportsman" for the *Atlantic Monthly*—now that would be a monthly—in 1983. It was a bit of a departure from the standard Morton Martin Spell archival forced march across the legacy of the shuttlecock or the Abe Stark sign at Ebbets Field. First of all, it was a mere five thousand words. Second, it was personal. A re-creation of thirty hours he spent with the singer/movie star/corporation on an otherwise faceless day in 1947. It started at 8:00 A.M. as a round of golf in Palm Springs. Bing was looking for someone to ghostwrite a book of links lies. All Bing had was the title—"Golfing My Way."

"It looks like 'Going My Way,' but there's a tee with a 'l' and an 'f' on it trying to squeeze in there," Bing gushed. Mort was not completely uninterested in the project, and wouldn't let himself be until he and Bing had finished the round, and three more in the Grille Room bar. Then it would be time to humbly apologize and even more humbly give Bing a list of a dozen writers who'd work for less. And while he was turning things down, Mort would also refuse to accept the forty dollars Bing owed him for unsuccessfully pressing his bet on the back nine.

"You won't take my money, then we'll just have to invest it," Bing Crosby said. An hour later, they were in his private box at Santa Anita, two minutes before the start of the third race. Morton Martin Spell, whose entire method of handicapping consisted of picking horses whose names when scanned contained at least two dactyls and *no trochees*, had winners in four out of the six remaining races and was up $280. Bing had coattailed for the last three and was five thousand dollars to the good.

Mort did not mention Bing's windfall at the track in "Bing Crosby: Sportsman." Nor did he go into great detail about the booze, reefer, and call girls on the night charter they took to Chicago. Nor did he see any reason to involve the local police, who were kind enough to help everyone out of the Pump Room at 4:30 A.M. so Bing and his guests could be sure to get seven and a half hours of sleep and still arrive at Wrigley Field in time for the Cubs-Pirates doubleheader. Bing owned a piece of the Pirates and saw his boys whenever they were in Chicago, New York, or Brooklyn. Rarely in Pittsburgh. "You go to fuckin' Pittsburgh," was how he explained it to Mort. And how Morton Martin Spell wouldn't explain it in his piece.

The whole thing was written as a hectic, dignified paean. There are no men like this. There are no days like this. Anymore. But perhaps you'd like to meet such a man and have such a day. That was Mort Spell's premise. He excavated his recall and found every nuance of the Palm Springs course layout, every saddle cloth cover of the winners at Santa Anita, every song the sound of a post-war eastbound airplane engine reminded him of, every idiosyncratic twitch in the way Pirate star Ralph Kiner mimed his swing while standing in the outfield. He found all of this, and left behind the man he had outgolfed, outhandicapped, outdrunk, outfucked, and outbailed-out.

"Did the kid come by and take my shoes?"

"What shoes?"

"My golf shoes. I left them out for him to shine."

"Mr. Spell, nobody has been here except me. You have the one pair of shoes that you checked in with. And they're in the closet."

"Have people told you what a nice job you're doing filling in for the regular clubhouse attendant?"

Morton Martin Spell wrote it all so adroitly, nobody missed the Bing Crosby that "Bing Crosby: Sportsman" replaced. In fact, "adroit" was one of the epithets Mort used more than once. Spread out over five thousand words, it made a nice touchstone. Bing Crosby "rescued par at the 8th with an adroit chip" and was "ever-adroit as he marked his scorecard with an asterisk to remind himself of the great play in the field by the Cubs' otherwise-maligned short-stop Lenny Merullo."

When he wasn't being adroit, Bing was being deft. And when Bing wasn't being deft, he was being jaunty. And when Bing stopped being affable, which was never, he started being sagacious, which was always. Quite a man. Generous, classy, prudent. Just like Mort Spell's version thirty-six years later. Thirty hours in five thousand words. Mort reined the whirlwind just long enough to flick out all bets, belts, cops, and blowjobs. But it was still a whirlwind. Eighteen holes at Palm Springs to seven races at Santa Anita to a split at Wrigley in just over a day met the legal requirement for whirlwind in 1947. And still did in 1983.

Little problem, though. By the time in 1983 Mort had handed in the piece to the *Atlantic*, people didn't want to hear about Bing Crosby: Sportsman. They were too busy reading about Bing Crosby: Dad with a Right Hook. Earlier that year, Bing's oldest son, actor-by-nepotism Gary Crosby, had published a tell-all, welt-all account of his childhood that included everything except statistics for punches thrown/punches landed. The *Atlantic* gave Mort a more than generous kill fee and got his word in writing that he would not try to sell the piece for six years. Mort waited seven years, then gave it to the tournament organizers at the Bing Crosby National Pro-Am to use in their 1990 program. For free. By then, the public had forgotten Gary Crosby with the same disinterested verve that greeted one of his guest shots on *Police Story*.

When "Bing Crosby: Sportsman" finally surfaced in print, it was a scrawny 2,400 words. Some guy whose editorial background must have consisted entirely of ransom notes, autopsied the thing beyond recognition. Five times, Mort leafed through the program, wondering if pages had fallen out. Six races at Santa Anita were scratched. And the flight to Chicago, the Pump Room wisdom, and the doubleheader were reduced to Bing lighting his pipe and telling Cubs owner Phil Wrigley, "Maybe you should stop paying your boys in gum." The correct line was "Maybe Phil should stop paying his boys in gum," and was delivered to Mort, but this yahoo with a knife and blue pen later justified the switch by saying, "Hey, Mort, Bing's been talking to you the whole article. I thought we'd change it up at the end." Morton Martin Spell was not one to use the words "fucking" and "idiot" in any combination, so he excused himself and his eviscerater. "Too bad," he said to the phone after he hung up, "you could have saved another half-inch by cutting my byline."

Three months later, the Bertram Hargan Cup people called. Guess who the late Bertram Hargan's favorite singer/actor/child beater was? *(Buzz)* Time's up. . . .

Right. Time was up. Time for Morton Martin Spell, the only guy who still wore a hat in the press box, to let himself be honored.

"Would you hand me my typewriter? I have to finish the front of my piece on placekickers."

"Your what?"

"My typewriter. Over there."

"You mean the bedpan?"

"Right."

The trip to Los Angeles had been needlessly frill-free. The Award Committee had sent Mort two first-class tickets, which he immediately exchanged for one coach ticket. When the girl, some angelic volunteer, met him at LAX to help him with his bags and to the limo, Mort handed her a check for $2,860 and said, "Be sure to thank your boss for confusing me with someone important." He then helped her into the limo and hailed himself a cab to the Beverly Hilton. Which was fine, except the Award People had him at the Beverly Wilshire. The girl in the limo followed him and used the time to rehearse this tender lie: "Oh, Mr. Spell, I am so embarrassed. Nobody ever called to tell you we switched your reservation to the Beverly Wilshire. First, the mixup with the airline ticket, now this. I hope you can forgive me."

The only thing Morton Martin Spell liked more than being apologized to was being apologized to by a girl in her midtwenties. "They're damn lucky to have you," he said. And he let himself get into the limo.

This girl, Kristin, no Kirsten, that's right, Kirsten, was really something. When they thrice doubled back to the Beverly Hilton, first to get his glasses, then to get his hat, then to get his other glasses, which he was wearing, she said nothing. Oh, she talked, but she said nothing about what they were doing. She pushed her hair behind her ears and off the shoulders of her pink lizard-skin vest and acted as if perfecting this 1.8-mile loop on Santa Monica Boulevard at the height of rush hour were indeed her plans for the day. She knew little of Morton Martin Spell or his work, but was smart enough to ask him, "When was the last time you were in Los Angeles?" She sat back, smiled, pushed her hair behind her ears and listened to him reconstruct an old polo pitch in Bel Air while patting his pockets for whatever they would have to go back and get next. Three times, one for each loop, he looked past her and said to the limo driver, "How about our good fortune that Kirsten could make it today?" Between the $2,800 check, the limo and all the gratuitous praise, you would have thought this little girl in the pink lizard suit was getting the Bertram Hargan Cup. And that would have been fine with Mort Spell.

What little was left of Mort to debilitate was achieved by the flight out. Airline travel played havoc with his ears, and it was a regime no consulship of Valium and vodka could topple. Thanks to a shrink with a heart in triplicate, Mort took enough Valium to make absolutely no difference if he took two more. So much, he used the Latin neuter plural when describing his dosage. It was not fifty milligrams of Valium a day. It was "five *valia*." Five blue valia. Check that. Five periwinkle valia. Or ten canary valia.

The *valia* wordplay was one of those rare occasions when Mort would entertain himself. It was the third generation of a joke Alistair Cooke told him one night at P. J. Moriarty's. Julius Caesar walks into a bar. Tells the bartender, "I'll have a martinus." Bartender says, "Don't you mean a martini?" And Caesar says, "If I wanted a double, I'd ask for it!" A week later, Mort had Alistair banging the table and wiping his eyes with P. J. Moriarty's starchiest linen when he asked the waiter for a "vodkum" on the rocks. "Don't you mean a vodka, Mr. Spell?" You already know the rest. And it only got funnier the next III or IV rounds. Later, as they struggled with their coats outside, Alistair Cooke told Mort Spell it was the first time he'd been shushed since boarding school. They parted laughing, and Mort walked three blocks north, then three blocks south to retrieve his hat and glasses.

The pill his regular doctor had prescribed for his inflight ears did not work. And the Valium and vodka had made it not work faster. Somewhere over Cleveland, Mort complained to the stewardess and she returned with a piece of gum. Ten minutes later, she was back and said the other passengers in coach were wondering if he could possibly keep the gum and his dentures in his mouth at the same time. "No, but thanks for stopping by," he said. "I'll trade the gum for another vodka." Mort almost said "ga," but remembered he had only one piece in his mouth.

"Who was that nice man I played with this morning?"

"Dr. Banks?"

"No, the other one. Stockier fellow."

"Enrique the orderly?"

"Yes! That's the man. Get him back in here!"

"Did you wet your bed?"

"I owe him ten dollars. I gave myself a four on the 13th. Should have been a five."

"What 13th?"

"You're right. It was the 12th. Thank you for clearing that up."

He let Kirsten check him in at the Beverly Wilshire while he sat down in the lobby. That was the first time Mort Spell thought he might be dizzy. The bellman took his bags upstairs while Kirsten ran to the closest place to buy masking tape. This was some girl. She even offered to tape up the air conditioning vents in his room. Mort thanked her and said he was an old pro at taping up ducts. He might have said something like, "It's duct taping season." But he couldn't remember. That was the first time he couldn't remember what he'd said or where he was. The second time was after he swooned and fell off a chair in mid-duct tape. Which was also the second time Mort Spell thought he might be dizzy.

If you count the fifteen seconds he spent on the floor, Mort got in two naps before the annual Bertram Hargan Cup reception. Though the actual award was coughed over with the frequency of presidential inaugurations, cocktails and cold lobster were handed out every May 27 at Lakeside Country Club. Mort welcomed the reception. It would be drinks and lobster and a lot of "You're looking awfully well." His acceptance speech would be the following night, in the big ballroom at the Beverly Wilshire. He didn't have to speak at the reception, other than "You're looking awfully well." This he could handle. To this he could look forward.

Mort had been working on his speech for two months, or since the day after he was notified about winning the Bertram Hargan Cup. Before he left for the reception at Lakeside, he flipped through his forty single-spaced index cards for the first time. And it hit him, harder than the hotel floor after his fall. There was no mention of Bertram Hargan, no mention of Bing Crosby, no mention of Morton Martin Spell. It was forty-five minutes on Alistair Cooke's first apartment in New York and a trip his sister Dottie took to Scotland in 1969. It was not an acceptance speech. It was a living will.

To his credit, Mort decided not to panic. He still had a day. He would call up one of his ready supply of "great man" quotes and attach it to Bertram Hargan. Then he'd talk about Bing's kid (Nathaniel, not Gary. God, not Gary) winning the U.S. Amateur in 1981. Ten minutes. That would be plenty. He'd panic when he got back to New York. Okay, he'd panic when his ears started hurting on the return flight. Okay, he'd panic after he got back from the reception.

At seven-thirty, Mort remembered the thing he liked best about coming to California. The time change. Suddenly, it was 4:31 and he had another hour, twenty-nine minutes to drink gin. Mort had strict rules about this. No drinking before four-thirty P.M., except on Sunday. No vodka before six P.M., except on Sunday. No gin after six, except on Saturday. No alcohol with lunch, unless the waiter asked him if he would like a drink. No drinking during "Double Jeopardy," because the questions were tougher. And no drinking of any kind during the taping of air conditioning vents. Of course, none of these rules applied on days he was flying. Or on an airplane.

Things last went well right about a quarter to six. Kirsten, who had changed from the pink lizard suit to a silk blouse/black slacks combo that tragically hid her legs, accompanied Mort through the lobby and to the limo before she said good-bye and got into a much smaller car headed somewhere else. She promised to see Mort the next night, at the Award Dinner. And she promised to wear her legs.

"Hey, Morty! Let's go, buddy. The cold lobster's getting warm."

Morton Martin Spell, who hadn't been "Morty" since he'd helped liberate France, saw the back seat of the stretch filled with the kind of man who usually sat in the booth behind him at P. J. Moriarty's. Until the waiter moved him to another booth.

"Do I know you?" Mort asked.

"You better. I paid for your goddamn ticket. Chuck Hargan. Bert Hargan was my grandpa."

"Oh."

"Come on. Get in." Mort looked around for someone to move him to another booth. "You like Kirsten? She'll give you head for a hundred dollars, but you gotta pay for that. Don't go charging it to your room. Aw, Christ, I'll tell you what. You cashed in your ticket for coach, the hummer's on me."

Mort got in hoping Chuck Hargan would lower his voice. The driver was about to close the door.

"You got your speech, Morty?"

"No."

"Well, you better get it."

"My speech isn't until tomorrow night."

"Who told you that?"

"I just assumed I would give my acceptance speech on the night I accepted the award. I'm funny that way." Mort Spell had been stunned into sarcasm.

"Hey, Morty, we changed things four years ago," Chuck Hargan said while snapping his fingers at the driver to get the door. "My grandma went on forever about the old man at the big dinner. We couldn't get her off. It was embarrassing. We had a big show planned. Kenny Rogers almost didn't come out. I had to beg the guy. 'Kenny, Kenny,' I said. 'Give me a break. She's my fucking grandmother. So you don't do "Lucille." You do forty minutes. Cost me an extra ten thousand dollars to get that bearded country prick to stay. Finally, my grandma finishes, and I couldn't yell at her. Her husband died, it was a big night, and she's my fucking grandmother. So, I decided then and there that we give the award at the cocktail party, and we don't fuck up the big dinner. I got Frankie Valli *and* a comic this year. Stewie Somebody. You think anybody wants to sit around after dessert and hear a speech? I'm thinking of you here, Morty. I'm a big fan. I read you every month in the *New Yorker*."

"Well, I haven't quite finished working on my remarks."

"Oh," Chuck Hargan said to give himself the half second he needed. "Well, fine. Screw it, you got nothing to prove to these Lakeside assholes anyway. You don't know them, they don't know you. Scotch is scotch. Lobster is lobster. And you're getting your dick sucked on me when you get back. What's bad?"

"The point is—"

"And Frankie Valli tomorrow night! Come on. I hear you old literary fucks from New York can really party." The limo had already pulled well out onto Santa Monica Boulevard.

"My glasses!"

"Whar?"

"I left my glasses back at the hotel."

"Do you really need them, Morty?" Morton Martin Spell gave the kid the kind of look he probably got from Kenny Rogers four years ago when he asked The Gambler if he wouldn't mind waiting around. "Shit. Jesse, turn this thing around. Shit."

It took ten minutes for them to double back to the Beverly Wilshire, ten minutes for Chuck Hargan to pretend to wait patiently before sending Jesse upstairs to get Mort, eight minutes for the paramedics to show up. By the time Chuck Hargan power-walked into the big function room at Lakeside, all that remained was cocktail sauce, half a dozen Carr's water biscuits, and well whisky.

"What size shoe do you wear?"

"8½. Why?"

"Because I found a footprint in the bunker at the 11th. You know the one behind the green?"

"No."

"Right. I'm thinking of the 10th. Thank you again. You're especially sharp today."

"Thank you."

"Well, this footprint couldn't have been a women's size 8. More like a men's 10. A 10 Charlie."

"Who's Charlie?"

"Charlie. C. 10C. You know, people stop raking the sand traps, the whole course goes to hell."

"Mr. Spell, maybe you should try and get some sleep."

"I will now that I've been able to exonerate you."

There are two versions of what happened between the ambulance at the Beverly Wilshire and now, here at Mount Sinai, or the golf course, which would make four versions. According to Version One, Mort spent twenty-four hours at the Scripps Clinic, was fitted with a catheter, which he pulled out during the flight back to Kennedy and left in his coach seat pocket. He then took a cab back to his apartment, unpacked, passed out, and was found around two o'clock by his housekeeper, Sheila, who called 911. In Version Two everything is the same, except Mort stops for brunch at P. J. Moriarty's before returning home and leaves the catheter in the coat-check room.

Something with his prostate. That's all Mort knew. And he only knew that when he wasn't being delirious, which was almost never. So, he knew nothing. Maybe he'd let his hand occasionally slip under the covers and touch the catheter and let himself think that he might be in a hospital and there might be something wrong with him. But it was easier to think he was touching the plastic trim on his golf bag, and the only thing wrong with him was that he was opening the hips too much on his downswing. The pro would fix that when he came by.

"What time is it?"

"Five-fifteen."

"What can I get you to drink?"

"Nothing."

"You don't mind if I have one, do you?"

"Mr. Spell, where are you going to get a drink?"

"You're right. They're still renovating the Tap Room. Do you mind if we wait until six, when the dining room opens?"

"Are you hungry?"

"Not really. I had a hot dog at the shack by the 9th hole."

"When was that?"

"1955."

Mort was getting better. He would still need some sort of procedure on his prostate, but it had been twenty-four hours since Harold Lloyd had been in bed with him. Thanks to a shortage of space, Morton Martin Spell had to share his bed with the great silent film star, comedian Harold Lloyd. Lloyd, dead since 1971, had moved in on Monday, after Charlemagne had checked out. And how about this for a coincidence—Harold Lloyd was in for a prostate operation, too!

Mort had much more contact with Harold Lloyd than Charlemagne. In fact, you wouldn't have known Charlemagne had even been there if Mort hadn't said to his nurse, "Wasn't it nice that Charlemagne could take time out from his schedule to sleep here with me?" Mort's relationship with Harold Lloyd was much more evolved. There were three basic exchanges: (1) Mort laughing hysterically, stopping briefly to catch his breath and ask the nurse "Are you watching this?" before collapsing again in laughter; (2) Mort angrily grabbing his pillow and yelling, "Not funny, Harold"; (3) Mort placing the back of his hand to the side of his mouth and whispering to the space next to him, "Harold, do you have any Valium?"

Harold Lloyd did not have any Valium. Three days Mort had gone without. Maybe if he left the golf course and checked into a hospital, they'd give him some. Bad idea. He wouldn't be able to drink in a hospital. It had been three days since that as well. No, he was better off here. And now Harold Lloyd was gone. Damn. Why hadn't Mort asked Charlemagne?

Valium stays in your bloodstream for eight weeks, which means whatever was still coursing around Mort would have a longer run than the musical *Nick and Nora.* No wonder he was having such trouble sleeping. That's the first thing Mort thought whenever he woke up. "I'm having trouble sleeping." Actually, it was the second thing. The first thing he thought was, "Maybe I'll ask Harold Lloyd if he has any Valium."

"I'd like to get some sleep before I tee off tomorrow morning. I've been awake for the last three days."

"Mr. Spell, you were sound asleep when I left last night and when I came in for my shift today at noon."

"How am I supposed to believe you when I know you've been here the whole time?"

"I'm not here between midnight and noon."

"That's right. You were out cleaning the driving range. That's where I saw you."

"What?"

"By the way, damn nice job out there."

Here's the strange part. Golf wasn't even Morton Martin Spell's favorite sport. Or favorite thing to write about. The past was his favorite topic. And if, on his way to the past, there was a nice course, he'd play. He preferred ice hockey, jai-alai, any kind of rugby, even ski jumping. But you really couldn't look out your New York City hospital window and act like you were at the Forum or the Holmenkohlen. That would be nuts. A country club. A nice country club. Someplace where you're entitled to wait around for a putting lesson, a gin and tonic, a pair of shined shoes. And no one, especially no large black woman in the chair opposite your bed, asks you why you're waiting. That worked. Even in Downtown Delirium, Mort Spell was using his good mind.

He slept until 7:01, until his internal alarm clock, repaired by two falls, went off just as he heard the TV announcer say, ". . . And now, here's the host of *Jeopardy,* Alex Trebek!"

Both Single and Double Jeopardy were especially good to Mort. Not too much pop culture or that pun crap they liked to run at you. A lot of monarchs and painters, and second-stringers from the Old Testament. Final Jeopardy was so easy, he could have done it with his catheter closed. You had to give three of the four state capitals that shared the same first letter as their state. Mort got all four (Honolulu; Oklahoma City; Indianapolis; and Dover, Delaware), and when none of the contestants thought of Dover, he hid his own contempt by saying, "I think Alex is bitterly disappointed with everyone's play today."

His nurse got three right—"Who is Heather Locklear?" "What is a Mighty Morphin Power Ranger?" "What is Dy-no-mite!"—and each time Mort said, "You're much brighter than these charlatans." Finally, the nurse said, "What is a charlatan?" and Mort cracked, "I think you won another six hundred dollars," and pissed himself laughing. Which was the first time in three days someone other than Harold Lloyd had made him do that.

Mort continued to snap out of it during *Wheel of Fortune.* He ate his dinner—consommé, cello-wrapped salad, ICU chicken, apple pie—with great reverence. And for the first time in three days, did not push it aside and ask the orderly to read him the specials instead. He was trying to behave for Vanna White.

Morton Martin Spell, Yale '37, Cambridge '39, who had played squash on every continent except Antarctica, who smuggled two gloves to Cuba in 1964 and got Castro to show him how he threw a curveball, who had Jane Russell give him a skeet-shooting lesson, who had flattered enough Mrs. Sid Luckmans, Mrs. Jerry Wests, and Mrs. Al

Oerters to have a couple of them offer to meet him alone later for drinks, who when he and Bing split up the call girls grabbed the pretty one, had a stone crush on Vanna White. Going on four years now, and with enough two-dimensional contact he thought he might, just might, have a shot at her. He'd have to come up with a girl for Pat Sajak, but he had a shot. Maybe if he had been able to stay conscious in Los Angeles, they might have hooked up. But he kept his plans to himself. And because he kept his plans to himself, technically, technically, he had only been considered delirious for three days. The only thing the world heard from him about Vanna White was how "she does some damn fine work turning those letters."

"By the way, Vanna does some damn fine work turning those letters."

"I hear she's an idiot."

"You're rather cocky since your performance on Jeopardy."

How old was Vanna anyway? Thirty-two, thirty-three? A few years younger than Sheila, the woman who cleaned his apartment twice a week. And heh, heh, we all knew how things were going with Sheila. He'd heard something about Vanna being married. So? Sheila had been married. And we all knew how things were going with Sheila. Mort, of course, was terminally single. The only thing he liked about the idea of being married was you could use the line, "Hey, I'm married, not dead." The first time he heard the line was around 1946. Some hockey player. Maybe Eddie Shore. No, Shore wasn't that clever. The second time was 1947. Bing. Somewhere over Nebraska.

Maybe he'd go out there in a couple of months. Vanna looked like she played tennis. He could do one of those celebrity tennis studies, like the one he wrote in 1971 about Lee Remick. "A Quick Set, Off the Set." Lee had been a little standoffish, especially after their opening exchange:

LEE: You want to watch me play tennis? What, did Hepburn turn you down?

MORT: Yes.

He would not make that mistake this time. Vanna White was his only choice. Without Vanna, there was no story. Some publication—*Tennis, Tennis World, Tennis USA, Tennis Illustrated, Tennis Monthly, Tennis Magazine Compliments of the Delta Shuttle*—would buy the piece. And at his price. He'd take his nephew, the actor, with him. To drive him around. And when Mort gave the word, to get lost.

Pat Sajak, nice enough man, but why didn't he let her talk? What was he hiding? Why was he so threatened? And for Mort Spell to take time out from being eternally threatened by women to notice someone else was threatened by them, that was something. He'd let Vanna talk. He'd let her talk all night. And not just for the magazine piece, either. He'd let her talk during dinner, after dinner, in the elevator, in the shower, during sex, and a half hour later, when they had sex again.

There was only one thing missing. His erection. What was this, this item, in his prick? Where did it come from? Oh, that's right: Someone had given it to him. But funny, it didn't look like the Bertram Hargan Cup.

Maybe this nice-looking man in the white coat could help him. This learned man looked up from his clipboard. He did not know that Mort Spell called every nice-looking man he met for the first time "doctor."

"Hello, Mr. Spell."

"Hello, doctor."

"Well, I see you're doing much better this evening."

"I could still use some work with my grip."

"Something wrong with your hands?"

"Well, according to you, they're five degrees off."

"Mr. Spell, this is the first time we've met."

"Then who did I pay sixty-five dollars to this afternoon for my lesson?"

"I'm filling in for Dr. Banks. I'm Dr. Cahill. You're in Mount Sinai Hospital."

"Well then, I'm bloody well not paying sixty-five dollars for a lesson."

Morton Martin Spell moved the back of his hand to the side of his mouth and asked the nice-looking man he called doctor what the thing in his prick was. Dr. Cahill told him it was a catheter, and Mort was satisfied. He figured this was what he'd spent the sixty-five bucks on.

Dr. Cahill had some questions, but at this point, he could only ask Mort if he was comfortable. He couldn't ask Mort if there was anything he needed, because he knew Mort would say something like, "I'll take Valium for a thousand, Alex." And it was much too early to ask the question anyone who was able to read Mort Spell's chart should pose, "How the hell did you make it here?" He didn't want to scare whatever was not scared. And he didn't want Mort Spell to say, "How'd I get here? Same as you. Drive and a six-iron."

Dr. Cahill told Mort he'd stop by again around 9:30 for another chat after he finished his rounds. Was that okay? "I'd like that very much," Mort said. This kind of thing—doctors stopping by after their rounds to chat with a seventy-five-year-old delirious man—does not happen. Not even a little. Not even in places where people might think it would happen. Like Iowa. So, it's pretty easy to understand why anyone would think Dr. Blair Cahill was just another lying sack of shit trying his best to get through the night filling in for Dr. Banks, the regular lying sack of shit. And when 9:30 came and went, and then 9:45, they would have been right. But when Dr. Blair Cahill walked in at 9:50 and apologized for being late, they would have been chagrined. Luckily, Mort Spell experienced none of this. He had forgotten Dr. Cahill was coming back for a chat. So, imagine how thrilled he was to have this nice-looking man visit him in the middle of the night. And once Mort figured out he was the same nice-looking man as before, well, what were the odds of that? First, at the golf course, now here at some hospital.

Blair Cahill was the type of nice-looking man who made people constantly nudge each other and whisper, "Is that someone famous?" He knew this happened and it visibly embarrassed him, which made him even better looking. He was twenty minutes late getting back to Mort Spell's room. That wasn't bad for Blair Cahill. He was late getting everywhere, which is what happens when the people you're with don't want you to leave. It was 9:51 when he sat down for his chat with Mort Spell. He had promised to meet his wife, Dr. Lesley

Cahill, outside the ER when she finished her shift at midnight. He'd be late for that, too.

Dr. Cahill excused the nurse, and Mort told her to make sure she got some help cleaning up the driving range. He sat down and offered Mort a cough drop. It was one of those eucalyptus throat bombs that Mort wasn't too crazy about, but it was as close as he'd get to a drink. Or a Valium.

That was the first smart thing Dr. Cahill did. The second was his first question to Mort, which he had formulated during the rest of his rounds. It wasn't "How the hell did you make it here?" It was "Where were you before you came here?" Actually, it was "So, Mr. Spell, where were you before you came here?"

"So, Mr. Spell, where were you before you came here?"

The combination of a nice-looking man giving Morton Martin Spell a cough drop and asking this question, this question *without* a wrong answer, is beyond disarming. It's that "I-don't-think-anyone's-ever-treated-me-like-this-my-whole-life" feeling a person experiences a dozen or so times his whole life. That's if he's not Morton Martin Spell. If he is, it's an invitation to start talking and stop being delirious for a while.

Two hours and fourteen minutes later, Dr. Cahill spoke for the second and last time. He asked, "Is there anyone else you'd like to talk to?" Mort said, "The actor." Dr. Cahill, who felt like he was jerking his fingers back from the slam-bound window of coherency, was sure Mort was back talking about Harold Lloyd again. He wasn't.

Harold Lloyd's name came up right away. Mort said, "Do you know the actor Harold Lloyd? He's dead. I don't know why I thought he was here." Once that was out of the way, Mort relaxed like a star witness about to set the record straight. He got to finally deliver his acceptance speech for the Bertram Hargan Cup. The speech *he* wanted to give. Alistair Cooke's first apartment in New York. His sister Dottie's trip to Scotland in 1969. Then he re-created that day with Bing in 1947 as the Crosby Pro-Am program had not. And the *Atlantic Monthly* would not. Palm Springs, Santa Anita,

Chicago, and glimpses of flesh and handcuffs in between. The director's cut. He closed with two stories about his father, Jacob Spell, and would have gone on except the eucalyptus and 134 minutes of yakking must have triggered some latent chunk of hemo-Valium and suddenly, he was looking at a real night's sleep.

He told the two stories about Jacob Spell that were all anyone needed to know about their relationship, and made anyone want to know more. Both took place on ships, neither one the steerage-equipped bacteria liner which had ferried Iakov Silvitsky to Ellis Island in 1901 (a good story for another time). The first was in 1938, when Jake Spell accompanied his kid over to Cambridge. Their second night at sea, he bursts into the state room.

"Kid, I met someone on the boat you can pal around with. He's just like you. He's going to Oxford, and he's a chemist, too!"

"Dad, I'm not going to Oxford. I'm going to Cambridge," Mort said. "And I'm not a chemist. I know nothing about chemistry. I'm a writer."

"Well," said Jake Spell, "you really fucked me on this one."

The second Jacob Spell story sailed eight years later, 1946, and alone. Jake had returned from two months in Europe on some wifeless business. The ship docked in New York and he met his son, ensconced and struggling in Manhattan, at the Oyster Bar for an hour before his train home.

"I met a writer friend of yours on the boat."

"Who?"

"Some guy. Ernie."

"I don't have any friends named Ernie."

"Ernie Hemingway."

"You mean Ernest Hemingway?"

"Yeah. Ernie. You know him?"

"Well, of course," said Mort. "He's the greatest American writer of this century."

"He's a souse. And he didn't know you."

Mort Spell liked to end with stories about his father. You close with your best stuff. It was smart. It was convenient. Not as smart as

Mort Spell during Final Jeopardy, and not as convenient as the fact that Jake Spell was now dead twenty-three years and not around to interrupt or correct him. The Jake Spell stories belonged to Mort. Seventy-five and alone since he learned to walk, he had finally landed a speaking part in his father's life after years of extra work. It was his best stuff, and the only thing he could not write. If the world had bestowed on Jake Spell the kind of celebrity he had deeded himself, Morton Martin Spell could have played Sandburg to his old man's Lincoln. He had that much material. It would have been a nice career. Travel, good hours, good pay, and maybe, maybe a thank you that he would have let himself hear.

Mort laughed again at the chemist and Ernie Hemingway bits. You know what? That's what his acceptance speech should have been. Fuck Bing. And fuck Bertram Hargan. And fuck the grandson, Chuck Hargan. And fuck Frankie Valli and the comic he rode in on. And, if everything went as planned, fuck Vanna White. Fuck Vanna. Fu . . . Va . . .

Dr. Cahill had to meet his wife. He still had five minutes left before his eleven-minute margin of error closed, after which Dr. Lesley Cahill could legally bust her husband's balls for being late. He fished out another cough drop and startled Mort out of drift-off as he stood up and it cracked against the floor.

"Is there anyone else you'd like to talk with?"

"The actor."

"Ah . . ."

"My nephew, the actor."

4

"Get down! Get down!"

He didn't.

"Out!"

He pretended to angrily grab the ball from the catcher, but the kid just smiled and rolled it back to the mound. End of the inning.

"Didn't you hear me tell you to slide?" said Roy.

He grabbed his glove. "Yeah. I thought I had it beat. Too bad. That makes it only an eight-run lead."

"That's not the point, College Boy."

Thirty-five years old, and they still called him College Boy. He tucked in his "Roy's Pizza" jersey. And his head. "Sorry, Roy."

"Don't worry," Roy said. "This won't cost you anything."

College Boy did not slide into home plate after June 1 on Diamond #4, Heckscher Fields, Central Park, Manhattan. Before Memorial Day, it was fine. But after, the right-handed batter's box on Diamond #4 looked like something Dad had started in the backyard to give the family ferret a proper sendoff. By July, a sherpa was needed just to get out of the box. By then, College Boy was batting lefthanded, and it would still be another week before enough league commissioners would give enough cash to The Dirt King to allow the entire home plate area at Diamond #4 to be resurrected completely above sea level. Fucking guy.

Enough. Don't get College Boy started. He wasn't going to slide into home plate and get his ankle swallowed or slingshot his hamstring. Not today, June something. The 4th. Not for the greater glory of—Tuesday afternoon, New York Restaurant League, look at your shirt, shithead—ah, Roy's Pizza. Roy's Original Pizza. Roy's Original Pizza after the out-of-court settlement with Ray's Original Pizza. Not today. Not with an eight-run lead. Not after two doubles and a home run. And not for fifty dollars.

And not, especially not, when he still had over a dozen more fifty-dollar bills to make that week. No. When you're a softball ringer, there's only two things that close your wallet. Rain and injury. Fortunately, rain only postpones the money a few weeks. Injury, that's just good-bye. You ain't getting paid. Try and catch me. And you can't. Busted wheel.

There's really only one injury. The legs. The wheels. You make your money hitting and fielding and throwing and hitting some more, but in between all that, it's all wheels. The wheels are your fortune. The best thing a softball ringer can hear that first time up every game is a couple guys in the field yelling, "Good stick! Good wheels!" Or, if you're College Boy, "Good stick. Good wheels . . . still!"

College Boy jogged out to left-center field, trying to recall the last time he'd been thrown out at home. Never. Sure, it was June and he wasn't sliding and The Dirt King's an asshole and it's an eight-run lead and bip bip bip bip bip. But he wasn't lying to Roy. He thought he could make it. He thought he could make it to the point where he didn't think about it. Didn't have to. He never got thrown out at the plate. Never. All wheels all the time. Sometimes, he'd slow up between third and home to draw a throw so the other runners could move up. Decoy. Make them think they had a shot. Slow up, check the relay man's motion—he's coming home, he bit!—*boom!* Wheels! "Safe!" Always thinking. Well, sure. He was a college boy.

Final score: Roy's Pizza 13, Il Vagabondo 6. They score a run in the bottom of the seventh on two walks and a bloop single over shortstop College Boy had no chance of getting. None. Not even fourteen years ago, when he first showed up in the park and the first Spanish guy called him College Boy. When the wheels were still under warranty. Rookie ringer. He broke fast, always did, but the ball was too shallow and the runner on second was off, some kid with good wheels. He picked it up on the second bounce and felt the heat when he threw it in to third. Dull, fast heat. Hot, then gone. On the back of the right leg. The hamstring. Like the flicker of a dashboard indicator light. Hot, then gone.

But not forgotten. It was 5:25. He had forty-five minutes. He could stretch the hamstring for forty-five minutes before he had to leave for the subway to the ferry to the bus to the park, where he could stretch for another forty-five minutes to overcome the stiffness from the subway to the ferry to the bus to the park. In the last four years, he'd gone from a guy who was paid to play softball to a guy for whom softball supported his full-time occupation: Stretching. Specifically, stretching his hamstring.

What's it, Tuesday? Staten Island. Thank the fucking Lord it's Staten Island, thought College Boy. Which made him the only person who was grateful to be taking New York City public transportation to Staten Island during rush hour on a summer weeknight. Ever. He was not thankful for the schlep. Shit, Rikers was less of a schlep. He was thankful for the destination. Tuesday night, 8 o'clock, Stapleton Modified Fast-Pitch. No bunting, no stealing. And on this team, "T. J.'s Tavern," he played third. Not the outfield, his usual ringer realm. So, no bunting, no stealing, no wheels. He'd stretch forty-five minutes before, then between every odd inning. After the game, he'd get a lift into Manhattan from Julio and do Epsom salts in the tub till Carson's monologue. The next day, he'd stretch a half hour after he got up, an hour before the 1 P.M. New York Press League game in Central Park, and an hour after. And between all that and a six-Advil dinner, he'd nurture his hamstring back to 90 percent. That would be enough, and that would be right around the time he'd been arriving in Queens for his 7 P.M. game. The Bayside Elite Softball League. Windmill. Three-man outfield. Bunting. Stealing. Wheels required. No exceptions.

When was the last time he'd shown up five minutes before a game? When his entire warmup consisted of double-knotting his spikes and shaping the bill on his cap? Had to be ten years, but it felt like never. Never, like the last time he'd been thrown out at home.

Twenty-four, twenty-five years old. Born limber. College Boy. Roll out of some bed, maybe his own, grab the converted Prince Tennis tote bag with all nine jerseys (He was only playing for pay in nine leagues back then. A nascent legend.), devour the sidewalk and whatever the vendor with nobody on line was selling as the crow flew to Central Park. Maybe, maybe he'd stop to eat along the way. But that was only if the sign read DONT WALK. And only if he didn't feel like showing off his wheels against oncoming traffic.

Those days, when he swore his batting eye was better with a hangover and he didn't fuck with a batting eye that worked. When four hours sleep and two No-Doz guaranteed he'd tag and score on a routine fly. From second. When the only muscle he ever pulled was late at night, in the company of Manhattan Cable Channel J.

By 1984, already seven years ago, his body had begun to send him first notices of delinquent care. So, he, College Boy, began to stretch. And what had looked like $40 for ninety minutes of running around in Central Park for seven innings metastasized into a pre-game war against spasm that built up faster than Nixon's Cambodia. By then, College Boy was getting fifty dollars a game, but the Cost-of-Ringering increase barely covered what he now had to carry in his equipment bag. The Prince satchel had died years ago from overuse and lack of space. The streamlined days of toting nine jerseys, a glove, spikes, six tokens, and maybe a condom around Greater New York had vanished like Crazy Eddie. Now, you saw College Boy's bag before you saw College Boy. Huge. One of those black nylon hockey gear U-Hauls with "Cooper" in white rubberized letters on the side where it might as well have said "Bekins." With the padded-leather/sheepskin shoulder strap he'd picked up at Nevada Bob's Discount Golf House for sixty dollars. He never figured out how much of his stretching was devoted to counteracting the effects of just lugging this thing, Bagzilla, around. Softball was his livelihood, but College Boy knew when he showed up at the field, at least forty-five minutes before game time, he looked like someone who should have Freddie Couples and a gallery walking alongside him.

He had thought about getting one of those fold-up luggage carts that every third person at the airport seemed to be pulling, but then he remembered how much he hated every third person at the airport. He had thought about getting two lighter bags and dividing his week. Monday through Wednesday, Thursday through Sunday. Nah. Okay, how about a Central Park bag and a Queens-Staten Island-Brooklyn bag? And go home in the middle of the day? Like some fisherman? No thanks. How about a bag for every day of the week? Well, that was just silly. How about getting up fifteen minutes earlier and just packing for that day's games? Okay, stop right there with the subversive thoughts. No. Bagzilla lives. It was meant to be slung over College Boy's shoulders. Like the weight of the world, plus five pounds.

And once he set the thing down on the bleachers and provoked its main zipper to screams, opening Bagzilla for business, he looked like someone who could have used a stock boy. Thirteen jerseys, an extra pair of white baseball pants, an extra pair of gray baseball pants, two gloves (infield and outfield), three bats (slo-pitch, fast-pitch, windmill), spikes, six hats, four batting gloves, three pairs of white tube socks, extra shoe laces, a sweatshirt, a turtleneck, a windbreaker, a light jacket, a decent shirt/pair of pants/dark socks if he had to be somewhere, two towels, two clean pair of underwear and an umbrella.

That was Aisle One. Aisle Two: Glove oil, a lighter, and three wine corks (for applying burnt cork under his eyes to cut the glare), twenty pieces of Bazooka original, deodorant, shampoo, Cruex, Desenex, baby powder, hairbrush, two pens, three crossword puzzles, notebook, address book, family-size bottle of Advil, family-size bottle of Excedrin, No-Doz, Chlor-Trimeton, Vicks 8-Hour Nasal Spray, Nytol, extra-strength Pepto-Bismol, trial-size Mylanta, Tums, Imodium, vitamins B1, B6, B12, C, E, and Super Mega-one multis, Bactine, Tiger Balm, Sportscreme, ice bag, Band-Aids, ace bandage, thirty packs of Equal and two 32 oz. bottles of Gatorade—one lemon-lime, one citrus cooler. One of the guys he played with on the team from the Improvisation in the Monday morning Performing Arts League, a comic, Jon Hayman, came up with the best line:

"Hey, College Boy, I just went through your bag. The card section's a little weak."

The lock-zippered back pocket held his watch, wallet, keys, sunglasses, tokens. There was no room anymore for a condom. Under his free shoulder, he tucked the *News* and the *Post* like some laughable counterweight. His 1991 New Year's resolution had been to go the entire season without making this noise when he saddled himself with Bagzilla: *"Unhumph!"* He'd made it through Week Two.

But what could he take out? Go ahead. Tell College Boy one thing he doesn't need in there. Try. Two Gatorades? Okay, you pay two dollars for sixteen ounces in the park, *if* the guy shows up, instead of $1.79 for thirty-two ounces in the rest of the universe. Advil *and* Excedrin? What is a human being supposed to take an hour after four Excedrin haven't worked? Crossword puzzles? What else is there to do on the Staten Island Ferry twice a week, sight-see? Six hats? Okay, four went with other jerseys, one was the lucky Angels cap. The other was for slumps, when the Angels cap wasn't lucky.

Friday was Laundry Day. By then, College Boy had sweated through ten of the thirteen jerseys and both pants. The underwear and socks were replaced by strict rotation. Every day, or every day after a teammate said, "Whew! Who opened the Dumpster?" He had only one game on Fridays. The 6 P.M. Wall Street League at Heckscher. He'd finish at the radio station by ten, do the laundry, pick up whatever health and beauty aids Bagzilla had coughed up during the week, eat a black-and-blue Romanian tenderloin from the coffee shop next to the Laundromat while everything was in the dryer. Which would still leave four and a half hours for his weekly five-milligram Valium nap. Half a blue. A whole yellow. Two whites. He couldn't remember the last time he'd seen a white Valium. When had Uncle Mort stopped taking them? When had he stopped taking them from Uncle Mort?

Friday was also Vague Legitimacy Day. He had to be at the radio station, WLLS ("Wheels-102"), by 6 A.M. And by 6:05, when the news ended, he had to be in his chair. The once-a-week in-studio mascot chair. Then, for the next three hours, fifty minutes, College Boy laughed at everything Dan Drake said on the air. Especially the stuff that wasn't all that funny. For this noise, which he was good at, and the occasional line or two in a sketch, which he could deliver just north of amateur, he was paid $125. After taxes, $101.14, but 125 AFTRA dollars before taxes. Just enough to put him in the union. Just enough for health benefits. Just enough for a union card, which insured he could play unhassled in three show-business-related leagues Monday, Wednesday, and Thursday. Just enough so when people asked him what he did, he could say, with Vague Legitimacy, "I'm an actor." That's what he could say, because AFTRA had no category for what he really was at Wheels-102. A laugh ringer.

He got two hundred dollars a game in the Wall Street League. It had been fifty dollars, like everywhere else, but six years ago he, College Boy, was the object of a spirited bidding war between Goldman Sachs and Morgan Stanley. He went 4-for-4 for Morgan in the championship game, along with five RBIs and two SportsCenter catches in the outfield. After the game, some old guy in a suit, Goldman maybe, came up to him as his arms were about to be swallowed by Bagzilla.

"What do you do for Morgan Stanley, College Boy?"

"Work in the mailroom."

"You're a little old to be working in the mailroom. It can't pay much."

"Well, how much does your mailroom pay?"

"Seventy-five dollars."

At that point, another old guy in a suit, Morgan perhaps, redirected the discussion his way. It went $100, $150, $200, until Goldman or Sachs said, "Fucking keep him." That's when they started outlawing ringers in the Wall Street League. That's when College Boy started working in the mailroom at Morgan Stanley. One day a year. Three thousand dollars. To be paid in fifteen cash installments of two hundred dollars, April–August. Eighteen, if Morgan Stanley went all the way in the playoffs. And they always did. $3,600. The only guy in Central Park who could make that kind of cash for one day of real work was The Dirt King. Fucking guy.

College Boy learned a valuable lesson from Morgan Stanley. Take care of your investment. For two hundred dollars a game, you got a two-hundred-dollar game from College Boy. He showed up an hour and a half early, stretched, pitched batting practice, gave tips to whoever didn't want to throw or swing a bat like an investment banker, coached third when he wasn't up or on base, and generally high-fived and ass-patted these disdain-filled nouveau geeks like they were managing his portfolio. Or like he really gave a shit. It was the most money he made all week and the jersey he liked wearing the least. By far. It was the one day he took off from being a ringer and worked his other job. Whore. Only a Valium nap could get him ready for this gig. And only four furiously gulped Wild Turkey and sodas on the way home chased it away.

But now it was still Tuesday and his wheels needed work. College Boy turned his hat around backward, as he had done ten years before any of the brothers, and went to it. Eight minutes of lunges. Then he hopped up. Two minutes of calf raises. Four minutes of hip stretches. Then back down. Two minutes of groin stretches. Back up. Four minutes of quad stretches. College Boy never knew he had quadricep muscles until 1985, when he caught both games of a doubleheader in the Astoria North Fast-Pitch League (Mondays, 7:00 P.M.). A month later, bowlegging home from the Broadway Show League (Thursdays, noon), he saw Tim McCarver, the Mets broadcaster, out in front of the Regency Hotel on Park and Sixty-second.

"Hey, Tim, big fan, great job," said College Boy.

"Thanks."

"Can I ask you something?"

"Sure."

"You caught over 1,000 games in the big leagues in 20 years."

"1,387."

"When did your quads stop hurting?"

"They haven't."

The last twenty-five minutes were devoted to the hamstrings. Ten minutes on each, then an extra five to the one the judges (calfs, hips, groin, quads) decided was the most deserving. Alone in foul territory on Heckscher Field, Diamond #4, College Boy hurdled in place, while two women's slo-pitch squads straggled out and ignored him as only women could.

He saw The Dirt King over at Diamond #3, filling in the hole in front of the pitching rubber.

"Hey, Ernie," he yelled. "How about saving some of that for Diamond #4?"

Ernest Giovia, The Dirt King of Central Park, straightened up to his full five feet four and one half inches, put his ringed hand to his mouth and yelled back, much louder, "Hey, how about sucking my dick?" So much louder, the women's teams stopped straggling and began to glare. Glare, until they realized they might piss off The Dirt King. So, they stopped and went back to ignoring College Boy.

He finished with the hamstrings. Better. Wheels stable but guarded. He threw in two more minutes of lunges. For the rhomboids. He'd learned the lunges from Julio and they quieted his spasming upper back as Tylenol with codeine had not. But occasionally, the beginnings of a toothache back there would holler. Like today. He'd have to ice it down on the ferry. For an extra buck, the guy at the snack bar on the Staten Island Ferry filled his ice bag after he bought an overpriced Diet Coke. What a racket. Until then, Bagzilla would be confined to his left shoulder.

Thank God for Julio. Julio Rentas, "Papa J" to his fellow ringers, was a Swedish Institute-trained massage therapist when he wasn't sending opposing outfielders scurrying. One afternoon, as he and College Boy shared a between-game joint, one of those great-looking women with a stroller in the park wheeled by, then stopped and came back.

"Julio?"

"Yeah?"

"Peggy."

"Yeah?"

"Last Thursday at five."

"Oh right."

"Well," she said, "you probably didn't recognize me with my clothes on."

College Boy reaggravated his rhomboids first when he threw his head back laughing, then when he fell off the bench. That's when Papa J showed him the lunge and prescribed another joint, to be used as directed in the bathtub that night. Healed, he went 2-for-2 in the second game. Two home runs, two intentional walks.

Before Papa J laid on hands, College Boy had entrusted his rhomboids to a Fifth Avenue chiropractor, the type of guy who went into skeletal manipulation after he realized there was too much integrity selling aluminum siding. For $240, he cracked College Boy like one of those old commercials for Bonamo Turkish Taffy, then told him to walk for ten minutes, twice a day, on a hard floor, wearing one boot. For two weeks, or until he had another $240. On Day Ten, he woke Rachel at 1 A.M. when he clop-clopped outside in the hall. When he came back in, she was just finishing buttoning her blouse and preparing to silently storm out.

"I forgot to do this a second time," he said.

Nothing.

"Are you leaving?"

She grabbed her bag.

"Are you not talking to me?"

Rachel wheeled and gave the doorknob a pre-slam grip. "I don't talk to stupid people." Slam.

On Day Twelve, Julio showed him the lunge. Shit. For $240, he could have scored an ounce and a half of pot.

The ice felt good on the ferry. He lay back on the bag, and his restricted movement prevented him from doing a crossword or flipping through the *News* or *Post.* So, he just stared at tomorrow's entries for Belmont. Hardly a sacrifice.

That was the other item usually tucked in Bagzilla's lock-zippered side pocket. OTB tickets. Unripped OTB tickets. Unripped until eleven that night, when he would call the Off Track Betting hotline and find out if he had won the ninth race triple. College Boy knew just enough about handicapping horse races to know he didn't have a fucking clue. But he knew just enough about chance and probability (an elective junior year which he tamed for an A-minus) to develop a low-risk, high-yield investment system which could potentially net him thousands of tax-free dollars a year. And who better, who better to take the gambling out of gambling than a thirty-five-year-old man leaning on an ice bag on his way to Staten Island whose idea of planning for the future was deciding whether to set his VCR to tape the Yankees or Mets before he left his apartment?

College Boy didn't even like horses. But he liked numbers. Loved them. He could update his batting average before the ball dropped into the outfield. But he did not like all numbers. Only numbers that made sense. And because only he, College Boy, knew which numbers those were, well, you have an idea how much sense this would make to the rest of the world. Which was fine with College Boy. He had a deal with the rest of the world. He didn't have to explain which numbers made sense, and the rest of the world didn't have to explain the popularity of soccer, ABBA, or *The Road Less Traveled.*

But College Boy would tell anyone his system if they asked. And if they didn't ask why. It was very simple. He only bet during softball season. He only bet on the ninth race at Belmont. He only bet the trifecta, a wager in which you had to correctly pick the first three horses. He only bet one-dollar boxes, which meant the three horses he picked could finish in any order. He only spent a maximum of thirty-six dollars per day (thirty-six, *good* number), which bought six one-dollar box tickets. And, here now is The System: he only picked combinations of horses whose numbers added up. 1-2-3. 2-3-1. 3-2-1. Need more? Okay, here are all the possible combinations (based on a nine-horse field):

1-3-4 (1-4-3, 3-1-4, 3-4-1, 4-1-3, 4-3-1); 1-4-5; 1-5-6; 1-6-7; 1-7-8; 1-8-9; 2-3-5; 2-4-6; 2-5-7; 2-6-8; 2-7-9; 3-4-7; 3-5-8; 3-6-9; 4-5-9.

Simple. To College Boy, numbers that added up made sense. It meant the universe had an order. And if that order perhaps translated into a $586.20 payout, well then, on that day, the universe had shown its spiritual, nurturing side as well.

College Boy spent $216 a week trying to restore order to the universe via the ninth at Belmont. He had been doing this for the last five years. When he started bagging two hundred dollars a game from Morgan Stanley, his teammates chirped in with all kinds of unsolicited investment advice. He was so grateful to be making the extra dough, he messed around with some shit he still didn't understand. He might even have made 8 percent on his money. But it was Wall Street. Their universe. And 8 percent was a number that made no sense to College Boy. Meanwhile, he spent that year transcribing every winning trifecta at Belmont, Aqueduct, and Saratoga. In 1985, at Belmont Race Track, the numbers in the triple added up 38 percent of the time. The payoffs ranged from $26.20 to $6,656.40.

Of course, six tickets didn't cover all the combinations. You had to have the right numbers when they came in. Just like any other schmuck. That's when the chance part came into play. That's why in the last five years, College Boy and The System had grossed total winnings of . . . $313. And that's only because he had hit for $4,180 five years ago. And only because an OTB clerk had punched him a ticket for 1-2-4, rather than 1-3-4.

College Boy looked again at the results of Monday's ninth. 8-5-6. $748.40. There were no tickets in Bagzilla's lock-zippered side pocket today. Belmont was dark Tuesdays. The universe was closed.

Twenty minutes with the ice was enough. Any more and he'd just be feeling sorry for himself. College Boy spent the last few minutes on the ferry with his white baseball pants around his ankles, rubbing Sportscreme into his hamstring. If you had to work your wheels with analgesic, better to do it in the privacy of public transportation. Not at the ballpark. Sure, you could stretch. Go nuts, stretch your brains out. But don't let them see you taking a pregame palmful of Advil, like some over-the-counter Nick Nolte in *North Dallas Forty*. Don't let them hear the peppermill grind of a waiting ice bag. Don't let them smell Tiger Balm. Don't fuck with their image of you, The Ringer. They're entitled to it. They've paid for it.

And not just their image of The Ringer. Your image, too. College Boy bought the ringer ideal as his thirteen teams bought and paid for the ringer reality. The difference was he never let go. He knew it was over once the game ended, so why leave? Where else can a guy succeed six and three-quarters out of ten times, as College Boy did, and be twice as good as everyone else?

Okay, fuck the numbers for a second. To be good, really good, at the one thing you do. To do nothing else. To not—*not!*—be a fraud. Who wouldn't want that?

And so he rang, romping in Heckscher and three other boroughs, and felt the collective exhale of all just by his showing up. *College Boy's here!* Just show up, put a team on his back and let the game come to him. Then get your money. Don't give anything away. Then go show up at the next place. Don't stay too long. And don't let them see you hurt. The ringer philosophy of life. Apply everywhere and laugh all the way to the AFTRA bank every Friday.

College Boy wasn't the first guy to get paid for playing softball. Just the first to market himself so relentlessly. Every year, the players that jousted with him in four of the five boroughs became younger, stronger, even faster. Their tools undeniably more plentiful. But none of them got more money. None.

The white thing helped. College Boy was, for the first and only time in his life, a minority. And he took advantage of it like that guy who forced the Bakke Amendment. The ringer market was overstocked with Puerto Ricans and Dominicans. Their sheer numbers drove their per game price down. And that Latin thing, that love for the game, that "I'll play for nothing all day" shit. A smart, cheap manager could really tap into that. The truly great young Latin players only lasted a year, two tops. Too frustrating. Too embarrassing. Softball? Didn't matter how fast the pitch came in. Clemente never played fucking softball. They might try to come back years later, but by then there was a job, a family, a drug habit, or a belly they couldn't get out from under. Maybe they'd play once a week. They couldn't guarantee. College Boy guaranteed.

After thirteen years of helping some slob festoon his bar, restaurant, gas station, auto showroom, or office lobby with the kind of phallic tributes only available in championship trophy size, College Boy had become a trophy himself. Lord of The Ringers. Part icon, part good luck charm, all wheels. If you were tired of your team going 8–6 and losing in the first round of the playoffs, tired of eating shit from the guys at O'Hurley's or Al's Sunoco Station or Goldman Sachs, tired of carrying around your ordinary, tribute-less penis, you gave College Boy a call. He guaranteed you the big hardware in three years. And he always made good on his guarantee.

Of course, some fellas didn't want to want to wait three years. That's when College Boy set up a budget and made a few calls. Papa J at first. Ant'ny at short. Hector out of detox and on the mound. A couple of hungry twenty-dollar-a-game Spanish kids. And maybe two or three guys who actually worked at the bar, the restaurant, the gas station, or the office. By the time the trophy showed up, the total ringer tab came to $4,000. College Boy would deliver it personally and the guy, the slob, would immediately raise it above his head. (*"Look what I bought, Mommy!"/ "Very nice, dear."*)

With his benefactor's hands in the air, College Boy swooped in for his second payoff. That's when he'd convince the guy to shell out another two grand for jackets. You know, those stylish nylon windbreakers ("Ale 'n' Hearty, Yorkville Softball, Div. II Champs, 1984") that inspired the line from every woman over eighteen: "You're not going out wearing *that*, are you?" College Boy had his pitch down and away: "I've got a friend at Gerry Cosby's. He'll do forty jackets for two thousand dollars. You give fifteen to the guys on the team, sell the rest here at the bar (restaurant, gas station, office) for eighty dollars. You'll make your money back and have free advertising. Every guy I've done this for says it helped business. And most of them end up ordering more. Have I steered you wrong yet? Just make the check out to Gerry Cosby, C-O-S . . ."

And it did come to $2,000: $1,000 for the jackets, $400 for College Boy's friend to write up the appropriate sales slip (whose bottom line was always some bargainy figure like $1,983.67), $600 for College Boy's standard shipping and handling charges. The extra money would pay his rent in December, around the time College Boy would stuff that fiscal year's windbreaker into the closest winter coat collection barrel.

The guarantees he made were restricted to Manhattan. In Queens,

Brooklyn, or Staten Island he just showed up and played ball. Just a mercenary with no wife and a sixty-pound bag to support. Everyone in Brooklyn, Queens, and Staten Island already had a trophy. Everyone out there knew how much a windbreaker really cost.

The Staten Island Ferry squeezed into the dock. Shit. He forgot to buy bananas. College Boy's extra stretching session at Heckscher had forced him to rush to the ferry and pass by the fruit stand at Fifty-seventh and Eighth. He couldn't take six Advil on an empty stomach, and all they sold in Stapleton Town Park after six was beer and pot. College Boy lived on bananas during his softball day. Gatorade in solid form. Bagzilla's produce section was empty. He could gut it out and let his wheels operate ibuprofen-free. Or Plan B. Six Advil, plus twelve Tums. It had kind of worked once two years ago. Oh no, it hadn't. Too late.

The bus dropped him off at Stapleton Town Park at 7:10. College Boy, first guy on the field. Again. The local kids, with two scuffed-up hardballs, one bat, and almost enough gloves, ran around in daylight's last licks. They still had twenty minutes before the big guys showed up and chased them off. College Boy had fifty minutes till game time. Perfect. Forty-five to stretch, four minutes, fifty seconds to take some balls at third, the last ten seconds to find a piece of food, something to cushion Plan B.

The stretching went well. He only muttered "Good Christ" three times. The bonus time in Heckscher less than two hours ago had helped, and the yapping of his rhomboid took his mind off the hamstring. Around twenty-of, the bulk of the T. J.'s Tavern team showed up, carrying the bulk of T. J.'s Tavern under their arms. The guys from T. J.'s never brought enough beer to get drunk, just enough to blow a two-run lead in the bottom of the seventh.

It was College Boy and Papa J's job to get the lead to at least three by the seventh. Where was Papa J anyway? The guy was amazing. He was at least ten years older than College Boy, yet his entire regimen of stretching consisted of bending over his bag looking for rolling papers. Papa J was one of the two great things about playing for T. J.'s Tavern. The other was the uniform.

Of the thirteen jerseys in Bagzilla, T. J.'s Tavern was the only one which stayed folded all week. White/white, button front, Michigan navy blue piping around the collar and sleeves. Navy blue double-stitched tackle-twill Old English style "T. J.'s" over the left breast, just like the Tigers home uniforms. Navy-blue double-stitched tackle-twill 8-inch high number on back. 2.

Number 2. The pay scale varied, the wheels went different places, the rhomboids dropped in unannounced, Bagzilla cleared space for new apparel and sundries. But the number on every jersey was always the same. 2. Fifty dollars a game. Number 2 on the back of the shirt. That was the minimum price for College Boy. There was no discussion. Sometimes, a manager would say, "But Joey's been wearing 2 for years." And College Boy would smile. "Well, if Joey doesn't want to give it up, he shouldn't." He'd smile again. "But I'm really silly about this." And then he'd start to walk away and continue until there was an arm around him. Joey. The jersey would still be sweaty. "Good luck number?" Joey would ask.

"Something like that."

"Well, I never had any fucking luck with it. I hit .218 last year. Here."

Something like that. His first year as a ringer, 1979, College Boy made sixty dollars a week. He should have made ninety, but he dropped out of a league on Ninety-sixth Street after one game. He went 0-for-4. He wore number 12. There was no 2. That guy, Billy, had moved, and taken his jersey. Nobody had a new number for him. Or College Boy.

So, it had to be 2.

2.

Just another number that made sense.

"Come and git your love. Come and git your lo-ove . . ."

College Boy did not have to turn around. Which helped because he was in mid-lunge.

"Papa J."

He stopped singing. "What time is it, amigo?"

"Ten of."

"Shit. What the fuck is Papa J gonna do?"

"You could stretch," said College Boy.

"Shit . . ."

"You could take some batting practice."

"Don't need no BP."

"I think I saw a couple of girls behind the bleachers. You could work on your rap."

"Don't need no work."

"Well, that leaves blowing me."

"I think I'll stretch."

Papa J leaned over his bag, looking for rolling papers. *"Come and git your love. Come and git your lo-ove . . ."* He pulled out something wrapped in foil that thudded like ethnic food.

"What's that?" College Boy asked.

"Cuban sandwich."

"Let me have the top piece of bread."

"I'll let you have a bite."

"I don't want a bite. I need a piece of bread."

"How am I gonna eat this, bro?"

"Like a pizza."

"Can't do it, Freddy." Freddy was not College Boy's name. Freddy was what Papa J called everybody when he wasn't calling them bro or amigo.

"I'll give you a buck for the bread."

"Five."

Plan B—the Advil/Tums quinella—was about to seriously start not working.

"A buck and a Valium."

"Qué color, amigo?"

"Yellow."

"No agua?"

"Blow me."

"Okay, a buck, a yellow, and *you* blow *me.*"

"Deal."

"All right," said Papa J, sealing the transaction with a slow, soul shake. "And we ready for Freddy."

The Staten Island game was kind to College Boy's wheels. Seven innings at third base, which was like a vacation anyway, and very little work on the basepaths. He saw to that. College Boy came up four times and finished 1-for-2. He walked in the top of the first and trotted in five pitches later on Papa J's long home run. (Papa J sang "Come and Git Your Love" as soon as the ball took off.) His deep sacrifice fly in the third scored T.J.'s sixth run and a well-planned line drive to third in the fifth was caught before he could take a step. When College Boy walked back to the bench, he could swear his right hamstring was thanking him.

In the top of the seventh, T. J.'s Tavern led, 8–3, and two guys got on with two outs. Shit, he had to bat again. College Boy figured he'd aim another line drive third base-way and act like this load pitching for Red's, Jimmy, or Timmy, had his number. But the guy tried to get cute with a change-up, and College Boy waited the half-second longer it took before teaching Jimmy or Timmy a lesson. The ball hit the gap in right-center like a rock on a frozen pond. An easy home run. A triple if you had no wheels. Yet when the throw finally came back in, College Boy, at never more than a lope, was on second.

That's when Morales, playing left field for the other guys, started.

"Hey, what's College Boy doing on second? You okay, College Boy? You on second. What happened? Were you carrying that fucking bag of yours on your back?"

Without turning, he knew it was Morales. He'd heard that bogus Pacino "Scarface" accent for five years, in six different leagues. Morales was a ringer. And ringers could give shit to other ringers. Maybe that was all he was going to say. Maybe he'd shut up.

"Hey, College Boy." No. "Something wrong with your legs? They gonna have to take you out back and shoot you."

College Boy rarely responded. Almost as rarely as he slowed up at second on an easy home run. "Morales," he said, "you *start* for this team?" Ringer shit. Like that.

"Hey, fu—" and then Morales had to chase down a fly ball for the third out.

College Boy waited for Morales to run in, and they put their arms around each other, as ringers do, as they walked off the field. No hard feelings. Just trying to make a supplemental living. See you tomorrow night in Bayside. See you Saturday for the doubleheader at Heckscher. See you Sunday for two more at Riis Park.

No hard feelings. Piece of shit. Take it easy on one long ball, and Morales, that prick, was all over him. And with a racehorse reference, no less. Take him out back and shoot him. Fucking Morales was onto him. And Papa J with the "old man" bullshit. Whatever punishment lurked beneath his hamstring, whatever muscular comeuppance he was trying to stave off, was nothing compared to the pain of someone being onto him. Thirty-five years old. Playing fifteen games a week when guys ten years younger played seven, eight tops. Fifteen games a week, sixteen if he got up early enough on Saturday to bag an extra forty dollars in Felipe's nine A.M. pick-up game on Ninety-sixth Street. Forty dollars. That would make $890 for the week. $890 for running around. $890 for not stopping.

Halfway down to first on that sure home run. That's when he felt the heat again. On the back of the wheels. He just slowed, seamlessly, and eased, loped into second. Like that was the idea all along. Like he didn't want to rub it in to Jimmy or Timmy. The two runners were coming home. Nobody was paying attention to College Boy. Nobody was onto him. Except Morales. And that was enough.

Everybody got paid in Riis Park on Sunday. The official name of the league was Brooklyn Major Fast-Pitch. But everyone called it what it was. Riis Park Ringers.

All ringers. All there. All waiting for College Boy to get to a place from which he couldn't stretch himself free. All onto him. And his wheels. Still June. Still three months left on the ringer calendar. And College Boy needed a bunch of rainouts to get right. A bunch.

T. J.'s Tavern won, 9–2. No, 10–2. No, 10–3. Right, 10–3. And they beat Sam's. No, Sal's. No, Barney's. Some bar. Some bar with red shirts. Red's. Red's Cadillac Grille.

Pretty good. The game had ended over five minutes ago and College Boy still remembered who he had played against. Shit, thirteen leagues a week, the victory was to go a whole game without looking at his shirt to remember who he was playing for. Fifteen games a week and still only June, he barely knew the names of half his two hundred teammates. It would be the first of August before he stopped calling every other player "Big Guy." College Boy knew a little about women, okay nothing, but he knew one thing about men. Men loved to be called "Big Guy." Every guy. Gay guys absolutely loved it. Call a fag "Big Guy" and you've given him permission to do one of three things: talk about his dick; do his "butch" impression; or grab another fag and say, "Guess what he just called me?"

Some leagues were easy to remember. The Press League (Wed., one o'clock) had the same six teams every year. Although, there was an embarrassing moment in 1987, when College Boy ran out to center field with the *New York Times* team for the league opener against the Associated Press and then ran back in when he realized he was playing center field for the AP. And had been for two years. The same thing had happened in the Broadway Show League (Thurs., noon), but that was understandable. *Les Misérables* vs. *Ain't Misbehavin'*? It's too close, even after remembering to look at the front of the uniform jersey. College Boy hadn't, but he recovered and got a big laugh when he ran in from the outfield and yelled, "Sorry I'm late. I went to the wrong theater."

There were things, other lines, that College Boy wanted to say all the time on the field. Funny stuff. But he couldn't. Every time some self-important actor in the Performing Arts or Show Business League went down on a called strike, College Boy was dying to yell, like some casting director, "Thank you!" But he couldn't. Or when a fat guy, any fat guy, came up and he was all set to cry out "Throw him a salad." But he couldn't. One time, the shortstop for *Cats* bobbled three ground balls in a row and College Boy was this close to saying, "It's *Cats*. He'll play with the ball for an hour, till he gets bored." But he didn't. He couldn't. College Boy was paid to do a lot of things on a softball field, and after hitting and fielding, number three on the list was *not* to ridicule the 95 percent who weren't being paid. And number four was to take whatever shit The Unpaid gave him for being a ringer, just a ringer. Whatever shit. Even if it wasn't funny. And other than, "I just went through your bag. The card section's a little weak," it never was.

On the other hand, ringers could give shit to other ringers. A couple of T. J.'s Tavern players were busy tossing their empties in the Dumpster behind the backstop. They let the metal top close with a sickly clang.

"Hey, Julio," said College Boy seconds into the reverb, "you dropped your glove."

College Boy and Papa J were making their way to Papa J's car, a 1973 Chrysler New Yorker working on its fourth odometer cycle, sixth paint job, and third interior carpeting. The kind of car you only got into blindfolded and at gunpoint. Or if you really need a ride back to Manhattan. College Boy dropped Bagzilla while Papa J began jiggling the passenger side door handle. Thank God it had been a short walk.

"New paint job, Papa J?"

"Yeah."

"What would you call this color? Lime?"

"No, bro. Mint Julep."

"And I see you removed the sign."

"What sign?"

"The 'Grand Marshall: Puerto Rican Day Parade' sign."

"Don't be doing that 'Chico and the Man' shit in my face."

"Sorry."

Papa J opened the door and College Boy began shoving Bagzilla into the back shag. "Thank you. I know how you old people hate to apologize."

"Fuck you," said College Boy.

"That's better."

He would have loved another twenty minutes to stretch in the parking lot. But that would have prompted at least three more old-man cracks from Papa J. And maybe another asshole remark from

Morales if he saw him on his way out. He didn't need that. What he needed was a week of rainouts.

He paid the toll for Papa J at the Verrazano Bridge. He'd bring the Valium tomorrow night, when they played in Bayside. College Boy for the Tom-Inators. Papa J for Rincon Bail Bonds.

"Fucking Morales," said College Boy.

"You let that guy get to you? *Viente dolares.* That's what he gets a game. I know. He's just a mouth. Calls me 'Whitey Lover.' Keep calling me 'Whitey Lover,' you twenty dollar *cunio.* Nobody listens to him."

"Did you hear anything about rain tomorrow?"

"No way. I ain't waiting till Thursday for that Valium, Freddy."

5

(Ring)

(Ring)

(Ring)

(Ring—click) "How ya' doin? . . . Good . . ." *(click—BEEP!)*

"Hello? Hello? I hate this message. You know I hate this message. How do you expect people to leave you messages when they feel like—"

"Hi, Mom."

"Oh, you scared me. Why do you wait?"

"Sorry. I was on the john."

"I hate that message."

"I know."

"What if you get an important call?"

"I don't get any important calls."

"Since when?"

"Since the last time you called, Mom."

"Don't try and be charming."

"Okay . . . how's this, better?" Dottie Sussman laughed, as she always ended up doing on the phone with her son.

"Harvey—" Her son, Harvey Sussman. College Boy.

"Mom—"

"It's Mort."

"Mom, I know. I had dinner with him two weeks ago Sunday, before he went out to L.A., and I haven't called him back to reschedule. I just forgot and I'm the worst person in—"

"He's in the hospital."

"Now I'm the worst person in the world."

"Hey, Job . . ." College Boy thought about singing *"Where you goin' with that gun in yo' hand?"* but he knew she wouldn't get it. And he'd be upstaging her hip reference. So, he just said what he usually said when he interrupted.

"Sorry."

"He's in Mount Sinai."

"How long's he been there?"

"Since last Monday."

"Three days?"

"No, I mean the Monday before that."

"He's been in the hospital nine days! Why didn't you call me?"

"I only found out last Thursday."

"Why didn't you call me then?"

"First, I didn't want to bother you until I knew something."

"What did you find out?"

"Nothing. I thought you'd tell me."

"Why would I know?"

"Because he kept telling me I'd get a full report from you."

"Who?"

"Mort."

"I haven't seen him."

"I know that now. But I thought you had. He's delirious, and he kept telling me you'd been stopping by."

"Didn't the doctor tell you he was delirious?"

"Yes, of course. But I didn't believe he was being delirious about seeing you. He sounded normal. Then, when I didn't hear from you for a few days, because you always call, I figured maybe he hadn't seen you."

"Well, he hasn't."

"I figured that out after he said to me, 'Do me a favor and put Dottie Sussman on the phone.' And I said, 'Mort, it's me. Dottie.' He did that like three times in one call and then I figured maybe he was a little crackers about being in touch with you."

"How did you find out he was in Mount Sinai?"

"I called his cleaning woman. She took him in Monday. I said, Helga—"

"Sheila."

"Right, Helga was the mother. So, I said, 'Sheila, how come you didn't call me to tell me he'd gone in?' She said, 'I thought your son would have told you.' And that's when I waited to hear from you."

"When do you want me to see him?"

"Well, today."

"Mom, what time is it?"

"Eleven." Wednesday. Press League at one, Bayside Elite Fast-Pitch at seven. Stretching in between.

"Is it raining where you are?"

"What?"

"I can see him around nine tonight."

"No sooner?"

"I can't. I've got an audition at one, then a thing at four, then I gotta meet this guy at seven."

"You can't change the seven appointment?"

"It's a big guy, Mom."

"Who?"

"You wouldn't know him."

"What's the audition for?"

"I don't know. Some product." Dottie Sussman didn't bother to pursue it. For fourteen years, it had always been "a thing" or "this guy" or "some product." It was like having a conversation with a drug dealer. Not that she knew any drug dealers, but if Dottie Sussman ever called a drug dealer and asked him what he was doing that day, after five seconds she would think, "This is like having a conversation with my son. Except my son doesn't sniff as much."

"Well, make sure you give me this many details after you see your uncle."

"Do you know what's wrong with him?"

"It's his prostate."

"I bet he left it at the hotel in L. A."

"He almost died."

"Sorry. . . . Have, have they operated?"

"Not yet. He's still delirious. They think it's probably the withdrawal from Valium."

"And alcohol."

"The doctor just said Valium."

"Mom, it's Mort."

"I'm more than a little worried about him. You know, he hasn't worked in almost two years."

"That's not true. He goes into the office every day. I called him there like three weeks ago."

"Well, he took retirement from the magazine at the end of 1989."

"Really? When did you find out about this?"

"Last Thursday. That's the other thing. When I talked to his doctor, Banks, he asked me to call *Civilized Man* and find out about the status of his insurance. That's when they told me he took retirement. I guess he had a fight with his editor—"

"About the piece on placekickers."

"Right. Well, I guess the editor—"

"Liebenthal."

"Right, that fascist. Well, he told Mort he had to retire. Luckily, he was there long enough to keep full medical benefits. They've been waiting for him to clean out his office, but he keeps going in, saying he has to take care of a couple of things and never starts to pack his stuff up. This has been going on for a year and a half. The receptionist told me."

"Marion?"

"She told me about the medical benefits. Sheila told me about the fight with Liebenthal. He needs to get out of there."

"The hospital?"

"New York. I don't think he can stay in New York by himself anymore," she began. "He's seventy-five years old with no job, no family, no friends, and poor health."

"What about Alistair Cooke?"

"You think Alistair Cooke gives a shit about him? He calls Mort at the last minute when *his* plans for the evening fall through. I don't know what he does all day and I don't know what there's left in New York for him. And he certainly isn't getting any help from his shrink."

"Dr. Levitz?"

"That bum. I'd like to get my hands on that guy."

"Me too. I could use some Valium."

"I think he's got to stop kidding himself," she began again. "I think we've all got to stop kidding ourselves."

"You mean about Mort."

"Yes."

"Because I think the kidding ourselves thing in general has been going quite well for us for a lot of years."

"Did I tell you what a big help you're being?"

"Sorry."

"He needs to get out of there, come here where he can be closer to the rest of his family. I'm not saying we throw him in a home. I can find him some places to look at up here, but I don't think he's even thought about moving."

"He hasn't thought about moving out of his office."

"I don't want you to have to take care of him, but I do need you to get this in motion. Talk to him, find out what he needs to do to close up things and get himself out of there. I mean, if we work quickly, we could have him here and set up by the end of the summer. Get him out of that shitbox of an apartment and into a decent-size place with a bit of a yard and some trees."

"I don't think his apartment is a shitbox."

"Well, maybe he'll let you have it." College Boy felt himself begin to cheer, then stopped like he was checking his swing. "I just think we need to move fast. I have a feeling if he fully recuperates in New York after his operation we'll never be able to get him out of there. You'll have to straighten things out with his accountant, his lawyer, that bum Levitz, his other doctor—"

"Whoa, Mom. What time is it?"

"Quarter after." Five minutes before he resumed being College Boy.

"I'm a little under the gun here. I think we're getting way ahead of ourselves. We don't know what happened. We don't know what's going to happen. Nobody has really talked to Mort face to face. There may be no operation. He may not want to leave New York. He may have plans of his own. I'll go there tonight and speak with him, but right now, I've got like four minutes to call Mort and tell him I'm coming. I'll call you back after I see him."

"Okay, dear. His number at Mount Sinai is (212), well, you know that, how silly. I always do that. I completely forget you live in—"

"Mom—"

"JL5-6147."

"—6147. Thanks."

"Good luck on your audition."

"What? Oh, right. Good-bye, Mom."

"Good-bye, dear."

(beep-beep-beep, beep-beep beep-beep)

"Hello?"

"Mort?"

"This is your sister Dottie's kid."

"Am I glad you called."

"Really? How are you?"

"Fine."

"That's great."

"Fine, now that I'm back here."

"Where were you?"

"I was abducted last night. This large black woman and two men. They held a knife to my prick and took me naked down to the subway. And this was very clever. They took all my money, and invested it."

"Mort, I'm going to come see you tonight. Around nine."

"Good. We'll watch Johnny Carson together. You know, he's been talking about me. Every night this week. Where have you been?"

"I was out."

"So was I. I was down in the subway. Did I tell you about that?"

"You did."

"I wonder if Carson will say anything about it."

"He usually mentions the big items in the news."

"Oh, I think they've hushed this up pretty good. They're very clever. But then again, you seemed to know all about it."

"So, I'll be by around nine to see you tonight."

"—"

"Mort?"

"—"

"Uncle Mort?"

"You're looking awfully well today."

"Did somebody just come in?"

"Not that I know of. But I am expecting my nephew."

"Well then, I won't keep you."

"Well, good-bye then."

College Boy heard the sound of a phone receiver bouncing on the floor.

He'd have to take a cab.

6

"You know, they just released the official figures. Forty-six Americans were killed during the Gulf War. Forty-six. That's not a war. That's Labor Day weekend on the New Jersey Turnpike. . . .

("Ah-hah HAH, clap clap clap, ah hah-hah ha ha")

"I was thinking about this. I was watching a tape of the *Today Show*. I can't watch it live because I'm doing this program, this piece of phlegm which we hock up every morning. You know, long moments of awkward silence interspersed with chunks of lame comedy that make you pine for the moments of awkward silence. . . .

("ha-HAH!")

"And sycophantic laughter . . .

("Ah-HAH-HAH-HAH!")

"By the way, it's Friday, and as you know, on Fridays we have 50 percent more sycophantic laughter. You remember that song from the '40s: 'Sycophantic laughter, ba-da, ba-da-da . . .'

("Ba hah-hah")

"I'm a little tired, a little poofed by the end of the week, so my friend, my good friend, my brother-in-law, my next-door neighbor, my common-law wife,

("HAH!")

"College Boy stops by and helps out Dr. Blob and Carl, who stopped trying to laugh and suck up to me in 1981 on the advice of their union shop steward. Isn't that right, boys?"

"I'm sorry, Dan, did you say something?"

(Snort)

"Hey, Danny, keep it down, we're trying to read over here."

("HAH! ha-HAH! Ah ha ha ha . . .")

"I'm gonna guess what you're reading is not a rave review of Tuesday's sketch about Mayor Dinkins. What was it called?"

"Man-Dinko."

"Bravo. Could you boys maybe get a few more people writing me hate mail? Good Lord, do I look like David Duke?"

("Hah!")

"I don't know. Take off the sheet."

("Bah-HAHHAH!")

"Good one, Carl. Nice going. How to wait till quarter of ten on Friday. You know, a lot of people say David Duke still has ties with the Ku Klux Klan, but he's changed. Now, he has a much higher thread count. . . .

("heh")

"Higher *thread count.*

("Whoa-ha ha HAH! Eh-hee, hee heeeee!")

"Can I continue? So, I'm watching a tape of the *Today Show* and I figured why I never made it as a serious broadcaster on television. Radio, pfft, of course, radio. Come on, who we kidding? What's the sense talking? Radio, I'm Brando. And we're talking Streetcar Brando, Waterfront Brando, not that landmass that was in *The Freshman* last year. But television? I had some shots, you may have heard me refer to them from time to time."

"Jesus."

"That's enough, Blob. Anyway, I had some shots, but nothing happened. I blamed my management, the networks, the fabric of society, general envy. By the way, that was one of my favorite Richard Widmark World War II films, *General Envy*. Richard Widmark, Dan Duryea as the wise-guy sergeant, Millie Perkins as Anne Frank . . .

("Hah hah hah. Hee-hee, hee-hee.")

"Anyway, I never really understood why. And I'm watching the *Today Show,* and it hit me. I finally figured out why I never made it on television. I have no gums."

"You have gums."

"No, I'm talking the big TV broadcaster gums. Like Katie Couric . . .

("Jesus-ahaHAH!")

"Have you seen these things? Have you seen them? Look what I'm asking. Come on. It looks like she's got a quarter-pound of Boar's Head ham wedged up there. . . .

("HAH-ee-hahhaha")

"I never noticed her gums."

"What are you, nuts, Carl? Now, as we all know, and people have taken great pains to point out, I am not the best looking man in New York."

"You're not the best looking man in this room."

("hah-HAH!")

"Well, that's only because it's Friday and College Boy's here. . . .

("Sheesh, hah.")

"And Katie Couric couldn't be cuter. Cute like a puppy. As a matter of fact, I'm sure she has some puppy in her. . . . There's the teeth, which are fine, and then like a half-acre of slick, pinkish meat, which is stopped only by her nose. Don't get me wrong, it's attractive.

("Da-HAH-ha!")

"Do you remember Pinkish Meat? You're a little young, College Boy, but he played alto sax on the original version of Brubeck's 'Take Five'. . . .

("Ha-HAH! 'Take Four,' right? Hah!")

"Hee, hee! College Boy! Nicely done. That would have worked so much better if your mike had been on. . . .

("Heh heh-HAH!")

"I'm telling you, I really think I'm on to something here. Show some of them gums, things start to happen for you in that business. Gums and, of course, a huge head.

("Hah hah heh-ha.")

"So that's my problem. My gums aren't big enough. And I'm not corrupt."

"Enough."

"What?"

"Not corrupt enough, Dan."

"Carl, don't make me turn College Boy's mike on. . . .

("Yeah!")

"See what I did there? I threatened you. I have to do more of that, on a bigger scale. I have to do more threatening—Is it do more threatening or be more threatening? But I'm not good at this. As you know, I'm an extremely private man who shares a modest life with my two dogs, Zinfandel and Zima. . . .

("Hah-HAH-hahaha.")

"I work a blistering twenty-hour week here at the station, and that's with only twelve weeks off, mind you, and the rest of the time is devoted to my two charities, Big Cousin, for boys who don't have a cousin, and Veal on Wheels.

("hahahahahahahahaha . . .")

"What I'm saying, and if you follow what I'm saying, call in and explain it to me, is that I need some tips on how to become really corrupt. Just a complete, greasy sleazebag with his hand in everyone's pocket."

"How is that going to help you make it in television?"

"Good point, Carl. There's nobody like that in television. What was I thinking?

("Ah-hah! HAH-HAH, ha!")

"But I've really got to step this thing up. Like I said, I need some tips. And I'm willing to ask for help. Who's the most corrupt person in New York?"

"Gotti?"

"Well, ahem, let's not go nuts here, Carl. Just because a man makes ten billion dollars a year from one 1,500-square foot plumbing supply warehouse in Queens, that does not necessarily make him corrupt. . . .

("Hah heh heh. What about The Dirt King?")

"The what? The Dirt King? Did you say The Dirt King? Who is this guy?

("He controls—")

"Turn on his mike!"

"He controls, he controls the all the dirt in Central Park. If you want a hole filled in on one of the fields, you have to pay him."

"Come on."

"And that's to get the good dirt, which he has locked up in different locations."

"Is he with the Parks Department?"

"No, the Parks Department reports to him."

"So, he's with the city government."

"No, he's just The Dirt King."

"I think we may have a winner here. The Dirt King."

"Hey, what about Man-Dinko?"

"Dr. Blob, there's still time to fax that joke over to K-Rock before Howard goes off the air. . . .

("Dah-HAH-HAHH!")

"Just attach it to the end of your résumé."

("Hahahahahaha" clap clap clap, clap clap clap)

"Is this what you mean by doing more threatening, Dan?"

("HAH hah-HAH!")

"I think I'm really on to something here. I do this thing, where I'm the Corrupt Guy, for a couple of months. Okay, a year. Then, when I have enough money—you see where I'm going with this. And if you see where I'm going with this, call in and explain it to me—when I have enough money, I fly down to Mexico and get a gum job."

("Hah hah HAH hah HAH HAH!")

"I think you can still get a gum job in Times Square for twenty bucks."

("Bah-HAH!")

"Carl, in the Yellow Pages, under 'stations, radio,' I'll need the fax number at K-Rock. . . .

("Heh heh HA-heh")

"Does The Dirt King have a name?"

"Yeah. Ern—"

"What? Commercials, then news? Are we coming back? No? Tell Pretty Pipes, what's his name, Larry?"

"Jason."

"Tell Jason to hang on for a few minutes. What do you mean no? Then take it out of Sportsphone Boy's show, what's his name, Larry?"

"Steve."

"Right, Steve. I can't believe it's the first original thing we've done here in five years, The Dirt King, and we've got to go. Just give us his name, College Boy.

("Ern—")

"TURN ON HIS GODDAMN MIKE! What? We're hopelessly late? This blows. Five seconds? This is Dan Drake on WLLS, Wheels-102. See you Monday. Stay tuned for pinheads. . . ."

("HAH! —")

• • •

"Is this fucking guy for real?"

"The Dirt King?"

"Yeah."

"Yeah, he's a real guy."

College Boy walked down the corridor at WLLS with Dan Drake, trying not to watch everyone scurrying to get out of their way.

"And what's his name?"

"Ernest Giovia. Ernie G."

"Can we get him on the show?"

"Are you fucking kidding me?"

"Would it kill you to ask him?"

"Danny, I don't know when I'll see him, and besides that, he's a complete asshole. If I said, 'Hey, Ernie, Dan Drake wants you to come on his morning show. How about it?' He'd say, 'Lemme ay-ask you someding. What size pants do you wear?' And I'd say why, and he'd say, 'I wanna know where you get your balls big enough to ay-ask me someding like that. When you tooawk to me, you're either asking for dirt or asking for a rake up you ass. If you're asking for dirt, it's five hundred dollars. The rake is free.'"

"Seriously?"

"I heard him say this like five years ago to a friend of mine who asked him if he was going to put down some foul lines before July 4."

"Well, you gotta do this guy."

"The Dirt King."

"Yeah, with that voice."

"When? Next Friday?"

"No, Monday."

"I got ball Monday morning."

"What time?"

"Ah, ah, nine."

"You're lying. I'll get you out of here by eight-thirty. But you've got to be here by five-thirty so I can look at the script."

"What script?"

"Just give me two pages of stuff this guy says, like the rake up the ass thing, and questions for me. No more than two-three pages."

"Danny, I can't write."

"You think any of us can? It's not writing, it's radio. 'Man-Dinko.' You think that was writing? 'Let me fill your pothole with my mayoral probe.'/ 'Oh, Man-Dinko . . .' I swear, I'm going to kill Carl and Blob. That's the kind of crap you come up with in college after you've run out of bong water to drink. Man-Dinko. Give me a break. Once a week, I go through this shit with them. 'Oooh, Dan, this bit is great. It's edgy stuff.' Okay, I say. You boys are the producers. If you really think it's funny and clever, go nuts, but this time you're taking the call from the station manager. You're answering the mail. You're taking responsibility. 'Yeah, yeah. Sure, Dan.' They finish putting the thing on cart thirty seconds before we go on, I don't get to hear it, and I have to trust them. I mean, twelve years we've been doing this show. So, I trust them. They throw it to me. 'And now here's our Wimbledon preview,' I say, and then it's two full minutes of Monica Seles grunting on the toilet. Carl and Blob are back in Nutley by eleven, and I'm here till five, apologizing and trying not to get sued. So, that's the kind of writing that goes on here. Think you're up to it?"

"Really? Monica Seles grunting on the toilet?"

"I've never been more proud."

"Christ, Danny, I don't know."

"College Boy, I don't want to have to bring this up, which means it's the next thing I'll say."

"Not the charity softball thing. . . ."

"No."

"Good."

"But do you remember the charity softball thing?"

"No."

"When I saw you playing for the WABC guys."

"And I wasn't supposed to be playing for them."

"And you weren't supposed to be playing for them. And you hit those two bombs, even though you weren't supposed to be playing for those pricks. And I never said anything."

"Danny, you never shut up the whole game."

"What did I say?"

"'Isn't José Canseco late for his other game? I thought Curtis Sliwa was just a singles hitter. Isn't Davey Johnson going to be angry at you? Who's your favorite idol besides yourself?' Shit like that."

"Well, it was all for charity."

"Meanwhile," College Boy played what he thought was a good card, "you've completely forgotten about the last inning."

"My triple?"

"Your shallow pop fly that I pretended to lose in the sun so you could run the bases."

"And you ran behind me trying so hard to tag me."

"But I just wasn't fast enough, was I, Danny?"

"Eat me, College Boy."

"Speaking of which, who gave you the banana after your blood sugar dropped off the table from running the bases?"

"So, I owe you now?"

"No, the once a week thing here is enough."

"Yeah, sorry to pull you out of the park, the only place you're comfortable."

Ugh, he would have said. But instead: "So, you want two pages of stuff this guy, The Dirt King, has said?"

"Jesus, just make up some shit, and I'll fix it here. Just get it to me a half hour before we go on. Can you stop thinking about yourself and help me out here a little? Would it kill you? Would it fucking kill you?"

"Is there any money?"

"You're trying to fuck me, aren't you, College Boy?"

"No, Dan, I'm not trying to fuck you. But there's a lot of people here who'd like to see you go down."

"AH-HAH! HEE-heeeeeee! Very funny. Like to see me go down. What a complete lunatic I am. Hah! Don't worry, I'll take care of you. Hey, where you going?"

"I gotta do laundry."

"I remember doing laundry."

("Heh heh heh . . .")

7

So this was what they meant by slowing down. You stare at a six-inch TV, read *New York Magazine* when you specifically asked for the *New Yorker*, and three times a day walk numbly up and down a too-short corridor wearing twenty-year-old loafers with no backs and a cotton tunic incapable of closure, like you're rehearsing for some bizarre Commencement. One hand coaxes the light metal pole on wheels that holds your catheter bag. The other hand, with no pocket to hide in, looks for something to do. Like the rest of you.

He shouldn't have yelled at the nephew. But why didn't the kid shave? How long could it take to shave? And maybe the line "Put on a coat and tie when you come to see me" was a little excessive. No. Maybe the line after that, "Have a little class. Stop cutting corners. You've been doing that for years and people are beginning to talk." Maybe that was excessive.

Thirteen days without a drink. Pretty damn good. Two days since the large black nurse quit. Good. He was well rid of her. She was okay at first, but as is the case with service people, once you ask them to actually do something, that's when the trouble starts. One thing. Asked her to do one thing. An errand. Ten minutes. She couldn't do it. Not allowed. Who's she working for anyway? And where does it say "No liquor allowed"?

And what was with that enormous duffel bag the nephew had? Well, at least he got off a good line there: "I see you got your orders. When do you ship out?" Hey, wait a minute. How many bottles could he fit in that duffel bag? Who needed the black woman anyway? The nephew would come through for him. The kid always did.

Now, if only he'd come back with the duffel bag. If only he'd come back, period. Shouldn't have yelled at the nephew. Why had he done that?

His prostate swelled some more. This time with justified indignation.

The kid should know better. He let it slide the first two visits. Wednesday, the kid shows up at nine-thirty, nine-thirty at night, sweaty, wearing an Angels cap. Unshaven. With that duffel bag. Nobody told him he was coming. Nobody. You'd think he would have called. So, he let that go. Played the noble host. Would have offered the kid a drink, but he had nothing around. The large black woman. What was her name? Gertie? No, Sadie. There was nothing around to offer the kid because Sadie wouldn't run one errand for him. Ten minutes. Not allowed. Well, that's the world today. No real service people. You want Gertie or Hattie, you get Sadie. He was well rid of her. He'd yelled at her, too. Something like, "Stop extorting me with that bedpan and give me some answers!" She had it coming. Like the kid. Came by yesterday morning with croissants and marmalade. Sure, those you can bring in. He didn't say anything about the Angels cap, or that he kept calling him "Uncle Mort." Or that he couldn't stay for lunch. The kid had an audition.

The kid. He had to stop calling him the kid. He had to be in his thirties by now. Dottie's kid. Harvey. He never called him Harvey. Okay, once. Years ago, at P. J. Moriarty's, when the kid first came to New York. They were having the carrot salad, and he said, "Harvey, see if you could use your powers of urban diplomacy to get us some dressing." And the kid gave him a look, and then a big, "Sure, Uncle Mort." Really leaned into the "uncle" part, too, like a stroke on the varsity eight. That look he figured out immediately. That was the "don't call me Harvey" look. He caught it. Pretty good for a guy who'd never had any children. Pretty damn good. And he was right. "Do me a favor. Drop the 'uncle' crap, kid. You're in New York," he said when the kid came back with the waiter and the dressing. That's when the kid said nobody called him Harvey. And that's when they made the deal. No "Uncle Mort" for no "Harvey." Even up. If there was a third party introduction involved, okay.

What could you do? But the deal. That they stuck to. When the kid called him, he'd say, "Hi, Mort. It's your sister Dottie's kid." When he called, it was "Mort Spell here. Is this Dottie's kid?" Or "Is that you, doctor?" Or "Am I speaking with the Eastern Seaboard's number one expert on the AFC Central?" Or "Is this the Sid Fernandez Weight-Loss Clinic?"

When they were together, they didn't call each other anything. Just went back and forth. Laughs and drinks and sports talk and carrot salad. Not like Alistair Cooke. Everything with him was, "Well, you know, Morton. . . ." Like he'd taken a one-day course in how to keep someone's attention. There was nobody else at the goddamn table! Please. Alistair Cooke. Another one who hadn't called. Well, he was well rid of him, too.

Maybe that's why he yelled at the kid. The kid kept calling him "Uncle Mort." Like he was visiting a sick relative. Maybe the kid was nervous. Let's give him the benefit of the doubt. He was nervous. He *was* visiting a sick relative. Okay, so the kid misfired. But even if you are palsied with fear, even if it's the terror that clouds your vision like a thumbed box score in the *Times,* there's no reason to show up at a hospital, a goddamn hospital, unshaven and without a goddamn jacket and tie.

Honestly, if they hadn't hidden his clothes, he'd be wearing a jacket and tie. Well, a jacket. The black woman, Sadie, she'd hidden his clothes. The other day, before she quit. He asked her to leave so he could dress for dinner, and she handed him the bedpan and walked out into the corridor. Always with the bedpan. That she could do. He put on his white J. Press pinpoint oxford shirt and the mid-tan tweed jacket from some long-extinct Madison Avenue clothier who'd finished the first draft of Chapter 11 around 1962. He eschewed the year-round gray wool trousers from Chipp. Bad fit. He'd have to get the pants let out for the catheter. Enzo would take care of it. Maybe the black woman would run the pants down there for him. Do that one goddamn errand. He didn't see any "No Alterations Allowed" sign around. In fact, he thought that's what Sadie was doing at first, when she stormed in and grabbed the trousers off the bed. Then she demanded the jacket and shirt and he figured she was going to have Enzo give them a whack with the steam. But when nothing came back two hours later, then nothing still a day later, he knew she'd hidden everything. That's when he came out with the "Stop extorting me with that bedpan and give me some answers!" line. Pretty good line. Pretty damn good line, for a guy who hadn't had a drink in eleven days. Now thirteen. That was the worst thing he said. The worst thing he said that he understood. (There was another remark, something about being robbed on the subway—"And don't think you're home free on this, Hattie!") She threw the tie at him before storming out. Good. Now the tie hung around his bare neck, knotted with a serviceable four-in-hand, resting on the cotton tunic. Good-looking tie. Pheasants on a navy field, symmetrically stained. All in all, he had handled the whole thing pretty damn well.

And then the kid came in this afternoon, *avec* stubble, *sans* croissants, and said, "Hey, Uncle Mort, what's with the tie?"

At least I'm wearing a tie, you wise-ass cur. Had he said that? Well, you could hardly blame him for snapping a bit. *Go climb a gum tree, kid.* Right, that he said. *I might find your concern touching, I might even have you talk to that Viennese thief, Liebenthal.* Was Liebenthal Viennese? *Perhaps you might ask Sheila how I'm holding up.* No, he hadn't mentioned Sheila. Couldn't have. Nobody knew. *Get a second opinion on the state of my prick.* Oh no, he had. *I might even tell you a few stories about your mother, Dottie, who goes through life as if she's giving the world two strokes.* Giving the world two strokes. That was good. He had to remember that. *She's never finished one goddamn thing I've written. "Oh Mort, what a gripping first paragraph. . . ." But I shan't. I find it hard to give a thoughtful response when you clearly care more about the black woman. By the way, I know you gave her the croissants.* What? *You've shown up the last three days like I'm something to check on the way to your locker. For Christ's sake, kid, pick up a razor at the goddamn gift shop! You're making me look bad. And put on a coat and tie when you come to see me. And especially when you plan on having this discussion with me.* No, that wasn't excessive. *Have a little class, kid. Stop cutting corners. You've been doing that for years and people are beginning to talk. Close the door on your way out. I'm well rid of you today.* That was.

"Mr. Spell?"

"Yes?"

"I'm your new day nurse. My name is Marva. Your nephew hired me. I'll be here one to ten every day. I'll stay till midnight tonight, because I'm starting so late."

"Narva?"

"Marva."

"And you're from someplace in the Caribbean?"

"Yes, Trinidad."

"Do you know the runner Hasely Crawford?" He had been there. Hasely Crawford, running in Lane One, had upset a strong field to win the hundred meters at the 1976 Olympics in Montreal. He had pulled away in the final forty meters and stumbled across the finish line, ahead of Jamaica's Don Quarrie and the robotic Russian Valeri Borzov, the defending Olympic champion. The World's Fastest Human hatched from a country of perhaps but no more than a million people. It was the first gold medal of any kind for Trinidad and Tobago.

"I know him because everybody in Trinidad knows him. I was already here in the States when he won. But he's still a hero."

"You're looking awfully well today."

"Thank you. Your nephew told me to tell you he'll be here tomorrow morning at nine." He should warn her not to steal the croissants when the kid shows up. Wait. She won't be here. "And he wanted me to give you this."

"You open it."

A tie. Hunter green, with a silver-stitched rendering of some building. MSH. Where was this place? It was too modern to be a university, too large for the clubhouse at Forest Hills. Christ, why does everything look like a goddamn synagogue? The same building was on the plastic bag. MSH. Mount Sinai Hospital. The kid had bought him a tie in the gift shop.

"You dropped the note on the floor."

"That would be great if you could pick it up and read it to me. I lost my glasses."

"They're right here on the floor."

"Hasely Crawford is damn lucky to have a friend like you."

"Sorry, they were all out of razors."

"You can borrow mine."

"No," this new black woman said. "That's what the card says."

He'd laugh later. The tie fit well. Pretty damn well. He'd show it to the other patients on his late afternoon walk, which should be around now.

"I think I'll take my walk now, Marva."

"Would you like me to go with you?"

"No thank you."

"Would you like me to take your other tie to the cleaners?"

"That would be damn nice."

"Anything else you need while I'm out?"

The loafers felt good.

"I think not."

8

"Before we get into the situation with your uncle, I'd like to talk about our last session."

"That was five months ago. What about if we talked about the stuff we couldn't talk about for a year because all we talked about was this fucking move of yours?"

"We could talk about that."

"Really?"

"You know, Harvey, I'll be honest. I'm still very hurt that you left me."

"Fuck."

Saturday night. College Boy on the 6:05 Hackensack local. New Jersey Transit had lost big coin on this voyage. $5.80 round trip, and College Boy virtually had the entire coach to himself. It had been just him, Bagzilla, three girls snapping their gum and a guy poring over a shopper for the Sears in Hackensack like he was six credits short for his degree in Craftsman Tool Appreciation. College Boy had flipped through the *Daily News*, which on Saturdays was half the thickness of the Sears shopper. Friday's 9th at Belmont—9-1-7, $432.20. Fuck.

Saturday night, and College Boy is on the bus to Teaneck. Going back into The Tank. Tank was College Boy's word for psychotherapy. Tank, being short for Think Tank. Shrink was everybody else's term.

Well, at least Dr. Bettles had agreed to see him, even if it meant shlepping way the hell out to Teaneck. Considering all those

Saturday mornings when he had overslept or opted for Felipe's nine A.M. money game, this was damn thoughtful. A turning point in the relationship. Bettles's word, not his. There was no "relationship" between him and Bettles. None. Just like every other relationship College Boy had ever had.

Maybe Dr. Bettles was just curious about Uncle Mort. Maybe he was being thoughtful because he hadn't seen College Boy in five months. Maybe he was being thoughtful because College Boy had finally broken down and was coming to him. Gary Beitleman of Teaneck, New Jersey.

"What's with Beitleman? I thought your name was John G. Bettles."

"Bettles is my New York name, Harvey."

"Christ. So, what do I call you?"

"Doesn't matter. Remember the time you got angry at me about your name, Harvey?"

Early on, Month Three of their nine-year dance, College Boy had asked Bettles to call him Suss. Suss Sussman, the nickname that had buried "Harvey" through Curtis Junior High, Lynn South, and college, after which he moved to Central Park and became College Boy. Suss. "Hey, Suss." "How's it goin', Suss?" "Get laid last night, Suss?" He loved being College Boy, but he was still okay with Suss.

For the next six months, this had dominated every session. *"Why do you prefer to be called Suss?"/ "I just do."/ "Why is it so important?"/ "It's not. I just prefer it."/ "Don't you like being called Harvey?"/ "I just don't like the name."/ "Your parents gave you the name Harvey. Tell me about that."/ "You'll have to talk with them."/ "I'd rather talk with you, Harvey."/ "I'd rather be called Suss, Dr. Bettles."/ "But why do you prefer to be called Suss?"*

"Okay, call me fucking Harvey!" he'd snapped, and with that, he had given Bettles the first of four buttons to push over the next six-plus years. Buttons two, three, and four became: *"Remember the time you got angry at me when I asked about your gambling?" "Remember the time you got angry at me when I asked how long you thought you could play softball?"* and *"Remember the time you got angry at me when I told you I was moving my practice to Teaneck?"*

•

"Go with 'fuck.'"

"What?"

"Before. When I said I was still hurt that you left me, you said 'fuck.'"

"Aren't we supposed to be talking about *my* feelings? Isn't that the fucking idea?"

"Fucking idea."

"Christ. I come out here to talk about my uncle and we're right back where we were five months ago!"

Actually, they were back where they were a year ago. Five months ago, Bettles had moved to Teaneck. But this was after seven months of trying to convince College Boy to join him out here. At eighty dollars a session. When he'd only paid twenty-eight at the Astor Place Institute for Psychotherapy. For two sessions.

"Go on."

"Every time I tried to talk about things that were bothering me, like some old thing with Rachel, you kept bringing it back to fucking Teaneck. *'Why don't you try it in Teaneck?'* Like the Chamber of Fucking Commerce."

"You mentioned the chamber of commerce in our last session. After you broke my ashtray."

"Before."

"Now, which one was Rachel again?"

"She worked at Macy's. Wanted us to move in together."

"Yes, I remember. The one who rolled off you and said, 'Well, *I* came.'"

"No. That's Trish. Rachel I still keep in touch with. We're still friends."

"Tell me, Harvey, when was the last time you shit in your pants?"

Good Christ, College Boy thought. Not *this* again. With a ringer's logic, College Boy's strategy with Bettles had always been to keep fouling off pitches to prolong his half of the inning. For he knew that once he stopped, Bettles would quickly and irrevocably change the subject. He'd yak for thirty-five minutes about Rachel's latest disappointment, pause to reload, and Bettles would stop lighting his pipe and ask, "How long do you look in the toilet after you flush your shit?" He'd give an unedited account of the time his father forgot to pick him up at the bus station, and he sat there three hours with 101-degree fever and no money until a janitor woke him up and gave him a dime to call home, and Bettles would wait a respectful two minutes before asking, "Does your mother still give you an erection?"

"The last time I shit in my pants? You mean, other than right now?"

"You still see Rachel?"

"Every once in a while. She has a baby daughter named Callie. Sometimes I stop by with a present. Stay for an hour or so."

"When you saw her last, what did she say?"

"Same shit. *'Take off your cleats. This could have been yours, Suss. When is College Boy going to graduate? What are you so afraid of? Uh-oh, it's been an hour. You don't want to get too attached. Better take off. Time to run. I wish I could have been more patient with you, Suss. But I'm happy now. I like my life.'* That kind of stuff."

"You called it shit. 'Same shit,' you said."

"So what if I did?"

With Bettles, it was all shit and Mommy, Mommy and shit. Like some Freudian Cuisinart, Bettles processed anything and everything into a bowel movement or an Oedipal moment. For the sole purpose, College Boy was sure, of pissing him off.

"Nice girl."

"Too nice for you."

"I didn't say that."

"No, I did."

"Can we talk about my uncle?"

"You met her on a train?"

"Trish was the train. Rachel I met at a wedding. A guy on my Bayside team."

"This was . . ."

"A few years ago."

"I'm surprised you went. You so rarely socialize. College Boy is on many teams, but he is a part of no team. He is a team unto himself."

"Yeesh."

"The groom was . . ."

"Jimmy Boyle. Catcher. Could never get the number of outs right. *'Okay, two down, no, I mean, nobody out.'*"

"This Jimmy Boyle. Did he look like your mother?"

"Christ. You know, this is the shit that stopped me coming here in the first place."

"'Shit' again. Interesting . . . I thought you stopped coming because I moved to Teaneck."

"That too."

"I remember. You were quite angry when I told you I was leaving the Institute and moving to Teaneck."

Men are usually equipped with one of two seminal delusional thoughts. The first is "She digs me," the second, "I can take this guy." Some men are outfitted with a deluxe set, which contains the same two thoughts but with interchangeable genders: "*He* digs me."/"I can take *her*." College Boy had never entertained either bon-machismo. Until nine years ago, when Dr. John G. Bettles hunched into the waiting room at the Astor Place Institute for Psychotherapy and creaked out his name, "Uh-ah, Har?vey Suss?man?"

I can take this guy, thought College Boy.

This delusion lasted all of one session. Session number two began with Bettles asking, *"Why don't you lie down on the couch?"*

"Why?"

"This is therapeutic analysis."

"Nobody told me."

"I'm telling you."

And College Boy lay down, Bettles out of sight behind him, and went back to being a man who never thought, "I can take this guy."

"Yes."

"'Yes' what?"

"I was angry when you told me you were moving to Teaneck. But really, I was pissed at how we stopped doing anything here. All of a sudden, it was zero fucking progress."

"Did Rachel know anyone at the wedding?"

"Just the maid of honor. They hired her the last minute when the singer fell through. Jesus. A voice like that and she's buying housewares for fucking Macy's? I never got that. You do what you do best."

"Like you playing softball."

"Damn right."

"Remember the time I asked you how much longer you thought you could play softball?"

"No."

"You got very angry."

"Yeah, well . . ."

"She had a nice voice?"

"Unreal. You know that song from *Godspell,* 'On the Willows There'?"

"No. Perhaps you'd like to sing some of it."

"What? Um . . . Anyway, she sang the shit out of it."

"Right, 'the shit out of it' . . . Sex with Rachel must have been strange with her rolling off you and saying, 'Well, *I* came. . . .'"

"That was Trish. Most of our first date she spent telling me how her mother couldn't understand how she could have sex before marriage, and most of the second date explaining how all that stuff about her mother was something she had to get out of the way before we could have sex. We did it six times that first night. She said she was going to call in sore to work Monday. People like that, like her, they just talk about doing shit like that. The next morning at the Seventy-seventh Street subway, the train was full. I said, 'Let's wait.' What did I know? But she was gone. She jammed herself into the last car with all the other people on their way to work. I couldn't handle that. Took a nap on the platform for an hour and a half. A cop woke me."

"Six times? Impressive."

"You think so?"

"You certainly do. You took great pains to mention it."

"If I thought it was impressive I would have mentioned it eight fucking years ago. It's just what happened."

"You must have felt the need to show her up after she had rolled off you and said, 'Well, *I* came.'"

"That was Trish!"

"Your mother's name is Trish, isn't it?"

"No, it's Dottie. Dottie Sussman."

"That's a first."

After eight-and-a-half years riding the couch, College Boy finally felt he was making something resembling a bit of progress. He had come to understand that he and Trish or he and Rachel had not hated each other; they had a *dynamic* they were *playing out.* He had considered exploring the notion that being a softball ringer fed both his *grandiosity* and his *infantilization.* He had even allowed for the cringe-inducing possibility that spending two hundred dollars a week trying to hit the triple at Belmont was the *fiscal* equivalent of *diarrhea.* Of course, attending the twice-weekly fourteen-dollar sessions at The Institute, as he had for the last two years during the softball off-season, was the fiscal equivalent of a really good morning dump. Just ask Dr. John G. Bettles, API Therapist/Arbiter of All Things Fecal.

"So, then she gets a big promotion, I told you this, and we go out for Indian food at this place overlooking the park. My last hundred dollars. She grabs my hand and says, 'Your patience has paid off, Suss. I'm finally making enough for us to get a decent place.' I didn't panic all that much. I mean, I don't think she saw it. I just told her I wasn't interested. Just like I wasn't interested in getting whatever a real job was. She said, 'Well then, fuck you.'"

"Was that before or after you came back from the bathroom?"

"What?"

"Go on."

"No, that was it."

"It's been, what, five years now? And you stay in touch?"

"Sure."

"She called you?"

"Yeah, but I called her back. And, like I have to tell you, it wasn't easy. Still isn't."

"And no relationships since then?"

"Um . . . not counting Robin Byrd? No."

"You seemed reluctant to talk about Trish."

"No, you kept changing the subject."

"Like now."

"What do you want to know?"

"Was she pretty?"

"Gorgeous. Like a young Phoebe Cates. We met in the smoking car on a train to Greenwich. What a voice. She would say the word 'man' like *'mahhhhnnn.'* Great. Sexy as hell. I just sat there and let her yak the whole ride. I'm a good listener. What does that take?"

"We're a little hostile, Harvey?"

"What do you mean?"

"That it doesn't take much to be a good listener. You're implying that I don't know what I'm doing."

"Shit."

"There's that word again. So, she rolls over, says, 'Well, *I* came,' and then dumped you. Is that correct?"

"No. I told you. We dated for two years. Casually. It was like I was on call. Couple times a week I'd take her out so she didn't have to be single. Never had to pay, which was great. Never had to call her, which was insane. Unheard of. She'd call me, always twenty-four hours in advance, and I had to be available. She was a fashion photographer's assistant, so she had all kinds of connections. We got in everywhere. Didn't even mind the softball ringer thing. In fact, she thought it was cute, unless a game ran long and screwed our chance of getting a table at the Mudd Club or Café Central. Then it was, 'What the fuck is wrong with you?' Actually, with Trish it was pretty much always 'What the fuck's wrong with you?'"

"What was wrong with you?"

"I don't know. And I don't know why, but one day she called—it was *'The Tunnel. Ten o'clock. Pick me up. Get some new shoes'*—and I just said no. It was in the winter, too. Off-season, so I could have used the free meal. But I just couldn't do it anymore. Couldn't take the whole thing. It became too much of a charade, even for me. Like a competition over which one of us was less willing to commit."

"You play ball, Harvey. What the hell is wrong with the Mets?"

College Boy rose up from the couch with a "What are you, fucking soft?" look on his face. For Bettles, the present normally served little purpose, except when he said, "Our time is up." The past, that was where the action was. The future was where the money was. In Teaneck. At eighty dollars a session. Pay to the order of Gary Beitleman. Bettles scribbled on his notepad, then tore out the page and handed it to his patient.

"Here are the names of two geriatric psychiatrists. They're both very good. I'm glad you came." College Boy stuffed the paper in his pocket. "This situation with your uncle must be very tough on you. You're reaching out, and I don't know if you've ever reached out to me."

"Well—"

"But our time is up."

"Come on."

"You're right. We've got another minute." They faced each other. "Harvey, I don't want you to take what I'm going to say the wrong way. You have the emotional maturity of a four-year-old who's embarrassed by his own penis. You are covered with the feces of your gambling, which we conveniently never discuss. You avoid relationships, preferring to wipe yourself with people. I've counseled convicts, rapists, and murderers who are more in touch with their feelings toward their mother than you are. Analysis is your only hope. Real analysis. Four days a week. In Teaneck."

Like those cops everyone's heard of, but nobody actually knows, Bettles had beaten him up and not left a mark. He pushed the four big buttons, and found a few new ones. . . .

College Boy sat on what was left of a dilapidated bench, waiting for the next bus back to Port Authority as darkness fell without a clue over Teaneck, Vienna-on-the-Hudson. The bus wasn't due for another 10 minutes. He could still do it. He had time. Cross Teaneck Road, walk back two blocks to Gary Beitleman's house. Drop his Gap Easy-Fit khakis and unload right there. Just a huge shit. Leave a dump that would be the envy of every Rottweiler and bullmastiff in the Teaneck-Hackensack-Ridgefield Park metroplex. A turd the most hardened municipal worker would refuse to clean up. *Pay to the order of Dr. John G. Bettles.* Now that—to come out here and drop a load on Dr. ShitMommy's lawn—that might make riding New Jersey Transit for four sessions a week worth it.

But Harvey Sussman, College Boy everywhere else, stayed put. Sitting on a bench slightly less broken than himself, like a guy who still had choices. A guy who wasn't, as some thought, down to his only hope.

9

When he finally put the key in the bottom lock, it was 10:45. The return bus had coughed into Port Authority by nine. And although he was cross-country-drive tired and still sticky with the Teaneck-Bettles glaze, College Boy kept his next appointment and met Julio Rentas at the Improvisation on Forty-fourth and Ninth. There, on College Boy's 50 percent ringer discount, they ate, drank, and smoked weed with the comics to celebrate Papa J's forty-sixth birthday. The same thing they had done four weeks earlier to celebrate Papa J's forty-fifth birthday.

He left the door open as he dropped Bagzilla on the couch he stopped folding out in 1987. He walked seventeen feet and retrieved a twenty from the tape slot on his VCR. That left eighty dollars in Hiding Place A. And he was back out the door. If he caught every break, he could be home from Mort's apartment with groceries in time for the first shitty sketch on *Saturday Night Live.*

Before their dress code dust-up in the hospital Friday, Mort had given College Boy a vague bunch of keys (*"You'll find the right one. You're a bright man."*) and a short list of things he needed from his apartment. There were three items on the list: his checkbook, which could be found in one of the four drawers in his desk; the half-eaten box of Droste chocolates in his refrigerator; and any and all pairs of glasses which College Boy found in his desk or refrigerator. College Boy was more than up to the errand. He knew what a big step it was for Mort to ask anybody for help. And he knew an uninterrupted Valium run when he saw it.

College Boy started on the wrong end of Mort's key chain and went through two Medecos, two Schlages, and three Russwins before hitting upon a toothless, nameless piece of glint that looked like something a tourist might dig up at an Apache burial ground. Thank God, Mort was one of those Manhattan deadbolt decoyists, who used the other locks on their door for display purposes only.

Mort Spell liked to joke that he lived in a "one-and-a-half bedroom." He said that hoping you'd say, "There's no such thing." That's when he could say, "Well, I passed out in the hallway between the living room and my bed last night and got eight hours sleep, so I'm counting it." He wasn't lying, and he wasn't wrong. The six-foot by three-foot hallway, besides giving the impression that Mort had tunneled from his studio into another apartment, was damn cozy. Mort loved the hallway. Eddie Foyer Jr., he called it. Or the Aisle of Black. The walls were lined with gushing thank-you letters from President Eisenhower, Joe DiMaggio, Bob Cousy, Mrs. Don Budge, Bing, and Ernie Hemingway. Letters that could only be read in daylight, between 11:00 and 11:20, when the sun elbowed in and no one was there. Except Sheila.

College Boy was still young enough to think this floor plan (seven-by-four-foot terrace, five-by-five-foot closet, 14.5 cu.ft. refrigerator) was high-living, but wise enough to know the place was not worthy of half the writer of Morton Martin Spell. The kitchen had barely the counter space to fit four wire-handled Chinese take-out containers. The living room horseshoed three hair-oiled chairs, a couch, and a kidney-shaped desk around the threadbare landing strip on the oriental rug where Mort practiced his golf swing. The bottom third of the bathroom door smiled from its thrice-daily collision with the toilet bowl. The bedroom seemed spacious, but only because you had to enter through Eddie Foyer Jr. . . . It all explained Mort's standard reply when he was asked why he never married. "I never found a girl who could fit in my apartment." If only College Boy could come up with a line that clever. Five years now, and he still had no line. It might be easier to come up with a girl.

College Boy was too busy being grateful all the lights were on to think it was odd. He grabbed the Droste chocolates and found the checkbook and three pairs of glasses in the first desk drawer he opened. He heard the moaning on his way to the bathroom. At first, he thought it was coming from him, excited over his impending Valium score. Then College Boy realized he didn't squeal. Never. Not even when the triple came in at Belmont. He looked diagonally through Eddie Foyer Jr., through the open bedroom door, and saw a woman he assumed to be Sheila, riding some headless, shoulderless man like she had a shot at place money.

He stood there—five seconds? a minute?—until he frightened her. Nah, he hadn't frightened her. She gave a quick surprise intake of air, smiled, and raised her left index finger like she was about to get off the phone. The headless guy didn't move until she said, "Uh-oh . . ." By then, College Boy was closing the front door. That's when he heard, "I thought you said this was your place."

Well, now.

College Boy absentmindedly ate two Droste chocolates as he walked crosstown and tried to be outraged by what he had seen. Somewhere between Madison and Fifth, he came to this conclusion: It's damn tough, impossible, to be outraged when you have an erection.

She was probably close to forty. If she was any older, then Bravo. Author, author. This was an eternally great-looking woman. Not gorgeous. Just great looking. The body was well thought-out. It moved like an athlete and a restless kid. The same breasts they probably teased her about in ninth grade, the slim God's gift of a waist, and a gym-free round ass. Five, maybe six pounds overweight, but not an extra half-ounce of self-consciousness. The ample nose a dumb girl would have begged Daddy to fix. Eyes that acknowledged you were watching diagonally across the hall, but could still act surprised. The smile was easy, experienced, piercing. And red hair. The official hair of great-looking women. Red. Who cared how much help she got out of the bottle? Lots of red hair. And all of it worked.

And, even though at the time they weren't doing anything except elegantly supporting the bouncing rest of her, good legs. Good wheels.

Well, now.

College Boy heard Sheila's first message during an *SNL* commercial break just after he put away his Sunday provisions. The voice did not quite fit the rest of her. The voice sounded a little too beaten. A little too misunderstood. The voice sounded like it might be married. Her second message came around two A.M., while he was in conference with Robin Byrd. This voice was calmer, resigned. And the apology sounded more like an intro to an apology. It made nice background music to the flickering Ms. Byrd. Nobody ever apologized to College Boy. Well, no woman. He slept better than great.

The best part about Morton Martin Spell's being in the hospital was what it did to College Boy's Sunday. It killed it. By the time he returned home from the doubleheader in Riis Park, showered, shaved, put on a coat and tie, and made it up to Mount Sinai, it would be seven P.M. By the time he returned home for good, it would be at least ten-ish. Maybe half past ten-ish. And just like that, Sunday would be dead, and another week come and gone without self-confrontation. Beautiful.

Now it was nine-thirty A.M., College Boy still had an hour and a half before his life was forced to resume. It felt like the only hour and a half he'd had all week. The quarter pound of nova and two half-sour pickles from the Regency Deli that had somehow remained intact during his crosstown walk home. The Sunday *Times,* fresh orange juice, and three everything bagels from the deli downstairs. For $6.50, he could do-it-yourself two nova and onion sandwiches. He had the onion in his refrigerator. Onion and a half-jar of Skansen Matjes Herring, which would be mated with the third everything bagel when he got home from the hospital. Mort had hipped him to Skansen Matjes Herring ("By the way, kid, Matjes is Danish for 'Jew,'" he'd say.). And buying the *Times* Saturday night. And all the isolation-soaked bliss of a Manhattan Sunday.

The only nonsports conversation he remembered having with Uncle Mort was at P. J. Moriarty's right after he moved to New York and just before their first cocktails arrived. The conversation was three lines. Mort insisting that he read Alexis de Tocqueville's *Democracy in America,* him saying okay, and Mort saying, "I think that bastard Pat Moynihan stole our drinks." The only thing College Boy retained from de Tocqueville was the notion that there was no such thing as true freedom because one was always forced to make a choice. Unknowingly at first, then knowingly, and then finally settling in with the arrogance of delusion, he had been proving de Tocqueville's point in reverse for the last fourteen years. Nothing but choices, and in the end true freedom, which turned out to be College Boy alone.

He would not tell Uncle Mort what he had seen. That he knew. What he would tell Sheila, Mort's cleaning woman, the next time he saw her—that he hadn't worked out yet.

The nova was a color that College Boy had never seen. Past sunset, heading toward coral. Not orange. Shit, the orange juice. That was orange. Not red. The tomato he thought he still had in the refrigerator. That had been red, and it hadn't been there for two weeks. College Boy's refrigerator was everything Bagzilla was not. Onion, matjes herring, Smuckers Butterscotch Sauce. Iced tea steeping in a Gatorade bottle since the S&L scandal. That was it. Not even the jar of desiccating mustard every unmarried man was required by law to have.

His machine clicked. Another message from Sheila (*"Please call me. I have to talk to you. There's a very simple explanation. . . ."*) That made three.

Wait. He had seen that color red before today's nova. Last night. 301 East Sixty-fifth. Sheila's hair.

(*". . . Your uncle knows all about this. . . ."*)

Really, College Boy thought with his mouth full. My uncle knows that you fuck guys in his apartment while he's in the hospital? Guys who, judging from expressions like, "I thought you said this was your place," don't appear to be your husband? Exactly what part of the housekeeping process was this?

(*". . . So, all I'm saying is if you could just give me the chance—"*)

"Hello, Sheila."

"Oh, ah, hello, Mr. Sussman."

"What's up?"

"I'd like to come over and talk to you."

"Well, I'm on my way out."

"What time do you have to leave?" Nobody ever asked College Boy that question. It stunned him into the truth.

"Eleven."

"Well, I can be over there by ten-thirty. I live on Roosevelt Island, right by the tram. You're on the East Side, like Mort?"

"No, West Fifty-sixth. One-sixty-three."

"Well, I'm sure I can be there in twenty minutes. This will only take a second, but I'd rather not do it over the phone. Okay?"

"Uh, okay."

"Terrific. So, I'll see you soon. Do you need anything?"

"Yeah," said College Boy. "Some cream cheese."

So, scratch that shit about another Sunday without self-confrontation. But then, maybe this meeting might not turn out to be a total loss. Maybe College Boy could wise-guy Sheila into helping him with his current problem. Mort still needed a new shrink. The piece of paper with the phone numbers of Bettles's recommendations was now a crumpled crouton floating in some N.J. Transit chemical toilet. And Mort's former psychiatrist, Dr. Meyer Levitz, could not be reached. He was not out of town, just sulking. Some other doctor had decided to take Mort off Valium after he arrived at Mount Sinai. Without consulting Dr. Meyer Levitz. The nerve. Forget the fact that Mort had showed up with enough Valium in his system to get Liza Minnelli through a long weekend. Not to mention that when the admitting nurse asked him if there was any physician they should contact, Mort said, "See if you can get ahold of Linus Pauling. I'd like to play with him." When Dr. Levitz finally found out, three days later, from Sheila, where Mort was, he threatened to sue the hospital for interrupting his patient's "treatment." The world famous, time-tested, "Fifty Milligrams of Psychotropics a Day for Ten Years to an Old Man" treatment. Instead, he waited a week and sent Mort a letter charging him for two missed sessions and giving official notice that he was no longer responsible for his mental health.

College Boy found out about the letter yesterday, Friday afternoon, when he called Dr. Levitz from the lobby of the Albert

Einstein Pavilion at Mount Sinai, moments after Mort had kicked him out of his room. Something about not shaving. Levitz hopped on the line immediately because his secretary thought College Boy was a referral. "Mr. Sussman, I can see you at five-thirty today. I'll need a credit card and the phone number of your pharmacy," he accommodated. That was until College Boy's second line, "I'm Mort Spell's nephew."

"Your uncle is no longer a patient of mine. I sent him a letter terminating our treatment."

"So, you won't see him or talk with him?"

"It's out of my hands."

"But *you* ended it. He still thinks you're his psychiatrist."

"Your uncle is a very sick man," Dr. Levitz said. "I don't know what he's doing in that hospital."

"What do you mean?"

"I'm sorry. That's confidential."

"Well," said College Boy. "What can you tell me?"

"He still owes me for two sessions."

"I'm sure he'll take care of that."

"Tell your uncle I'm very disappointed in him. He should have called me."

"He was delirious."

"And whose fault is that?"

"I don't know. He was in severe withdrawal from Valium."

"Excuse me. What did you just say?"

"He was in severe withdrawal from Valium?"

"Why doesn't this fucking tape recorder work? Shit! Mr. Sussman, will you testify in my negligence suit against Mount Sinai Hospital?"

"Ah, no."

"Well, in that case," said Dr. Levitz, "I'll have to cancel your five-thirty appointment."

There is no rejection in life quite like a canceled shrink appointment, even if that appointment never existed. Or especially if it never existed.

The downstairs buzzer jumped his heart. 10:17. Forty-three minutes before his life was forced to resume. Plenty of time. For the first time, ever, College Boy was not polite. He didn't ask. He opened the door and saw the half-smirk behind her sunglasses. And he pulled Sheila in by that slim God's gift of a waist and threw his mouth at her. She dropped the cream cheese. He was right. He knew what she had meant last night, with the smile and the index finger in the air. She meant "*you next.*"

There was no condom in Bagzilla, but College Boy found two in his medicine cabinet, in the empty Sucrets box next to the twenty-dollar bill. Hiding Place D. He used them both on Sheila. Before the second invasion, Sheila playfully said, "Well, well. Young stud." Well, it had to be playful. He felt neither young nor studlike. What he did feel was the rare relief of being in the company of someone, who, like him, enjoyed what had happened but couldn't wait to get the hell out when it was over.

There was some time in between, not a lot, for her to sit up on the couch, fold her T-shirt in her willing lap and explain what College Boy had seen last night. The true story. Occasionally, okay, a couple of times a week, she, ahem, entertained. Referrals only, please. She had access to six apartments in the building, the six apartments she cleaned every week, and with the tacit help of the doormen and her overly forthcoming employers, she always knew who was home and who was away. She'd been using Mort's apartment since he'd gone into Mount Sinai. She felt bad. She'd been working for him two days a week for seventeen years since her mother, Helga, got sick and turned the business over to her. The cleaning business. The other business had only been up and running for, ah, six years. And until last week, she had never used his apartment for anything that didn't involve a vacuum and disinfectant. She felt bad. Had she said that? Well, she did.

The second time took nice and long, and they both marveled at how sweaty two people could be on a Sunday at 11:04 A.M. . . .

Shit.

College Boy hustled Sheila and himself out like a guy who just said, "Quick, it's my wife!" He tucked his Prospect Pros jersey—Number 2—into the gray softball pants and rezipped Bagzilla as they rode down on his building's idea of an elevator.

"Ah, this is embarrassing," he said. "Do I owe you anything?"

Sheila laughed. Dusty. The laugh of the great-looking woman.

"Of course not," she said. "You're family." She kissed his perplexed cheek. "I've given your uncle a blow job every week for the last five years. I never charged him. I'm certainly not going to charge you."

Well, now.

College Boy's life resumed, ten minutes late. Another Sunday, this one killed in an altogether different way.

10

"You're looking awfully well today."

"So are you, Mr. Spell."

"Did you see my tie?"

"You weren't wearing it when you came in."

"When I came in here?"

"Yes."

"And just run by me what I'm doing here again."

"We're going to do the TURP procedure. On your prostate, Mr. Spell. We're going to take care of you."

"I've had this done already."

"When?"

"Nineteen sixty-two, after Laver won Wimbledon."

"That was your appendix."

"You're awfully bright. Not many people know Laver won Wimbledon in 1962."

"We're going to put you under now, Mr. Spell."

"Run what day it is by me again."

"It's Monday morning, Mr. Spell."

"And what time is it?"

"Just after six."

"Do they know we're in here?"

"Yes."

"Good. That way we'll get our drinks. What did you order?"

"I didn't order anything."

"Right. I ordered for you. I hope you like gin."

"I'm more of a vodka man."

"Very well then. We'll switch glasses."

"Mr. Spell, I want you to count backward from one hundred."

"Thank you, but I'd prefer to count backward from Prime Ministers."

"That's fine."

"Don't help me unless I ask you."

"Don't worry. Okay, start up on the ketamine, John . . ."

"I asked you not to help me."

"Sorry."

"There's the new boy, John Major, then Thatcher. Well, that's over. . . Sir Anthony Eden . . . no, Wilson, Heath, Wilson . . . Harold . . . Harold . . . Anthony Eden . . . Churchill . . . Clement Attleeath . . . Heath . . . Churchill . . . Churchill . . . Churchillannnn . . ."

"Okay, I think he's under."

". . . MacMillan. Harold MacMillan . . ."

11

"And now it's time for a brand new feature on *The Dan Drake Show*. Something we call 'Ask The Dirt King.' That's what we call it now, but we're going to need something snappier. I don't want people thinking they've dialed up a seed show on NPR. Now, before we begin, I've been instructed to read this disclaimer: The Dirt King is appearing on this program without remuneration. The Dirt King is here to answer your specific questions about dirt and dirt-related issues as they pertain solely to the Heckscher softball fields in Central Park. The Dirt King does not work for the New York City Parks Department, the New York City Parks Department works for The Dirt King. The Dirt King is on no prescription medication that he is aware of. The Dirt King is appearing on this program without remuneration. The Dirt King has no criminal record in New York State. Do not ask The Dirt King about New Jersey, Florida, or New Mexico. Ask only about dirt and dirt-related issues as they pertain solely to the Heckscher softball fields in Central Park. If you have a problem with The Dirt King, it is your problem. If The Dirt King has a problem with you, it is your problem. Please refrain from beginning any question with the phrase 'Your sister.' No freaks. Lastly, The Dirt King is appearing on this program without remuneration. . . . Okay, sir, you have a question for The Dirt King?"

"Yes, if I was playing softball in Central Park and I needed some dirt to fill in the right-handed batter's box, where would I find you?"

"Can I ay-ask you someding?"

"Yes."

"Do you know me?"

"Ah, no."

"Then why are you trying to find me?"

"Well, I need some dirt."

"Can I ay-ask you anudder thing?"

"Yes."

"How do you play softball with that rake up your ass?"

"There's no rake up my ass."

"That's cause you didn't try to find me, *capisce?*"

"Okay, next question."

"Yes, I have a dirt-related question. How do I get dirt stains out of a pair of cotton Gap chinos?"

"Lemme ay-ask you someding? Where did you get this dirt from?"

"Heckscher Field, Diamond #2."

"Okay, step one, set your washing machine on the warm cycle. Step two, use nonchlorine bleach. Step three, remove that rake from your ass."

"Next question. Yes, the gentleman that sounds like the first gentleman we heard from."

"Ah, this is difficult for me to bring up, but last month, I severely twisted my ankle on Diamond #4 when I stepped in a six-inch hole running to first base. The umpires immediately moved our game to another field and ten minutes later, a man who I could still recognize in a photo array showed up and filled in the hole. My question is, can I sue the city?"

"Yeah, go nuts, knock youselves out. Even though this is technically not a dirt-related question, I do know a little bit about such matters as they pertain to those things in these areas. And lemme educate you, you—hey, over here!—that it is extremely difficult to file a lawsuit against the city with a rake up your ass."

"Okay, next question. Sir?"

"Yes. Last week, the charity I do volunteer work for had its annual fundraising softball game. You were nice enough to drop off some dirt on Diamond #1 after I gave you five hundred dollars cash. Unfortunately, you forgot to leave a rake."

"Did you check your ass?"

"No . . . okay, thank you."

"All right, that's enough. Join us next time for 'Ask The Dirt King.' We're horribly late for the news. . . ."

The only time Dan Drake was horribly late was when he was enjoying himself. The other way you could tell if Dan Drake was enjoying himself: He talked to you during the news break.

"College Boy," he said to College Boy, who still looked behind him to see if Dan Drake was talking to someone else. "We blew that one question. When the guy said 'How do I get dirt stains out of Gap chinos?' why didn't you say, 'Hey, you should be ay-asking yousself's how do I get that rake out of my ass?'"

"Nah, too forced."

And here's another way you could tell if Dan Drake was enjoying himself. If he talked about what happened during the news break when he went back on the air.

It would be 9:25 by the time College Boy unhooked himself from the WLLS studio building. Famous people, people like Dan Drake, all share a common trait. They tend to say, "Hey, where you going?" to people who aren't famous, aren't like them, and definitely have somewhere to go. And the people who definitely have somewhere to go wind up staying.

Of all the things Dan Drake liked about College Boy, and "Ask The Dirt King" was maybe 17th on a list of 20, what he liked best was that College Boy had somewhere to go. Which made him the only one at *The Dan Drake Show* who had somewhere to go. He didn't have time to let the icy good-byes from Carl and Dr. Blob, workplace sorbet, settle. It was 9:25, the Performing Arts League game started at 10:00, and unless he somehow discovered a way to change clothes and stretch in a cab, for the first time in five years, College Boy would be running into a game cold. Ice cold.

With nothing to do in the cab but project, the intricacy of the softball scenario College Boy tried to visualize made "Ask The Dirt King" seem childish and one-dimensional. His only hope was that his team, the Improv, would be away. That the game would start at least five minutes late. That the three guys ahead of him in the order would have long at bats but not reach base. That the only balls hit his way in the first two innings would be hit no more than six feet to either side of him. That he'd only bat once in the first three innings. And that, oh that this be so, he'd jump on the first pitch and hit a rocket right at someone so he could jog a few strides and give the big smile and finger-wave and the "I'll get you next AB, you SAG-carded clown" at the pitcher, then clap his hands for the other guys to pick him up with a big enough inning to get in ten minutes of lunges behind the bleachers.

That was the plan, and it almost worked out that way. Almost, like when your horses in the triple finish third, fourth, and fifth. That kind of almost. The Improv was indeed away against Warren Robertson, first place Warren Robertson, but that was the end of things breaking right for College Boy. The game started on time, and the wisdom of the first three Improv batters swinging at the first pitch, while yielding two singles, escaped him briefly, which is how long College Boy had to put on his spikes and adjust whatever appendage, real or aluminum, he could get to. The line drive he carved at the left-center fielder with one out in the first was handled like the editing of *Heaven's Gate.* Without discretion. College Boy had to bust it all the way to third against the better judgment of his hamstring. He felt it tug as he slid into third. The tug said "From now on, do *not* get on base unless you have to."

And College Boy listened. It was 5–5, one gone, in the top of the seventh when he hit the left field tree on Diamond #4 for a ground-rule double, a merciful jog into second. But then Manfrellotti, the last guy on the Improv who could drive him in, hit an outside pitch high and deep to right. High enough and deep enough for College Boy to try. Try to tag and score from second. He hadn't done it in a game since last August. Ten months ago, or, if you really want to get technical, another lifetime.

Everything held up. The hamstring screamed but the wheels remained axled, even when he juked the Warren Robertson catcher as the throw sailed up line. He had to start his slide late, and the sidestep veered him toward the pitcher and away from the right-hand batter's box-ditch-abyss, which saved his ankle and forced his body to stylishly bypass home plate, instead reaching back to whisk it with his hand. 6–5, Improv.

But College Boy lingered, which he never did. His right hand in particular, which lay seductively behind him just past the plate, and just long enough for the catcher to think he still had a play. That must have been what happened, because the next thing College Boy heard was himself saying, "Fuck! Get off! Get off!"

His Improv teammates, led by Manfrellotti, rushed to mob College Boy and triumphantly escort him back to the bench. But it was a two-part project: Rolling the 180-pound Warren Robertson catcher off his right wrist, then picking him up. The first high-five confirmed College Boy's diagnosis. Sprained. Badly. At least a week off. He might as well have left $850 under the catcher. That fucking load.

You can wise guy your way around bum wheels, but the wrist, the right wrist—the wrist that triggers the buggy-whip torque of your bat and unhinges the slingshot follow-through of your throwing arm—well, there is not enough cocky misdirection in Softball Ringer Nation to act like your goods are undamaged. You can play with pain. You are not supposed to play with an injury. Starting now. Right fucking now.

And by right now, College Boy meant immediately following the bottom of the seventh.

Any doctor will tell you when you play with an injury you run the risk of aggravating it. Or reaggravating it. It's an interesting term, "aggravating." It seems like a hopelessly cute way to describe the possibility of making a physical condition worse. Another euphemism from the profession that expunged the word "pain" from its lexicon and replaced it with "discomfort." Doctors. They can be so, so, what's the word? Aggravating.

The point is, you don't play with an injury because you run the risk of really fucking up your shit. College Boy knew that. He knew better. And as he trotted out to left-center field for the last of the seventh, he added this moment to the ever-growing list of situations about which he knew better. Belmont triples. Bourbon and Valium. Ambition. Red-headed allure.

"Hey, College Boy, what are youse, fuckin' nuts?"

It sounded like his conscience, but louder, dumber.

"Lemme ay-ask you someding. You don't think I don't own a fuckin' FM radio?"

The Dirt King, over on Diamond #6, was tamping what was left of the area in front of the pitching rubber.

"You don't think dat?"

College Boy waved like he'd get back to The Dirt King. Waved with his right hand. Just enough to tell himself, "ow . . ."

"Yeah, yeah. Go ahead and wave. You keep doing that 'rake up the ass' shit, like it's a fuckin' joke. You tell that half-a-fag DJ this ain't no fuckin' joke, College Boy. This is my life. I am that fuckin' guy."

College Boy stared straight ahead. The Warren Robertson cleanup hitter cued a 2–1 pitch foul.

"Hey," said The Dirt King, "not so fuckin' funny anymore, huh?"

The catch was a great one. In College Boy's top ten all-time? No, but up there. And it might have squeezed into elite leatherdom had it been the last out of the game, but it came with none down in the seventh, which still left the tying run on second with two harmless fly balls to Manfrellotti to come. That robbed some of the drama. The rest was robbed by The Dirt King laughing on Diamond #6 and yelling, "Hey, College Boy, gimme a quartah to call the fucking wagon."

There are three ways to catch a sinking line drive: the sliding basket, the flat-out dive, picking it up on the first hop after it drops in front of you. Option number one, the sliding basket, is not available on a ball hit to your left or, as in this case, your right. Option number three is never available when you're getting fifty bucks a game. That leaves what it leaves.

The one thing with which an injury cannot compete is instinct.

College Boy launched himself at the end of a furious forty-foot run. Fully extended, the Rawlings Pro 1000 infielder's glove, too small for everyone else, backhanded and agape. The flat-out dive. Option number two, like the number forever on College Boy's back. A flying hypotenuse between ball and earth. His timing, like his math, perfect. Instinct. Just as it was instinct to try and cushion his post-catch landing with his hand. His right hand.

Broken. Not just aggravated or reaggravated. Livid.

Still on the ground and pre-writhe, College Boy backhanded the ball with his gloved hand, like a jai-alai player at the end of the one match point that isn't fixed, to Rackham, the shortstop. And they almost caught the runner scrambling back to second. Well, that's what it sounded like. When your eyes are blind with pain and shut down like the rest of you, indefinitely, all you're left with is what you hear. A safe call from Butch the ump. An "aw, fuck!" from Rackham. Butch calling time. A couple of guys who sound like they're standing over you asking if you're all right. Someone who sounds like you saying yes. A laugh-dipped pierce from The Dirt King about calling an ambulance. The fucking wagon.

The worst part about The Dirt King's remark was this: It wasn't a bad line. Funny, actually. Funny on levels The Dirt King wasn't aware of, and he was the one who fucking said it. Just the notion of The Dirt King asking College Boy for a quarter, of *anybody* asking College Boy for a quarter then, just when the pay window had slammed, pinning his right wrist to the sill. The sign on the window, if a metaphor ever needed a sign, read CLOSED FOR THE SEASON. Funny. Not funny like *"Did you hear about the Polish guy who froze to death at a drive-in? He went to see* Closed for the Season." But the same punchline.

He did not want an ambulance. Maybe if it had been something with his knee. Maybe if he hadn't been College Boy. A dozen times a year, the wagon would sideslip down the dirt path behind Diamond #5, an unmarked detour off Central Park Drive, as if a couple of EMTs were trying to skip out on the check at Tavern on the Green. Onto the paved, too narrow walk that encircled Heckscher Fields. Ambling to wherever a small crowd of players had gathered and told each other, "Don't move him!" Always, fucking always, saving its screaming lights and blinding sirens for the last ten feet of the trip. Why? If you could answer that, you could figure out why, when the FBI goes undercover, it's usually under the cover of those bright orange jumpsuits with FBI stenciled on the back.

The wagon usually came in a half hour. Forty-five minutes if it was a new driver looking for the dirt path behind Diamond #5. Ten years ago, the first year of the ten o'clock Performing Arts League, College Boy's first year with the Improvisation, one of the bartenders at the club leveled the first baseman from Art New York on a close play at the bag. It was three years before they added the outside bag at first for the runner to prevent this kind of collision, but there's a good chance this was the incident that prompted the legislative response. The bartender broke the Art New York guy's leg, clean. The wagon was called and the small circle of players saying, "Don't move him!" gathered. The Art New York guy kept banging the ground, then covering his eyes to moan. In the middle of the wait, one of the Improv comics, Lawrence, wandered up to the circle, knelt down next to the Art New York guy, waited until after a particularly torturous moan, and asked, "If it doesn't work out, can I have your mitt?"

That's the first and last thing College Boy thought about whenever he saw someone down and waiting for the wagon. The first thing was Lawrence's line. The last thing was whether he had the balls to walk over and deliver Lawrence's line. He never did. He wasn't a comic, and a ringer can't be funny like a comic. A ringer can only be funny like a ringer.

Once a year, he tried to be funny like a comic. He'd get up on stage at the Improv on a winter Sunday night just before closing, with three or fewer customers and most of his fellow teammates in the audience, and stay up there just long enough to play in the Performing Arts League without being hassled. The Performing Arts League required all of its teams to have some connection with the performing arts, and all its players to have some connection with their respective teams. So, if you were going to have ringers, they had to be bootlegged. College Boy didn't mind the ritual nonsense. He always made it through the drill without remorse or exemption, which really distinguished him from the comics. A couple of minutes, a couple of new old jokes, more than a couple of bourbons, and enough clumsiness behind a microphone to reaffirm annually that he was funny like a ringer.

Manfrellotti and Rackham helped him off with his spikes, but ran screaming when College Boy asked if they'd help him carry Bagzilla up to Tavern on the Green. Butch the umpire opened the Advil bottle and unscrewed the cap on the Gatorade citrus cooler. College Boy popped four, took a swig, then backed it up with three Tylenol with codeine, and thanked Butch for keeping the part about his wrist being broken to himself.

He would wait until 1:05, when he could tell Buddy from Columbus Restaurant that he would be unavailable for today's 2:00 game. He'd either show Buddy his wrist or tell him he had a big audition. Screw it, he had an audition. And then he would wait until 1:15, when maybe, just maybe, Papa J would show up early enough to twist him up a couple of bon voyage joints for his cruise to the emergency room.

Papa J showed at 1:14. Some guys just live right.

"What's the closest hospital," he asked the cab driver, "Roosevelt, right?"

"Yeah."

"Then take me to Mount Sinai." And College Boy started giggling, like the second man who discovered irony.

Irony. Funny. Funny like a ringer no longer.

12

If anyone asked College Boy what happened to his arm, he would use the line from *The Big Fix,* the first movie he saw eleven times in a month on HBO. Actually, the private eye, Moses Wine (Richard Dreyfuss, post-Oscar, pre-rehab), had a different answer every time about the cast on his right arm, depending upon who asked him. But the exchange College Boy loved was with the ultra-left lawyer (Fritz Weaver. No, wait. Nicolas Coster. Fritz Weaver played the ultra-right evil industrialist.) who he tracks down teaching at Berkeley:

LAW PROFESSOR: What happened to your arm?

MOSES WINE: You know, same old stuff. Couple of cops hassling a black kid.

That's what he would go with. *Couple of cops hassling a black kid.* That was good. Maybe something different when Uncle Mort asked him. *If* Uncle Mort asked him. Don't forget, this was the same guy who thought the catheter on his hip was somebody else's gym bag. But just in case, College Boy waited by the nurses' station on the fourth floor until he came up with something to say about the cast. Arm-wrestling with Marty Glickman over a locker at the NYAC? No. *Indian* wrestling with *Jeane Kirkpatrick* over a locker at the NYAC. Okay, all set.

"Mr. Sussman, what happened to your arm?"

"Uh . . . I broke my wrist going for a ball."

"You make the catch?" Sheila asked. College Boy looked at her in full furrow. "Sorry. Wonder Boy, right?"

"College Boy."

"Who's Wonder Boy?"

"That was the bat in *The Natural.*"

"Robert Redford, right?"

"Yeah."

"Well," Sheila said, pulling her sunglasses to the edge of her nose, "honest mistake."

College Boy had to laugh, had to take her off the hook on which she had never really been.

"How is he?"

"Redford?"

"Give me a break here, Sheila."

"He's still out. They wheeled him up from surgery about an hour ago."

"He had the surgery?"

"Yeah, I thought you knew," Sheila said. "He called me last night at midnight to tell me to bring in his checkbook."

"But I gave him his checkbook last night when I visited him." College Boy refrained from adding, "You remember, I picked up the checkbook when you were converting his apartment into Mustang Ranch East." For a lot of reasons, mainly because it didn't occur to him until Sheila started talking again.

"That's what I told Mort, but he said, 'Well, I have to pay you and Dr. Levitz before the starter can hold my tee time, so you might as well come in.'"

"How much was the check for Dr. Levitz?"

"Five thousand dollars," Sheila said.

"He wrote a check to that guy for fucking five thousand dollars!"

"Actually, I did." And then Sheila explained how when she had come two hours ago, Mort's room was empty except for two checks and a note on his sliding tray table. The checks were signed in the same unsteady hand as the note, which read: *Sheila: Please make a check out to Dr. Levitz for five thousand dollars and to yourself for five hundred. I will testify on your behalf in court. Mort. P.S.: There's another hundred in it for you if you can find my tie.*

Sheila had decided to wait until Mort was wheeled up from surgery to ask if this was really the way he wanted to do things, but that had been over an hour ago. He was in, but still out. Deeply. Although, at one point, she thought Morton Martin Spell might be awakening when she saw him spring bolt upright in his bed and exclaim, "Ah! Sir Alec Douglas-Home!" before sliding back down. Alec Douglas-Home, whoever that was. Probably another guy who had a five-thousand-dollar check coming.

Sheila ended up making out the check to Dr. Levitz and stuffing it in the blank stamped envelope that not enough women keep stashed in their purse. She got Levitz's address from a NYNEX directory assistance operator who wasn't supposed to assist her that much. It was purely for confirmation. She had the address pretty well memorized from fifteen years of mailing Mort's bimonthly checks. She dropped it in the box across Madison in front of the Guggenheim Pavilion when she went to stretch her legs, her good wheels, before coming back to take one last look in on Mort, hoping he'd be with it enough to write out her check. She saw College Boy at the nurses' station when she got off the elevator on the fourth floor and had plenty of time to duck back in and slip between the closing doors of confrontation. But she knew he'd be caught off guard seeing her again, so soon. And if you knew Sheila, you knew she couldn't pass that up.

"You mailed the check already? How could you do that?" College Boy asked.

"I had a stamped envelope in my purse."

"Blank?"

"Yes."

"I never heard of that."

"Are you impressed?"

"Yes . . . I mean, no," said College Boy. "I mean, what is he doing paying that piece of shit five thousand dollars?"

"He probably owed him half of it, and gave him the other half in good faith. That's what Mr. Spell does with doctors."

"But I let the guy go!"

Sheila smiled quizzically. "Did Mort tell you to do that?"

"No."

"Are you making those decisions for him now? College Boy?"

"No, just that one so far. I'm hoping to work my way up to where I'm writing fucking checks for him."

College Boy was gang-shushed by the fourth-floor nurses' station. Sheila grabbed him by the elbow just past the city limits of his cast and led him fifteen or so feet down a less trafficked hall. She whispered unmistakably.

"Three things. First, I've never done anything for your uncle I wasn't told to do." College Boy smiled.

"Ah, I mean, I haven't handled anything of his I wasn't supposed to handle." College Boy looked like someone trying to keep a straight face who was sure he wasn't. He said nothing, just enough for Sheila to say, "Shut up!" She knew any other attempts to rewrite this line of reasoning ("Ask Mort about the *job* I've done.") would come off as yet another encore at the Theatre for Single Entendre. She'd move on to point two, and she knew he wouldn't mind, just as he didn't mind her hand on his elbow. Still.

"Okay, second. Judging from all the visitors he's had, it looks like you and I are all he's got here in New York. If you would like to do this alone, be the nephew, that's fine. I'll respect that. I don't know what your plans are, but that's a tough gig. That's a tough gig with *two* arms."

"I don't know," said College Boy. "I'm a little overwhelmed right now. I didn't plan on being here till tonight, but then I thought, hey, wouldn't it be funny to break my wrist, get it set here, and pop in for a visit? You know, one-stop shopping."

"And I'm sure you didn't expect to see me."

"No."

"Okay, so that was a surprise."

"That makes two if you're scoring at home," he said.

"And if you're scoring the surprises accurately, that makes it 2–1," said Sheila. College Boy hung his head as she let go of his elbow and started to walk back toward the nurses' station.

"What was the third point?"

Sheila stopped. "I think," she said, "we just made it. Tell Mort I was here and I mailed the check to Dr. Levitz. Tell him I'll be by tomorrow. Or don't."

College Boy grabbed her elbow.

"Ask me again what happened to my arm."

"Why?"

"Because I'm asking."

"What happened to your arm?"

"You know, same old thing. Couple of cops hassling a black kid." Sheila laughed. Dusty. The laugh of the great-looking woman.

"Okay," she said. "I'll tell him." She walked away like someone trying to keep a straight face, who didn't give a shit she wasn't.

• • •

Sheila was proud of herself. Not the repartee with College Boy. That was batting practice stuff. She'd been going toe-to-toe with guys since high school, especially the jock and near-jock. They'd ask her out and she'd say, "Sure. How about the library?" and watch them back off. That's when she was Sheila McCall, the most popular enigma at Astoria High. Did she really date black guys, or just like sitting with them in the cafeteria? If she wasn't gay, what was with all the hand-holding with the field hockey players? Was that really her dad lying in front of the Presbyterian Church? Why would she sign up for Mr. Benezia's advanced biology six months after slapping him? Didn't she know she'd be sent home for wearing hot pants? Where in all of Queens did she find Rothman's cigarettes? Why would anyone turn down a full ride to Cornell to pay for night classes at St. John's?

No. Sheila Manning (same girl, same initials, twice the wordplay) was proud of herself for having the courage to break a promise. The promise she made seven years ago when she walked out of Roosevelt. What were her exact words to herself? Who can remember, but it was something close to "I'll never walk into a fucking hospital again. Not even as a fucking visitor."

This was a bright girl. But for all her mental nimbleness, for all the bon-mot elixir distilled from equal parts high IQ and low self-esteem—clarified banter—when it came time to answer the Roosevelt Hospital Emergency Room doctor's first question, "How'd you get the black eye and broken nose?" the only thing Sheila Manning could come up with seven years ago was, "I walked into a door." Jee-sus. "I walked into a door." The Citizen Kane of domestic lies. The doctor was nice enough not to press the issue, other than tell her to "watch out for those doors," which hurt worse than her nose. If it ever happened again, Sheila would be ready. She'd say, "I walked into a euphemism." But it wouldn't happen again. It couldn't, because she was never walking into a hospital again. Not even as a fucking visitor.

When the bandages came off, Sheila was left with the tiniest bump in the middle of her nose. It kept her sunglasses up and gave her uncharacteristically toothsome face 20 percent more uncharacter. The bump, and a round-trip coach ticket to Mexico, would be her entire divorce settlement. And that was just fine. Ivana Trump fine.

The ex-husband, Jerry, backed off like the rare piece of male who knew he'd fucked up. That made twice he'd fucked up. The right cross, and a year and a half earlier, when he'd left Sheila for another man. Johnnie. Johnnie Walker. Yeah, yeah, like the scotch.

Jerry Manning had just enough AA in him, eight-and-a-half years clean and sober, to know when he went back out and picked up again, his word was no good. That's why he knew he couldn't tell Sheila this would never happen again. That's why he knew he had to let her go. This was his path, his journey, and all that righteous twelve-step shit that only makes sense in a church basement. Another place in which Sheila would never be seen again.

It took her just under a year before she could get the people living in her mother's apartment on Roosevelt Island out of their sublet. She kept a room at the women's hotel on Twenty-seventh Street, and when the caged skeeviness was too much, she would take whatever cat-sitting, plant-watering gigs she could get from her cleaning customers or anyone else at 301 East Sixty-fifth Street. Morton Martin Spell's building.

That was a little less than seven years ago, and that's when it had started with the referral clients. Not immediately. Sheila needed time to grieve the end of her marriage while not impinging on the celebration of her escape. So, fifty-six days.

And not on purpose, either. She was set up by Alexa Mulvoy, 16J, who had been asking Sheila to "Let me know when you're ready to hit the street again," since the day she had returned, papers in hand, from Mexico. Alexa, the Widow Mulvoy as she referred to herself, had been living alone at 301 East Sixty-fifth Street for fifteen years, since her estranged husband, Mike, had the bad taste and worse timing to walk off a subway platform two days before *her* round-trip ticket for Mexico arrived in the mail. The Widow Mulvoy had waited twenty-seven days ("Three for every year we were together.") before hitting the street, during which time she converted the second bedroom into a closet and the second bathroom into an office for her cat, Ratelle. So, to her, fifty-six days must have seemed like showing off.

The Widow Mulvoy gave Sheila Manning two numbers. Both Wall Street guys. Sheila opted for "Brad" because the other guy's name, Terry, sounded way too close to Jerry, the ex-husband, and she didn't want the assonance of disrespect. "Brad" (not his real name) met Sheila in front of the Beekman, where they were supposed to see *Once Upon a Time in America.* "Well," he had said, "you were right about recognizing you by your hair." That was all the wiggle room Sheila wanted. "I forgot to feed my cat. My building is right across the street. Do you want to wait here?" Much better than "I walked into a door."

"Brad" walked her into the Fecters' apartment and *Once Upon a Time in America* was seen by sixty-five other people. Most of whom didn't get laid. None of whom got laid twice.

Sheila could try and tell herself that she was equally surprised by the turn of events, but you don't buy a three-pack of condoms at

Tower Chemists across the street from the Beekman because you're worried they might not have them at the concession stand. And you don't bring a strange man back to your apartment fifteen minutes before a movie to feed your cat when it isn't your apartment, and it isn't your cat. Even if there is a cat, it ain't yours.

That was the problem. There was no cat. The Fecters were allergic, which, with a name like Fecter, shouldn't surprise anyone. This was a plant-watering/mail pick-up job for Sheila. The Fecters were in Boca for the entire month of January, like all good Fecters. They had left everything behind, including the cat they did not own. Wrong pad.

Sheila would be honest for the last time. "Ah, I don't have a cat."

"Brad" was suitably relieved. "Thank God," he said. "I'm allergic."

The sex was what you might expect from and with a Wall Street guy: A lot of excitement at the very beginning and very very end and no real credible explanation for what went on or why. The only thing that disappointed Sheila was her own level of cool detachment. Not nearly enough, but that would take some practice. She did appreciate being with someone who didn't pass out after he came. Except for the conversation, which seemed to be required, it was a nice change.

"Now I'll have to take you out for a much more expensive meal than I'd planned," said "Brad" while searching for his second sock.

Sheila leveraged. "No. Just give me the hundred dollars and get yourself a slice."

"What?"

"Come on," Sheila said. "Alexa told you I was a hooker."

"No, never."

"Well, then. I must not have been able to resist myself," she said, and laughed that great laugh. Another line much better than "I walked into a door."

That was it for "Brad," who could now answer yes to the question "Have you ever gone to a prostitute?" on those yearly "Thirty-five things to do before you're thirty-five" surveys in *Esquire*. But "Brad" would turn out to be "John Zero," the original source referral to the dozen or so guys who Sheila judiciously scheduled over the next six-plus years, no more than twice a week. Three times during the holidays or if she wanted to do some remodeling in her apartment. Her real apartment.

She kept the whole operation low-key and her appearance decidedly unescortworthy. Sweaters. Everyday slacks. Low heels. Just enough make-up for any straight guy to swear she never wore makeup. After six, she might throw on a scarf or refresh whatever perfume lay around whatever empty apartment was in play. She'd put on one of three stylish trenchcoats (white cotton, chocolate suede, black leather), her only real surrender to glamour. And then Sheila Manning would leave 301 East Sixty-fifth and go outside to wait, looking like the best-looking over-thirty-five woman headed for the supermarket, which she might have been, or the best-looking cleaning woman on Second Avenue, which she was. All rendezvous took place outside 301 East Sixty-fifth. In front of whatever Northern Italian restaurant was Grand Opening! on the corner. In front of the Beekman. In front of Tower Chemists. Sheila Manning never buzzed a client up to an apartment. Too Butterfield-8. She walked him from wherever they met to the service entrance at 301 East Sixty-fifth Street and they took the service elevator, usually riding with some delivery guy from China Fun or the Regency Deli. The doormen were never directly involved, but she tipped them anyway because that's what you do, even if you ain't a hooker.

After "Brad," her fee jumped to $250 and stayed there, with no cost of living increases. For $250, you got two jumps or two hours, whoever comes first. That line, "whoever comes first," always received the uncomfortable *"Hah, ho, heh, ihhh"* quasi-chuckle from every first-timer who thought he had an idea what the arrangement would be. Sheila liked uncomfortable. The uncomfortable man was the man who did not stay two hours. Which meant just about everyone. Sure, there was the occasional Wall Street wanker who'd realized he had stumbled onto this victimless Valhalla. That he could get laid and forfeit the second go-round for a diatribe about his boss or his wife or the less empathetic hookers in town. When she sensed the end of sex and the beginning of real intimacy—the yakking—Sheila usually suggested they head out for a drink. No sense taking complete advantage of 301 East Sixty-fifth Street. She'd come back to clean up the next day. The drink, by the way, never lasted longer than the end of Hour Number Two. Never.

Guys. The poor things. So misunderstood. All of them equally and in the exact same fashion. What were the odds? Ten years ago, Sheila had been at Catch a Rising Star with Jerry and she'd heard a woman comic do a bit about how you know you're dating a married guy when he has the Band-aid around his ring finger. "Cut myself shaving," the woman comic had the guy saying. And then she added the aside, in her own disdain, "Yeah, my razor doesn't understand me." Sheila loved that line, *"My razor doesn't understand me,"* like she loved few lines. Shit! That would have been perfect to say at the Roosevelt Emergency Room. "How'd you get the black eye and the broken nose?"/*"My razor doesn't understand me."* Then the doctor would have said, "Huh?" He would have misunderstood! It was too perfect. Why hadn't she thought of that? Well, it didn't matter. She wasn't going back to a fucking hospital ever again. Not even as a fucking visitor. Until this.

Five years of free blow jobs to Morton Martin Spell represented his reward for being unlike any man who had been in Sheila's life. Other than that, they meant absolutely nothing.

Sheila was not in the habit of lugging around too many memories from childhood, but going to work one October day with her mother at age five survived like a playground rhyme. She sat quietly at two strange tables, one eye on her crayoned lore, the other on her mother, humming some vague Irishy trill as she glided from room to room, the tumult of her antiseptic wake eventually settling down to the glassy, crisp stillness of clean. Helga McCall made two promises to her daughter: If she sat quietly and watched, the next time, she could be her mother's helper. And if she sat quietly and watched, at four, when Mr. Spell's apartment was finished, they would cheat dinner and head for Schrafft's on Fifty-eighth and Madison. The only thing a five-year-old knows about Schrafft's is that grown-ups become five-year-olds when talking about Schrafft's. Diligent, reserved people, people never known to exaggerate, people like Helga McCall, end up saying things like "Schrafft's is a magic place where angels make the best ice cream in the whole wide world."

By three, Helga was giving ETD updates. Sheila sat with her hands folded and eyes closed, trying not to look at the clock she couldn't read. Her mother began trying to recite the roster of ice cream flavors as she wiped down the roomy insides of the single man's refrigerator. At either quarter to Schrafft's or half-past peppermint stick, the fumbling around the front door lock started. Helga McCall let it go on long enough before saving another false alarm call to Trafalgar Locksmiths. She flicked the knob to the right and Morton Martin Spell came half-tumbling in like the cop who hit crosstown traffic and just missed the big vice raid. He came to a complete stop and returned to his original locked and upright position two feet past the narrow hallway to the bedroom. Eddie Foyer Jr.

"Well, that was too easy," he said.

"I'm sorry, Mr. Spell," said Helga. "I wasn't expecting you."

"Nor should you, and I apologize." Mort Spell saw Sheila for the first time. "I, I, hope I didn't make you look bad in front of your supervisor."

"This is my daughter, Sheila."

"Yes, um . . . Well, I shan't be here long. You deserve an explanation for this behavior. I need, what I need is both those items sitting on this desk here and then I'll be out of your hair. . . . By the way, you're looking awfully well today."

Sheila marveled at how this man treated her mother like he was working for her. And Sheila loved how he looked at her when he saw her looking at him. Frightened. It was a nice change.

"We're going to Schrafft's," Sheila blurted.

"Don't rub it in, kid," said Morton Martin Spell.

"Sheila, don't bother Mr. Spell."

"My mommy says Schrafft's is a magic place where angels make the best ice cream in the whole wide world."

"The angels make a pretty damn good hot dog, too, kid." Mort whisked a five-dollar bill out of his pocket and stuffed it in Sheila's crayon box.

"Mr. Spell, please don't do that."

Morton Martin Spell, dually startled by Sheila's beam and her mother's chagrin, grabbed a pair of glasses and a manila envelope and rushed for the front door. His front door. He poked his head back in, after he'd come up with something.

"I've owed her that money since the end of the war," he said. "Well, good-bye."

The door slammed and Sheila and her mother both giggled like twin five-year-olds. Twin five-year-olds headed for Schrafft's.

She would return to the Guggenheim Pavilion tomorrow during visiting hours. Around lunchtime. She'd bring a couple of hot dogs. Good ones.

13

"You the nephew?"

"Yes."

"Mr. Spell will be discharged Wednesday morning."

"Okay."

"Ten A.M."

"Fine."

"You can pick him up then."

"Okay."

"Or we can put him in a cab."

"No, I'll be here."

"You're very brave."

College Boy would ask the nurse at the admitting desk what that last remark meant later, when he got up the nerve. He knocked on Mort's door with his cast.

"Mort?"

"Oh, for Christ's sake. Those bastards roughed you up too, kid?"

"No, I . . ." The "two cops hassling a black kid" line would definitely be inappropriate here. Definitely.

"Kid, we're going over the wall. Get my clubs."

"Mort, you're being released Wednesday. And you don't have any clubs."

"Right. They're being regripped. I should have them back Wednesday."

"You're being released Wednesday."

"Well, that worked out quite well, didn't it?"

The first thing College Boy noticed was the tie. In a room which by its very whiff made the least convincing argument that its occupant was recovering, one would be hard pressed to find anything sicker than Mort Spell's tie. College Boy couldn't keep his eyes off it, which worked out because it made it seem like he was listening intently. Worked out quite well.

There are many cheap analogies you can make, and feel free to make them, but let's just say this: If Morton Martin Spell's tie was in a museum, several groups would be out front protesting the exhibit.

When did I buy this thing, College Boy asked himself, Friday? Yes, Friday. Today was Monday. Still. How can you do that much damage to one article of clothing in three days? But to be fair, the tie hadn't really been an article of clothing since shortly before lunch on Saturday. It had become a mottled swatch of bacteria basking on a field of defiance.

Mort's tie was now sheathed in plastic, which would be replaced after every meal, just as soon as Mort's hands could be strapped down. What had been a serviceable four-in-hand was now distilled to a straining polyp of silk that appeared trapped by Mort's neck rather than vice versa. It was a knot which could only have emerged from a struggle and could only be removed by court order or decapitation. Okay, maybe not decapitation, but had the Guggenheim Pavilion fourth-floor staff voted, that would have been the overwhelming write-in winner.

Two male orderlies finished cello-wrapping and left just after Mort could begin to try and tip them. And just before he said, "How about those folks at the Saran Wrap Company?"

"Mort, you can't be comfortable," College Boy said.

"Now?"

"Yes."

"I thought you were talking philosophically."

"I was talking about your tie."

"Because if you're talking philosophically, I agree." Mort cleared his cordoned throat. His mouth would frequently go dry from whatever they'd been giving him to detox from the Valium. This old school noose couldn't help. "No man can ever be comfortable. No free-thinking man anyway. I don't know about those jackasses at the University Club, who think I must be mistaken when I say 'Bring me another glass so I can get rid of all this goddamn ice.' Or Red Auerbach, who can eat—"

"Mort, the tie. It's too tight. It looks like you want people to ask you about your tracheotomy."

"I don't, but if they had some manners, they might ask."

"You didn't get a tracheotomy."

"Well," said Mort. "That worked out quite well, didn't it?" He put his hand to the side of his mouth and pointed to the aide, another ample black woman who would have had to have been in another room to be paying less attention to him. "Knows nothing about track and field," he whispered.

"See, I think—"

"You know Bob Creamer?" Mort interrupted. "He wrote the fine Babe Ruth book I loaned you?"

"Robert Creamer, yeah. That was thirteen years ago. I gave it back to you. And I gave you his book on Stengel for Christmas. In '87, I think."

"He wrote that book on Stengel?"

"Yeah."

"He's led a perfect life."

"So?"

"You made your point. I stand corrected," admitted Morton Martin Spell.

"Huh?"

"I'm pretty sure he could be comfortable."

College Boy asked the aide to leave and figured he had about an hour. To think he had any more time would be to admit he had nowhere to go on a late Monday afternoon, and he hadn't had nowhere to go on a late Monday afternoon since March. So he had an hour. He checked the watch he couldn't wear. Maybe he'd have a friend draw a watch on the cast, like Dreyfuss in *The Big Fix*. Who did he know who could draw?

For fifteen minutes Mort talked, mostly about how he wasn't

going to the Summer Olympics in Barcelona because he didn't feel like getting shoved by "those cretins" from NBC in Spain. Australia, well, that would be a different story. He didn't mind getting shoved in Australia. Better weather, nicer people, great golf courses, and they didn't have television there yet.

"Mort, I think they have television in Australia."

"You might want to check on that, kid."

Television had not come to the island continent when Morton Martin Spell was there for the 1956 Games. And that's where he was now. Melbourne. November, 1956. Just about the furthest point on the globe from a bed in the Guggenheim Pavilion. (Actually, the furthest point would be Perth, Australia's western port, but Mort had no business there. Then or now.)

Mort looked past College Boy and saw runners easing into blocks for the first heat of the first event of the decathlon, the hundred meters. There was "the fine Negro" Milton Campbell, silver medalist at Helsinki and back in the decathlon only after he'd failed to qualify for the 110-meter hurdles. Young Rafer Johnson, the world record holder nursing an injured left knee, would be in the next heat. So would Johnson's teammate from UCLA, C. K. Yang, now wearing the elegant white singlet of Taiwan. Due up to the starting line were a couple of Russians, Kuznyetsov and Palu. But Mort was savvy enough to know if either was going to be a factor, it would always be the Soviet with the more difficult last name. So, he'd keep his eye and eraser on Vassily Kuznyetsov. He and Palu were keeping each other company in a remote corner of the infield, just past the pole vault runway. "Their heads are down, like the world hates them." Thirty-five years later, Mort still spoke in the present tense.

The decathlon is ten events sadistically spread out over two days. Mort made it through recounting the first five events in just under thirteen minutes before falling dead asleep.

• • •

The nurse at the admitting desk gave College Boy a pair of scissors.

"You gonna cut that tie off, aren't you?"

"He's asleep now."

"You're very brave," she said. Again.

"Why do you keep saying that?"

"Honey, did you get a tetanus shot?"

"No."

"Then," the admitting nurse laughed, "you can't do this." She called behind her, "Tamara, take the desk for a second. We're going to circumcise Dracula's tie."

Now everybody was laughing. The admitting nurse, Sara, told College Boy the story of Dracula. He'd bitten his first nurse Saturday morning, when she tried to take the tie off before breakfast. "It was more snap than bite, with no real breakage of skin," she said, "and that's when we decided to cover it with plastic and not deal with it.

"Now with the orderly, Francis, there he got freaky. They had to get the tie off Sunday night, before the surgery. And Francis, he's always so nice, very quiet. Your uncle calls him 'Oscar.' He started to take Mr. Spell's tie off, and then I hear him yelling and calling for Preston, the other orderly." By now Sara had grabbed onto College Boy to keep her propped up and convulsed.

"Preston comes running, and Francis walks out of Mr. Spell's room. He keeps wiping his hand on his whites. There's blood—not a lot, but enough—and we're all a little, like, what's up with this ting? And then Francis, and this is when we all lost our shit, said, 'Old Mr. Belvedere-acting motherfucker bit me!'"

College Boy did not expect the 'Mr. Belvedere' line. He shrieked.

"That's what we all did!" said Sara. "And it's ten and everybody on the floor is pushing the call buttons and we're running around trying to get to them, but we're laughing. And then—" College Boy waited while she caught her breath. "I see Preston walk into Mr. Spell's room and say, 'Dracula, what's happening? Don't make me build no damn cross.'"

College Boy and Sara were now holding each other up. He was envious. Why had he missed this display? Where had he been

Saturday night at ten-thirty, when it all started? Oh, right. Getting Mort's glasses. . . .

"Did you get the tie off him for surgery?" he asked.

"Oh, sure," Sara said. "Preston acted like he was adjusting Mr. Spell's pillows, which he does every night, so your uncle suspected nothing. Then, once he was behind him, he leaned him forward and pulled the tie off before Mr. Spell could do anything. Preston is very quick. He may not look it because he's so big, but he's quick. He kept telling everyone it was a martial arts move."

"Tie-kwon-do?" College Boy was sure someone must have already come up with this.

"No!!!" Sara screamed, and ran back to the admitting desk. She grabbed three nurses and they went running into the ladies room. College Boy heard more screaming and the reverbed laughter of the bathroom. The muted toll of the call buttons from the other patients on the floor brought them staggering out. Sara still had the scissors.

"How did he get the tie back on? And why is it so tight?"

Sara wiped her eyes. "We were stupid. Preston should have given that thing to me and I could have burned it. But we're not allowed to destroy patients' property. So Preston put it in the closet."

"Didn't he see Preston put it away?"

"No. They'd given him a sedative by then."

"So, how—"

"That's what we were trying to figure out," Sara said. "I didn't come on until noon, and they brought him up after that. And he was still under. And he wasn't wearing no tie."

"That's what Sheila, Miss ah-Manning, said."

"What is she?"

"She's Mr. Spell's cleaning woman."

"That lady that was arguing over there wit you?"

"Yeah."

"I never seen no cleaning woman like that show up here. Ever."

"Hey, Sara," College Boy said, "what can I tell you?"

"What happened to your arm?"

College Boy hesitated. You can't do the "cops hassling a black kid" to someone whose black kid the cops may have hassled. "Nothing happened. I just don't want to get bitten."

Sara laughed and said, "Tell me 'tie kwon do' again." College Boy obliged and she pushed him towards Mort's room. College Boy held his uncle's head to the side, while Sara found a slightly slacky spot behind his right ear and clipped it with one sure stroke. The aide stood by the door like an alarm might go off. Mort did not move.

He had ten minutes to pick up another tie at the gift shop. He was actually worried they might be out of the blue ones, as if the Mount Sinai Glee Club had grabbed some last minute gig at the Ninety-second Street Y. He tried to get the cashier to charge the forty dollars to Mort's room, but was told the gift shop operates separately from the hospital. All of which forced him to run back up to the fourth floor and fish forty dollars out of Hiding Place F—inside the top of Bagzilla's aerosol can of Cruex. In the last three years, he'd gone through a couple cans of the jock itch spray but had always been careful to transfer the same red plastic cap with the two twenties crouched along the underside. Thank God the good people at Cruex hadn't changed the can's design. He hadn't hit up Hiding Place F since maybe 1984. For College Boy, this was like spending principal.

He got back to Mort's room in time to put the new tie in the closet and the gift shop bag and price tag in his pocket. His left pocket. Thanks to the cast, that was the only pocket College Boy could do business out of, and in a few short hours it had bulged to resemble a hip goiter.

Other than the Valium heists or the occasional eleventh-and-a-half-hour broken dinner date because of an "audition," College Boy was not in the habit of deceiving his uncle. But he considered all of that to fall under the heading of victimless crime. It was nothing to puff one's chest over, but it wasn't lying. Well, it wasn't lying to the man's face. He'd never looked his uncle dead down the barrel of his eyes and said, "No, Mort. You distinctly said 'Let's try the Four Seasons next time.' I thought it was strange, but you had your heart set on it. That's why I put on this suit. . . ." Dan Drake had a T-shirt he used to wear in the studio. Gray, with a grove of pine trees around a lake and over the left breast, in green loglike letters: "Camp Mindfuck Staff." Morton Martin Spell, decent, brilliant, and confused in ways College Boy could only aspire to, had never been introduced to the staff of Camp Mindfuck.

He woke frightened and went directly for his neck.

"Did Sheila find my tie?"

"I don't know. I just came in."

"Good to see you. You're looking awfully well."

"Thanks, Mort. Did you check the closet for your tie?"

"I might have gotten up and done that. Or Sheila."

"Was she here?"

"Yes. She and a couple of her friends from the track team were trying to find my tie."

"I must have just missed her."

"Of course you did," laughed Mort. "They were track guys."

"Let's look in the closet." College Boy smiled and displayed the new tie pinched between the tips of his cast-peaking fingers. "Looks like she went out and had it cleaned while you were sleeping."

"How about Sheila doing that? And while entertaining her friends from the track team."

"Hey, Mort, what can I tell you?"

"Kid, what happened to your arm?"

"Broke my wrist Indian wrestling Jeane Kirkpatrick for a locker at the NYAC." He forgot how easily he could make his uncle laugh sometimes. Just make up some shit with the right name at the end. Victimless crime.

"Let's have that tie."

"I thought you wanted to wait and dress for dinner."

"When did I say that?"

The aide walked back in and sat down.

"You know, Mort, I can't remember. Maybe I made it up."

"Maybe you're confusing it with the conversation you had with Jean Simmons at the NYAC."

"Jeane Kirkpatrick."

"That's right. I forgot. They don't allow women. Sorry."

The aide left because she couldn't read with all the hysterical banter. It didn't last long. The hysteria wore Mort out. College Boy, too. They both dropped off for another forty-five. College Boy usually needed a Valium to nod off that successfully in the late afternoon. But now, slumped in a straight-backed chair, drool puddling on the left shoulder of his Columbus Rest. jersey (which he had changed into out of habit and oblivious defiance to his wrist), Mount Sinai gift tie draped cluelessly over the entombed arm in his lap, really now, who was visiting who?

College Boy had a dream while he was asleep. The Dream. Same one he'd had since before he was College Boy. He's running down a long corridor. Fast, with the good wheels. There's an open window at the end of the corridor. Two-thirds of the way there, he realizes he's in the middle of a dream, and if he jumps through the window, he'll die. And somewhere he heard—and this is all as he's running—that if you die in your dreams, you die in real life. So, College Boy runs full tilt, Shemp-like, into the wall to the right of the window. The impact knocks him down, and always wakes him up.

College Boy treated The Dream pretty much as public domain conversation material. He never offered it up unprovoked, but if someone started in with "Man, I had such a dream last night. . . ," he followed up with the corridor and the window and the Chevy Chase pratfall. Rachel and Trish had both heard about The Dream on early dates. His parents knew. Julio Rentas heard it and stopped laughing long enough to grab the joint away from College Boy. *"No mas por tigo, amigo."* Dr. Bettles was told The Dream three times, and all three times he said the same thing: "Sounds like someone was on his way to the bathroom." Actually, he said that once. The other two times he said that, followed by, "Remember how angry you got at me the first time I said that?" College Boy was never shy about telling anyone. Two reasons: He thought the whole thing had a cartoon whimsy to it, however black; and, unlike the rest of his dreams, he didn't appear in either his underwear or with his pants around his ankles. That would have really curtailed the wheels.

Today, after however many years, The Dream had a slight twist.

This time, College Boy slammed into the wall, fell down, then was hit in the head with a chunk of plaster. When he woke up, he found his right arm in mid-descent back to his lap. Mort's tie lay on the floor.

"Kid, when did you get here?"

"I don't know," College Boy said.

"They must have drugged you."

"I don't think so."

"Well, find out who did it, and send them my way." College Boy, who had gone through most of his adulthood comfortably deprived of the ability to anticipate, knew Mort's next question. "Kid, you wouldn't happen to have a Valium on you for a prickless relative?" Well, the asking for Valium part, not the "prickless relative" flourish.

College Boy looked behind him, at Bagzilla, then back at Mort. He smiled the helpful smile of the staff. The Camp Mindfuck staff. "You must have been asleep, Mort," he said. "A guy came by and added Valium to your IV."

"Did you offer him a drink?"

College Boy held up his arm. "How could I?"

Mort, who had brightened for an instant, got suddenly serious and painfully insightful. "Right, your wrist. I'm going to assume you made the catch."

"Yes."

And then just painful. "And," Mort said, "I'm going to assume this happened before Lenny Merullo showed up."

"Ah, heh-heh, yeah."

Wow. Lenny Merullo. Wow. Fuck.

It was a reference to the tryout Mort had arranged long ago for his nephew. Lenny Merullo was the East Coast chief of the Major League Baseball Scouting Bureau. The same Lenny Merullo that had struggled at shortstop for the Cubs in the 1950s and specifically, in Mort's piece on Bing Crosby. Bertram Hargan Cup–winning piece on Bing Crosby. The same Bertram Hargan Cup once won by Rafer Johnson. The same Rafer Johnson. Funny how it all came together now. And it would have, but College Boy chose not to think further of that day.

"Let's have that tie," Mort said.

College Boy stepped on the front edge of the tie as he was trying to pick it up, leaving the dusty imprint of his Stan Smith Adidas and starting the sure parade of stains to follow.

Mort caught the aide's eye in mid–page flip. "And miss, let's get those Saran Wrap boys in here with the Zamboni. . . ." College Boy snorted with pleasure at Mort's hockey metaphor as he handed his uncle the tie. But Mort was no longer playing for laughs. He snatched the tie and in a voice grabbed from the nastiest badass in some General Population lockdown, screamed, ". . . RIGHT FUCKING NOW!" Loud. Dolby in an empty theater during the previews loud. College Boy leapt back, got cut off at the knees by his chair, and landed in the seat, slump side first, as if he'd been thrown by the force of Mort's voice. Which he had.

The aide rose slowly, wagged a finger, and ambled out in the direction of oncoming hospital staff traffic. The two orderlies ran into the room as Mort Spell here was putting the last touches on his new 100 percent hand-sewn silk noose.

"Oh. Hello, boys."

Oh. Hello, boys. Like nothing had happened. Worse than that. Like he had convinced College Boy nothing had happened.

"Mr. Spell," said Preston or Francis or whatever his name was, "we have to have a little conversation."

"Okay, doctor."

"I'm Preston."

"Okay, Oscar."

"Right." He started to cellophane Mort's tie. "Mr. Spell, we can't be running in here every time you start screaming like Charles Motherfucking Manson. Now, you almost made it through the day, so we ain't gonna strap you down."

"That's damn nice of you, Oscar." The other orderly pretended to check Mort's IV, then handed Preston a medication cup.

"Now, I want you to take this and order some dinner." Preston edged closer as he finished with the cellophane. His voice softened to beta level. "You have two nights and one day left here, Mr. Spell. And I still like you. We cool now. But you can't be having these outbursts. Because if you have one more, then me, Preston, Preston's gonna get angry. And when Preston gets angry, he puts cellophane on more than a motherfucking tie. . . ."

Preston shook Mort's hand, as if he knew how much Mort loved to shake hands. On his way out he turned to College Boy. "I don't know if we can get him another aide tonight, little brother." He was in the hall when Mort called behind him, "Oscar, if you see our waiter, send him over." College Boy saw Preston's body ragdoll in delight. It must take a lot for Preston to get angry, he thought.

Sara let both of them order dinner. Which made her nice, and clairvoyant. College Boy was starving. A pre-show bagel at the radio station was all he'd eaten in the last eleven hours, and the pillaging of Hiding Place F now rendered him virtually broke.

Shit. He'd forgotten to play the Monday triples. Watch it come in. Watch it pay big. Watch the universe have a good laugh on College Boy.

Supper was fine, only because it showed up. College Boy devoured his Salisbury Steak, beans, home fries, and airline-size salad. "You went through that Prague Roast like the Jews went through Miami," said Mort, his standard postprandial remark to his nephew. The biggest intra-meal compliment he ever gave College Boy was one night at P. J. Moriarty's when College Boy didn't order bourbon. "You drink iced tea just like Arthur Schlesinger," Mort said. "You squeeze that lemon like it owes you money."

Mort picked at his baked chicken leg, beans, and mashed potatoes and moved his salad around like an eight-year-old just enough to justify the assault on his and College Boy's dessert, a square of what only some guy in marketing would call Black Forest cake. It was an even-up trade, College Boy's cake for the hermetically sealed slice of white bread from the Fink (*"Fink Means Bread"*) Bakery. Before he passed it, Mort held up his piece and admired the packaging. "Maybe we can get the Fink people to come in and do my tie."

The two of them tried unsuccessfully to think of something equally witty until *MacNeil-Lehrer* came on. College Boy behaved throughout the newscast, which meant (1) not asking Mort to switch to Channel 2 at 6:25 to find out what the 9th race triple looked like, and (2) not asking Mort which one was Lehrer. He said nothing, yet Mort acted as if they were still in full conversation. At the beginning of each news story, Mort would hold his index finger in the air and say, "I'd like to hear this, thanks."

Mort hit his call button at the end of *MacNeil-Lehrer* to ask Sara if he could stand during *Jeopardy*. Right. He liked to stand while he watched the show. It had been a while since they had watched together. "Okay, Mr. Spell," she said, "but just stand. Don't be using your IV bag as a signaling button, like last week."

"Well, maybe if Alex Trebek would call on me I wouldn't have to signal with my IV bag."

Sara put her hand on College Boy's shoulder. "He used to use the nurse's call button, and for the first three days we'd be running down here every ten seconds. 'What is it, Mr. Spell?' And he'd say, 'Who is Moby Dick?' or some shit like that. So now, one of us comes in before seven and hides the call button for a half hour. Just until the show is over. He always has the aide in here, in case something happens, like with the IV bag, so it's no problem."

"Except tonight," College Boy said.

"Well, you're here. You stay for *Jeopardy*."

"Uh, yeah."

Sara got fake tough. "Hey, you don't think I let you have dinner because I felt sorry for you." He did, but why be right about anything female all of a sudden? "That was your pay. Sara's puttin' you to work. You can leave at eight, after *Wheel of Fortune*."

Mort was already on his feet, waiting to take his cuts at Single Jeopardy. The categories were much too modern, except "Running Mates." Sara leaned behind him and tucked the call button under the mattress.

"We got your uncle someone for later tonight," she told College Boy.

"She comes on at eight?"

"No, midnight, but he'll be fine. That Vanna White wears him out."

"Who was Estes Kefauver!" Mort began to grab for the IV bag, but thought better. Sara, Mort, and College Boy all waited as the contestants drew blanks.

"I'm sorry," smugged Alex Trebek, *"We would have accepted either of Adlai Stevenson's running mates: who was Estes Kefauver or John J. Sparkman?"*

Mort looked straight ahead and mumbled, "Sparkman."

"You go, Mr. Spell," Sara said.

"Thank you, Vanna." Mort waited until she was out of sight to put his right hand to the left side of his mouth and whisper, "She does a damn good job turning those letters."

"I'm sorry, the correct question, Who was William Miller?" Mort had turned away and missed "Running Mates" for five hundred, Alex.

"CUNT!"

College Boy dove across the bed and caught the metal IV bag holder, or whatever that three-wheeled apparatus was called, before it hit Mort or the floor. He backhanded the stanchion with his left hand while holding his injured arm out straight to the side, away from his body, away from impact, and hung on after the mattress threatened to buck him from his bellyflop. He wriggled off, then set the IV trellis, whatever it was, right and climbed over the bed to stand in front and guard the thing like it was on loan from the MoMA. Some catch, but no one was watching. Lenny Merullo had left. Left thirteen years ago.

The catch, and it was some catch, came not without clamor. But Mort did not react, and College Boy couldn't tell whether he was being ignored or unrecognized until his uncle turned around during the next commercial break.

"You've got a lot of nerve showing up now, doctor."

Go ahead. Try and leave at eight. Go ahead.

14

College Boy was bone weary from what had turned out to be a ten-hour shift at the hospital. Two hours in wardrobe, getting fitted for his cast, eight with Mort. Ten hours. How did the rest of the world put in that kind of time? And every day? And indoors?

What was so foreign about all this—about just sitting there as Mort fell asleep for keeps somewhere between Johnny saying "Welcome to *The Tonight Show*," and "I'm Johnny Carson, poster boy for term limits"—was the staying. Not the hours. The staying. More specifically, the not leaving. College Boy had spent the first half of his life guilt-ridden and the second half guilt-rid. You couldn't pull that "obligation" shit on him if you tried, and many, with and without the last name Sussman, had tried. So, forget that nonsense about hanging around because that was the very least he owed his uncle for all those meals and all those Valium and the big league tryout with whatshisname. Right, Lenny Merullo. He stayed because he didn't leave. That simple. And he didn't leave because whatever that mechanism, standard factory issue for College Boy, whatever that device was that turned his body into a compass and any door into magnetic north, had been jarred. It must have happened somewhere between the outfield ground on Diamond #4 and the Mount Sinai gift shop. College Boy would figure it out. But he wouldn't hurry. Because the staying, the not leaving, didn't feel that different. It felt like something he might have done before. And something—if a situation arose—he might do again.

So College Boy thought on the Number 6 downtown. *I might do this again.* Not much later, as he sat on the platform at Fifty-ninth

Street waiting for the RR to take him the last two crosstown stops, he'd look at his cast, lying too docile across Bagzilla and sniff more insight. *Well, sure I might do this again. What else am I gonna do now?*

The plan, the immediate plan, was to count the cash in the house, divide by the rest of his life, and be in bed by 1:15. It took eighteen minutes for the RR to come. Had he walked, walked like College Boy, he could have been at his front door by now. But Bagzilla always got 20 percent heavier after eleven P.M. And tack on another hundred or so pounds this night, after College Boy found a first-edition Tuesday *Post* with Monday's ninth race triple result:

7-2-5 . . .

paid . . . $2,984.60.

Would have had it, he thought. *Would have had it.* But his thoughts were traveling in twos, exactas, so they ran like this: *Would have had it. . . . If I have it, it don't come in.* Not bitter, just realistic. And so what? College Boy never played exactas. Just triples. And just not that Monday.

So, a little before one, and wrung out by hunger and self-pity, College Boy decided to treat himself to the elevator. The elevator in College Boy's building must have been installed as an afterthought because the thing could barely hold two people comfortably. Many a Chinese delivery kid would hand College Boy his chow fun and say "Why elevator so small? Why you not tell me to use stair?"

And the elevator made up for being tiny by being incredibly slow. Not even New York City slow, which is a tick above regular speed everywhere else. But slow. DMV slow. Harvey Kuenn walking out to the mound to make a pitching change slow.

College Boy rarely bothered with the elevator. It wanted little to do with him, and absolutely nothing to do with him and Bagzilla. All that, and the fact that College Boy's apartment was on the third floor of the eight-floor building. The last time College Boy had been on the elevator was Sunday. With Sheila. Damn chivalrous, especially since he was running woefully late—way past batting practice and perilously close to having ten dollars lopped off his pay—for the Riis Park doubleheader. (He ran off the Green and White bus in his spikes and ended up going 5-for-8 with two doubles and threw out the same guy—Rosado—at third twice, if you want to know. Even if you don't want to know.)

Had he used the stairs he would have seen the two of them, sitting on the flight to the fourth floor, yakking in a whisper. He would have smelled the cigarettes. Menthol. Kool badass Kings. He would have been able to imagine the exchange that must have taken place at least three or four times during the night. *"Can I help you guys?"/ "No, we're waiting for College Boy."/ "Yeah, we play ball with him and he left his bat at the game."/ "Yeah, we want to give him his bat."/ "Well, okay. See ya. . . ."*

Turns out the bat was for *their* protection. In case College Boy had one. College Boy had a couple, but you try telling two smoke-laminated slugs waiting three hours in your stairwell to hang on just another couple of seconds while you fish your whupping stick out of Bagzilla.

In the end, their bat was used to pin his throat to the wall. Worked out quite well, too. The exchange was brief. Quicker than the one College Boy would have been able to imagine had he taken the stairs. As he disembarked from The Little Elevator That Might, the two J.V. goons stood up and simultaneously flicked away their cigarettes, as if they were there for a casting call of his building's production of *West Side Story*.

"College Boy?"

"Fellas?"

"We have a message from Ernie G."

"The Dirt King?" College Boy, thinking more deftly than he had a right to, held up his casted right arm. "Sorry boys, that message was already delivered."

They were fooled for a few seconds. Whatever that amount of time it takes to put your key in the lock but not open your door. That long. Long enough to know it wasn't long enough. After that, the bat, the wall, and College Boy's throat got together.

"Well, then," said the bigger one, the one holding the bat and, as it turned out, a pretty fair loanshark *bon mot*, "Well, then, we'll just get a receipt." College Boy closed his eyes, and the smaller one, the one holding his left thumb, gave a clean jerk down, the same ferocious move the bag boy makes at the end of the checkout line. Paper or limb? College Boy did not make a peep. Fainting helped. The fellas were nice enough to open his door for him, throw Bagzilla inside, then slap him across the face so he'd be awake for their good nights. A full-service muscle call.

This is why I don't use a bookie. So thought College Boy just before he threw up, as he heard them giggling in the elevator, or because of the elevator. He rolled over and crawled elbows and knees almost across his threshold. Then he threw up on his otherwise all-weather doormat and thought, *No, this. This is why I don't use a bookie.*

He would need ice and cabfare to Lenox Hill. The ice was in the freezer, and there was a twenty-dollar bill in Hiding Place E. Under the doormat. What a break.

• • •

There's much better food here, College Boy thought. I have to remember that.

"Here" was the cafeteria at Lenox Hill Hospital. One of the women behind the counter had taken pity on him—three in the morning kind of pity—and cut his hot turkey sandwich into about fifteen pieces. Spoon-sized, which is what he had to use on his latest meal. Worked out quite well, as Mort would say. If Mort was here, he'd have said something like, "Damn fine invention, the spoon. No wonder they named a golf club after it." But Mort was not here. He was in the other hospital. One mile north and two arm casts ago.

There's much better food here. I have to remember that. That was the first thought, the thought that actually cheered and sated College Boy. It lasted all of three minutes, the time it took for him to devour the hot turkey sandwich. It was followed by the first frost of panic:

Oh my God. How am I going to jerk off?

Okay, College Boy thought. Settle down. He still had four free fingers and half the palm on his left hand. His "working" hand.

Guys had made do with less. Hell, his freshman roommate (when he actually was College Boy, just lower-case) hadn't even used his hands. Eddie Lonhoffer. It was an involved process whose main component was high-speed friction. No sense getting into it. Eddie Lonhoffer had made do. Show's over. Move along.

Move along. Sure, but where? Home? Again? Why not? How bad could it be this time? Maybe this time, he might actually walk into his apartment. Why not? His legs, the wheels, still worked.

Some guys just live right.

Part Two

15

If your goal is to be left alone, nothing will turn the collective back of the public on you like Parkinson's Disease.

A slight tremor, usually in the fingers or hands, is the opening metaphor for the rocking of your world. And like any good metaphor, it is sustained.

The brochure will tell you Parkinson's is a neurological disorder that can strike anyone over thirty. In the world of diseases, it is a mystery. A bad mystery, with little plot, no hero, and an end that drags out long enough to hopelessly point fingers in every direction. Technically—and anybody knows people never use the word "technically" unless they want to back up a really weak point—technically, no one ever dies from Parkinson's Disease. But everyone is lost.

College Boy first noticed the tremors in Mort's hands three weeks after his uncle was released from Mount Sinai. They were out at a Japanese restaurant, and he saw that neither of them was using chopsticks. College Boy had an excuse, the casts, but Mort was eating his sashimi by hand. Normally, Morton Martin Spell took great pride in his chopstick dexterity and never missed a chance to tease his nephew about how he grabbed his sticks too low. "You're choked up a little too much, kid," he'd say, "unless you're trying to hit that maguro to shallow right field."

College Boy became aware of the shaking when Mort switched from vodka to tea. Until then, it just sounded like any concerned drinker trying to help his ice along.

"What's with your hands, Mort?"

"They're idling."

"You should see someone about that."

"I'll talk to that fellow. I think he went to Dartmouth."

"Dr. Levitz?"

"You're awfully sharp tonight."

Since his release from the hospital, Mort had been confined to his apartment, except for six visits to Dr. Levitz, who was back on retainer with his Better Shrinking Through Chemistry Revue. To his credit, or his fear of litigation, Dr. Levitz let Mort know that his Valium days were over. College Boy, of course, volunteered to rid his uncle's apartment of the demon aqua and canary tablets before he returned home. Why risk temptation? More important, why risk the possibility of Sheila grabbing them first?

Levitz instead put his prodigal patient on Halcion, a sleeping pill Mort was not interested in until he found out fellow Yalie George "Poppy" Bush ('46) had used the stuff to help him sleep through the bombing of CNN during the Gulf War, and a dim sum of antidepressants and mood sculptors for which College Boy had no knowledge or use. Levitz saw Mort three times the third week of July before the doctor left for his psychopath-funded villa near Milan for two months. That's how good the man was. He could leave his patients in the lurch the last ten days of July, *all* of August, and half of September. During his second-to-last visit, Mort spoke of his anxiety about moving and mentioned the tremors in his hands. Dr. Levitz was curt. "Oh, for Christ's sake, I went through the same thing when I moved the office from Madison to Park. Could barely hold my scrip pad. Have a drink, Mort."

Two days later, when Dr. Levitz cattle-called most of his patients for his annual Getaway Day Special—ten minutes at the regular hourly rate—Mort shook and shuffled in at 4:20. Levitz looked up in the middle of trying on tennis shorts. "Mort, my friend, you got yourself Parkinson's Disease," he said. "I'll have Bernice call Graham the neurologist on the seventh floor. Try and see him today. He'll put you on the stuff, the dopamine stuff. Sudafed. No, not that. Sinemet. That's it. Get a wiggle on, Mort. Graham usually leaves by five."

Mort finally got in to see Graham on the seventh floor ten days later, who confirmed Levitz's diagnosis (while fully clothed) and prescribed Sinemet. By then, the tremors had progressed from occasional to steady, as if Mort was constantly trying to wave good-bye to Manhattan.

College Boy got both his casts off the next day, July 30, and then endured a rehab no physical therapist would recommend—a solid week packing up fifty-some years of Mort's shit. Sheila dropped by when she could to help and they left the rest for the big Irish guys from Liffey Movers. ("Which one of you boys was married to Bernadette Devlin?" Mort kept asking, always just before College Boy or Sheila could shush him.) Everything but the bed, two chairs, the living-room rug, a five-foot tower of *New Yorkers* from the early '70s, and the three-wood was loaded onto the van by noon, Wednesday, August 7. (Mort had another nineteen months on his lease.) Mort and College Boy were on their way no later than 12:15, after Mort had what could have been an emotional farewell with Sheila.

"Well, Mr. Spell," she choked out, eyes red as that great red hair, "between my mother and me it's been thirty years."

"Goodbye, Helga." And he was out the door and ten feet down the hall before he yelled back, "Ah . . . Sheila!" College Boy was still inside the apartment, and he gave Sheila the hug his uncle was incapable of, and one which he could only deliver as a messenger.

"You okay?"

"Yeah. Piece of work, isn't he?" she said. "Go take care of him. I'll lock up."

College Boy had never done his Mort impression for anyone outside his family. Who would get it?

"Goodbye, Helga." He saw the shock in her face and got half a shriek. Perfect. He might have heard her still laughing as the elevator closed. Then again, maybe crying, mistaken for her mother twice in the space of half a minute. Helga. The last person she had taken care of. He'd have to ask Sheila about that the next time he saw her. Maybe after he returned from unpacking Mort in whatever this new life was. That was the plan.

Other than Mort mistaking College Boy for Victor Mature twice (*"By the way, damn nice job in* Red Hot and Blue. . . ."), the drive to Massachusetts passed without incident. They stopped in New Haven for a late lunch at Sally's, the brick-oven pizza grail which had opened long after Mort left Yale and he'd been meaning to get to for thirty years. After College Boy had cut up Mort's two slices into workable canapés, mission accomplished.

This is the last time I do anything like this, College Boy thought. And then, as if looking for a reward, he wondered aloud if there might be a matinee at Milford or Bridgeport Jai-Alai that day. No such luck, but it did give Mort a chance to retell the story about the time in the early '70s when he stormed into William Shawn's office at the *New Yorker* after his jai-alai piece had been shelved another month and announced to the editor, "Mr. Shawn, I'm putting all my basques in one exit."

"That's a great story, Mort."

"Okay, Victor. Now tell us all about you and Hedy Lamarr."

Dottie Sussman had found Vinnin Estates in Salem, just up the street from Hawthorne Hospital, when everyone, College Boy included, was still under the impression that Mort could return to Massachusetts and live on his own with little problem, other than not knowing how to do anything. Dottie had her brother's tastes, which were her tastes but with more tan and burgundy, and decorated the white, two-bedroom cape house accordingly. Mort would pay $1,800 a month, almost four times his Manhattan rent, but would be only ten minutes from his sister in Lynn. And really, you can't put a price on being that close to the only surviving member of a family you had kept on a 206-mile tether for over a half-century.

We really should clarify, or qualify, do something, about what was meant by the remark that Morton Martin Spell didn't know how to do anything. By anything, that would be anything other than showering, dressing, hailing a cab, hailing another cab, making himself a drink, reading a delivery menu, and successfully dialing the restaurant by the fifth attempt. In other words, anything other than living in New York City, where the hermit-inclined are not only tolerated, but ignored.

That was the plan. College Boy would drop his uncle off at Vinnin Estates, set him up, build a lifetime of equity with his mom, then maybe get a ride back with the big Irish boys from Liffey Movers. Or, in a perfect world, work up some scenario where he could drive the Buick station wagon back to New York, keep the car, and make it seem like he was doing Mort a favor.

There's a term for this. Years ago, he'd overheard a woman in the Heckscher Field bleachers tell a friend how she convinced a bank teller to cash a double-endorsed, third-party out-of-state check by saying she was new in town and had to get some medication for her kid. A bank teller at a bank where she did not have an account. Cash for a kid she did not have. "I really dope-fiended her," the woman said to her friend. College Boy had never heard that expression before or since, but he pocketed that image, that notion, like that one Jews For Jesus pamphlet that seems reasonable. To dope-fiend. The pious simplicity of it. The implied bonanza that you don't have to be a dope fiend to dope-fiend, and it probably helps if you aren't.

Since then, during those half-moments when he would briefly, so briefly, examine his behavior, College Boy would inevitably wind up saying to himself, "Nice going, College Boy. You dope-fiended that *(choose one)* guy/girl/pitcher/landlord/Con Ed operator/horse race/clerk/waitress/teammate/family member."

Until recently, as recently as the moment when the softball season crashed against his wrist, dope-fiending was a muscle College Boy kept eternally flexed. It fit comfortably within the Ringer Philosophy of Life. So comfortably he didn't have to break it in. And it sprung his innate first step toward getting over. Getting Over. A wholly owned subsidiary of Getting By.

"You know, Mort, you have to change your registration and get new plates anyway. You might as well get a new car."

"Good point, kid. There's a Sunbeam I had my eye on."

Nice going, College Boy. You dope-fiended your delirious uncle. Then thought again, this is the last time I do anything like this.

The plan worked for all of three days. That's how long it took College Boy to figure out all the places he could not go anymore.

Heckscher Fields. *The Dan Drake Show.* His apartment. Actually, that took about ten minutes. The other three days were spent ducking Mort's landlord at 301 East Sixty-fifth, who wanted to make sure he knew how difficult it would be to legally assume his uncle's lease.

"I'm not running an SRO here, Mr. Spell's nephew, whatever your name is."

"Hey, I'm just here to pick up a few more things. My uncle's paid up through October, I believe. The garage, too. He'll be back. And I'll be gone Monday."

Dope fiend. Come on, he was College Boy. Given three more days and Sheila's knowledge of the building, he could avoid any overweight guy in a short-sleeved shirt. Never see daylight, order in, get the heads up from Sheila after they work out a *ring-ring, hang up* system with the phone. Do that for a month, and then it's "Oh, you didn't hear? Mort's back. Yeah. A week now. I was just bringing him some soup. . . ." Beautiful. All he needed was soup.

And cash. College Boy, his Prospect Pros jersey and uniform pants undeniably snugger, had the sincere sensation of driving himself to Riis Park for the Sunday Riis Park Ringers doubleheader. He pulled into the parking lot at ten-thirty. Ninety minutes to stretch when he needed a fortnight.

He was the second one to arrive. Felix, Felix Somebody, the Pros manager, walked over and gave him a hug.

"Look who's here."

"Playoffs, baby. Money time."

"You come to watch, College Boy?"

"Funny, man."

"No," said Felix. "I'm serious."

Shit. He forgot. "You frozen?"

"Yeah, man. We had to submit rosters last week for the playoffs. You know that." He forgot. "End of July. I was gonna call you, but the boys said your shit was still fucked up."

He forgot. HE FORGOT. Not College Boy. College Boy never forgot. This guy. The guy with the old man station wagon and the tight uniform. This guy. Harvey Sussman.

"Come on, Felix. Who's gonna check the fucking rosters?"

Felix smiled and College Boy knew he couldn't take back that last remark. All these guys did was check rosters. Check and be checked.

"Listen," Felix said. "Nellie will be here soon. I can ask him if he'll let me add you. He'll probably say it's cool. He likes you. Everybody likes College Boy."

"Great." He started to reach for Bagzilla. Jesus. Could he possibly drive this thing out to the bleachers?

"But I only got spots to pay twelve guys. Felix gotta make money, too. So, you'd have to play for free."

College Boy probably heard Felix say, "Or you could bet on the game with us and make some serious cash, man," squeezed in between the passenger door closing and the Buick station wagon's engine turning over. He stopped on his way out of the lot to commiserate with the early-arriving Julio Rentas and backhand him ten Valium through the driver's side window of that mint julep piece of shit held together by its inspection sticker. And he headed wherever nonringers go on a Sunday. Or any day. Whenever that was.

Some plan.

And that, sports fans, was it. The next day, he returned to stay in Mort's guest room at Vinnin Estates. Here in Salem. Just up the street from Hawthorne Hospital. College Boy, or Mr. Sussman as he would now be known in the nonsoftball world, would try to care about someone else for a little while and see how that worked. Take his mind off himself. Leave the dope-fiending to the dope fiends and not those of us who fall in love with idea rather than truth.

And speaking of the truth, who the fuck was College Boy kidding? He had driven Mort's Buick Century station wagon back to Salem only after he realized Manhattan had become too much of an island. He ran from three months of back rent, stored whatever the Buick wagon could haul in Mort's living room at 301 East Sixty-fifth, had Julio Rentas change Mort's bottom lock (Price: ten Valium), repacked Bagzilla with the maximum carry-on limits of the Federal Witness Protection Program, and left Monday morning at five-thirty after Dan Drake had given him a thousand dollars in cash and said even though the story had been endlessly entertaining, he had genuinely felt bad about the dislocated thumb. Five-thirty Monday morning. He was gone Monday. Just as advertised to the overweight guy in the short-sleeved shirt.

And here's the beauty part. Somewhere just over the Third Avenue Bridge, just ahead of the sun, College Boy thought, "You know, this is good. I could use a little time off." He had done it. He had actually dope-fiended himself. That's when he started crying. That's when he might have decided to "work on that."

So began this decidedly regional production of *The Odd Couple*. In the first week, College Boy made a thousand mistakes. A thousand. Bleaching a few colored socks. Running a tub too hot, too long, or without authorization. Getting the wrong morning ratio of instant coffee to faintly soapy water. Forgetting to take whatever that plastic bag of shit was out of the chicken before it went into the oven. Not to mention the capital offense: Too much goddamn ice in the three o'clock martini (*"Do I look like Admiral Byrd?")*. And we're not even talking about not dressing properly for dinner.

Of all the things in his life College Boy had not thought through fully, which, other than his softball schedule, would be all the things in his life, the concept of taking care of Morton Martin Spell was Stonehenge. And here's the problem: From Hour One of Day One, he had no chance to think about it. It was as if the moment he had pulled the Buick station wagon back into the driveway at Vinnin Estates that August Monday he had paddled himself into an undertow of responsibility and hard labor that sucked him to a place where, if and when his head finally came up, the horizon was more responsibility, more labor, more *"Christ, kid, when did Truman start rationing vodka?"* The notion of stopping and asking himself, "What the fuck have I gotten myself into?" was something to which he could only aspire.

You cannot go from talking about the Rangers over Czechoslovakian food every two weeks to living together. Well, maybe *you* could. It quickly dawned on Mort Spell that his nephew was neither a guest nor company, but rather, the only means by which he could survive privately, which is as close to living alone as a man who needs help taking a shit can get. And what dawned on College Boy was nothing. He was too busy.

College Boy was closed. He wasn't even College Boy anymore. His spirit went away, into cold storage, and the molecules inside his earth-bound body re-formed as a vessel. A vessel for whomever he was taking care of. His life, whatever that was, stopped. He was . . . closed.

His day was reduced to a blindingly mundane run-through of picking up, cleaning up, propping up, freshening up, cutting up, wiping up, waking up, cheering up, and cleaning up some more. Eight hours sleep was somebody else's headache and free time always smelled like a mistake. But every so often, when Mort went down for the night without a fight or an hour-long filibuster about Darwin's *Voyage of the Beagle*, when College Boy could collapse by himself before midnight in the one truly comfortable living room chair and keep his eyes open long enough to make it through Carson's monologue, he would hear something from Johnny that chronicled the passage of time. And it would scare the shit out of him.

Wait a minute. Elizabeth Taylor got married? Again? Where the fuck have I been?

If it wasn't on *Jeopardy,* ice, hardwood, grass, or artificial turf, he didn't know about it. The only time he saw a newspaper was when he gathered up a week's worth of *Boston Globe*s for the recycling barrel. The *Globe* tended to tilt a little provincial. College Boy remembered a *Boston Globe* parody in the early '80s whose page one lead was "Hub Man Dies in Nuclear Blast." That was about right. So, he didn't bother. But occasionally, as he walked the stack to the trash room, there'd be an unbreakfast-stained front page lying on top.

Magic Johnson has AIDS? Am I the only one who didn't know?

Yeah. Go figure. Someone else in the universe besides Morton Martin Spell was sick.

Okay, settle down. It wasn't as if College Boy had no contact with the outside world. His contact with the outside world amounted to furnishing his mother, Dottie Sussman, with updates and empty crockery from the casseroles and New England boiled dinners she'd drop off every ten days or so. But he was still a vessel. At best, he was Mort Spell's press secretary, and there was no room for a second client.

And for a while after he returned for good, however long that was, he had spoken with Sheila on the phone regularly. First from Vinnin Estates, then from a payphone in front of his primary source for take-out, China Sails. But that ended and he really didn't have to remember why or how. And if he did, he didn't have to let it in. Which was one of the few benefits of being closed. And College Boy was closed.

Occasionally, Dottie Sussman would suspend her guilt to pay her son some drive-by attention *("See how much better things are if you can get yourself some sun.")* or Mort might look up from *MacNeil-Lehrer* to acknowledge it all *("Other than rewriting my will, is there anything I can do for you?")*, but that was it.

Worked out pretty well.

There was one thing. Anger. Which was the one thing there wasn't. Oh, there was plenty lying around Vinnin Estates, but none of it belonged to College Boy. On or about Indian summer, by which time he had cut his weekly mistakes to ten dozen, College Boy was rousted from his morning dump by Mort screaming "Get away! Get away from there, you bastards! You goddamn prick bastards! Get away!" and pounding on the sliding glass doors that overlooked the communal back yard.

"Jesus, Mort. What is it?"

"Goddamn blue jays. On the bird feeder. Goddamn unwashed pirateering bastards. Where'd they come from? Some goddamn community college? Get out of here, you goddamn bastards!"

"Mort, I think they left."

"No thanks to you. And by the way, let me know next time you have Bob Oppenheimer or one of your other Manhattan Project buddies down here to rig the lock on this goddamn door!"

"You want me to check the bird feeder?"

"Well, I can't goddamn do it, can I? Get out there and chase those goddamn bastards, and be sure to take your time so my eggs can get good and cold."

"Let me redo the eggs, and then I'll go out there."

"I don't believe I said that. You bastards!" College Boy flipped the lock with less than one move. "You know," Mort flipped back, "I'm beginning to believe some of the things people are saying about you."

That day (was it that day?), College Boy tried driving around downtown Salem for fifteen minutes and screaming with the windows rolled up. When he returned, there was Mort, still looking out the sliding glass doors, but now swaddled in three blankets. "Kid, I think we missed a few air-conditioning vents," he said. So really, what was the fucking point?

And what was the point of whining, either? Why, when Mort, the sick one here, was capable of producing self-pity like there was money in it. And what was the point of giving it back to Mort when his uncle's flippancy throttle was wide open? Yeah, College Boy thought many times, that's it, make some sort of wise-ass remark about the tremors. Maybe something like, "Hey Mort, can you do any other impressions besides Don Knotts?" Good one. A real chest-puffer. Score one for the broke thirty-five-year-old male nurse with the mob landscaper after him.

And no shrink in front of him. Neither of them. Dr. Levitz sent his regards regularly through the Vinnin Square Pharmacy, and Mort, despite increasing difficulty swallowing (another complimentary gift of Parkinson's), seemed to prefer taking his emotional inventory in pill and alcohol form.

And for a while, College Boy was right there with his uncle. Then, in October, a little over two months into the Noble Experiment at Vinnin Estates, he stopped drinking. College Boy had been a twice-a-week warrior for years, but living with Mort Spell here turned every day into rushes from *The Thin Man* series. The Valium went shortly thereafter. That was not a conscious choice. College Boy ran out. The rest of his inherited stash was still at 301

East Sixty-fifth, in Hiding Place V, taped inside the fuse box. College Boy didn't want to go running down to Manhattan like some bust-out junkie. And he didn't want to call Levitz like he was some take-out joint and end up owing the doctor an explanation and a favor. He would have called Sheila, except the locks had been changed.

No bourbon. No Valium. And before you knew it, College Boy had new exposed nerve endings to go with his new life. He noticed them. Oh, these babies you couldn't ignore. It's hard to ignore anything when you're doubled over and nobody's punched you. Sure, College Boy was closed, but that didn't mean shit couldn't get through the one vent in Vinnin Estates he hadn't taped.

Three things helped College Boy through this period. And none of them had to do with telling anybody how he felt or what he was going through.

The first was jumping rope. Forty-five minutes a day, just like during the softball off-season, which was what this all was. Nothing says "fuck off" to an exposed nerve ending like a screaming quadriceps. And Mort loved the post–jump rope smell. College Boy would come back into the living room and after a few minutes, his uncle would yell, "You didn't tell me Jacques Plante [or some other 1950s NHL goaltender] was stopping by. Do we have any rye?"

The second thing College Boy stumbled onto by accident. During Week Two of Valium withdrawal, he gave in and called Julio Rentas. His former teammate was not at home, but he was treated to this outgoing message:

"Que pasa, this is Papa J. . . . No man, did you rip that? You fucking ripped it. No man, that's my last one. Shit. No, I'm all out, Freddy. Why didn't you let me roll it? Shit. Now Papa J gotta get out the fucking toilet paper roll. . . . (BEEP!)"

College Boy was laughing too hard that day to leave a message. And the same thing happened the next day. After that, he found himself calling at least three times a week to see if Julio had changed the tape. Papa J never did, so God knows how long it had been on there, Freddy. So, College Boy kept calling, long after he stopped calling for Valium. And it always made him laugh. And he never left a message, even though he wanted to say "Thanks" or "Eat me, amigo."

The third thing happened two weeks ago. A lunch with Mort and his mom at the Sussman ancestral home in Lynn was canceled after Mort had lost another battle of wills with the front steps. Those fucking steps. College Boy drove the ten miles to Lynn to grab the meal from Dottie Sussman (two courses, plus their usual palate-clearing argument about how he should get some help with Mort, just not from her). On the way back, for only the second time, he thought about rolling up the windows and screaming. Traffic slowed at the light in front of Pazik Liquors. Some sort of backup. What the fuck was it now?

By the time College Boy crept by, he saw a guy between five and a million years older than him, shrouded in mist from an overheated radiator on his van, emblazoned with the logo ROUTE ONE FUN. Waving and giving a "What are you gonna do?" shrug to each car he had inconvenienced, as he awkwardly shifted his weight. And smiling.

College Boy recognized the stance. Randy Zank.

Randy Zank was the best baseball player ever coughed up by Lynn South High School. Before College Boy was College Boy, he was just another kid in Lynn trying to catch Randy Zank. He couldn't. He wouldn't try. In June 1969, Randy Zank graduated from Lynn South and headed for the Mekong Delta, where they had a shortage of mythic figures. Six months in, the littlest piece of cartilage had lost to an even littler piece of shrapnel. He returned to Lynn, where he was greeted by the normal indifference extolled upon a Vietnam vet, plus the bonus resentment of a town cheated out of a big league career. The limp from his 5 percent Teflon knee was now barely perceptible.

"Zank!"

"Hey, Suss."

"Need any help?"

"Nah."

"How you been?"

"Can't complain."

Someone beeped, Randy Zank waved, and College Boy made the light. *Can't complain.* Since then, College Boy had that line all loaded up. If anyone asked him how he was. Mort, Dottie, Levitz, Sheila, Papa J. Anyone. *"How you doing?"/ "Can't complain."*

That was two weeks ago. It was now March. March, all of a sudden. Nobody had asked. Nobody would. And not because they didn't care. Because they knew. College Boy was closed.

16

Just after the first of the year, as his condition worsened and his defiance metastasized, Mort developed a bad habit of collapsing into easy chairs. Rather than letting the seat of the chair hit him in the back of the legs and slowly lowering himself down, the procedure diagrammed in every *Living with Parkinson's* handbook, Mort opted for what seemed less tiring. He would toss his cane to the side and drop shoulder first into the chair, which would have to brace for the rest of him. At first, College Boy was impressed. It was one of the few consistent efforts his uncle gave in a day. But quickly, he lost the ability to right himself in the chair and unless his nephew was close by, Mort might spend a half hour with his body position somewhere between fetal and trap block. When he wasn't exasperated, College Boy might walk in on his uncle and say, "Okay, Mort, hit that sled two more times and then we'll work on pass protection." And when he wasn't cantankerous, Mort would say, "That was awfully good. Now come get me looking like a big shot in this chair."

Neither of them had been anything but exasperated and cantankerous since mid-January. And the proper method of sitting had been their most consistent battleground. When College Boy threatened to turn the easy chairs against the wall and away from the television and have Mort sit in a straight-back model from the dining room, his uncle threatened to exhibit even less control of his bowels. ("And I'll do it, too. What do you young people say? 'Give a shit?' Well, *caveat emptor*, doctor.") When he found a place in Gloucester that rented one of those adjustable chairs that rises up to catch its incoming occupant, Mort complied for however long it takes a seventy-six-year-old to lose an attached remote control, which in Mort's case was about forty-five seconds.

And when College Boy did not politely lecture his uncle on the merits of sitting comfortably, when he would wordlessly come over for the fifth or sixth time that day and fulcrum the respected journalist and author right side up, Morton Martin Spell would use whatever strength he thought he had to jostle him emotionally. "Don't handle me like I'm in some Mexican jail," he'd say. "Let me get up and we'll settle this like we did in the service." Sometimes it was "Mexican jail," sometimes it was "Don't handle me, like you're looking for Bruno Hauptmann's phone number." But Mort was always offering to settle things "like we did in the service."

There are two laws of Parkinson's Disease. Law 1: People who have Parkinson's Disease fall. Law 2: There is nothing anyone can do to change Law 1.

So far, during College Boy's limited stint in the orbit of Parkinson's, he had discovered two types of falls. Rather, Mort had discovered two types of falls. Until Friday afternoon, it had been one. The semi-regular "I know what's coming and I can't stop it" fall, where everything happens in such slow motion you can provide narration. Two months ago, College Boy was in the living room around four A.M., trying to watch enough TV to fall back to sleep after a particularly willful trip to the john with Mort. He landed on Comedy Central and saw this comic, Jeff Altman, somewhere in the early-'80s, do a bit about how old people announce when they're going to fall. Altman, who College Boy recognized from Budweiser commercials, hiked his pants up just below his nipples and started rotating his arms backward and beginning his torturous final descent, complete with play-by-play. *"Oh boy, look out, here she goes, going down, hang on, look out, coming down, look out, here we go, coming in, May Day. . . ."* College Boy's laughter woke his uncle, who was angry for fifteen seconds, then suddenly grateful. He had to go again. College Boy, out of clean sheets and underwear, was grateful as well.

There were plenty of those types of falls, and Mort was always extremely cautious after each one, until five minutes after the bruises healed. Then it was "Mort, where's your cane?" followed by Altman's act, followed by a thud.

The fall on Friday was different. Its primary component was not the loss of equilibrium, but the glut of anger and frustration. In a pre-dusk "how to sit" argument, Mort followed up the "settle things like we did in the service" line by kicking College Boy in the balls. And not some accidental myoclonic jerk thing, either. A real rugby shot. College Boy rappelled off Mort's collarbone and staggered back to where he could bend over and hold his knees. When he caught his breath, he spat, "But you are in the fucking chair, Blanche," and left him there for as long as it takes a thirty-six-year-old to get ossified drunk for the first time in five and a half months.

The thing about stopping drinking, which College Boy had done a thousand times, is the time it gives you to think of scenarios over which you might drink again. Might. And even after you notice that your life has gotten a little more manageable, those scenarios will still arise, but you'll find yourself saying, "ah, no." "Ah, no . . . ah, no . . . ah, no . . . well maybe, ah, no . . . ah, no . . . six months ago, sure, but ah, no . . . ah, no . . . ah, no . . . ah, no . . ." And just when you've traversed every contingence and emerged dry, the seventy-six-year-old man you've been taking care of kicks you in the balls. Literally, and on purpose.

College Boy drove into the next town, Beverly, to the Tai-Waikiki, a Chinese-Polynesian restaurant just over the bridge. He hadn't been there in almost nineteen years, or since he'd been legal to drink at better places. The Tai-Waikiki had let older-looking athlete-types do as much underage tippling as they wanted. Two rules: You must order at least one appetizer and No Horseplay. The Tai-Wai's specialty drinks, Tiki Bowls and Headhunters, had been a sweet, easy introduction to the volumes that would follow. A few of those and a plate or two of pork strips would inevitably be offered in sacrifice before the porcelain god.

College Boy knew better now. Just one plate of pork strips, ten Wild Turkey and sodas. It had been a while since he'd driven drunk. But you know the old saying: It's just like riding a bicycle—into oncoming traffic with your eyes closed. That was all the excitement he needed. Seeing his sobbing uncle lying on the floor when he returned to Vinnin Estates, with a Mont Blanc pen stuck in his shoulder and his white broadcloth shirt looking like People's Exhibit B in a *film noir* murder trial, that was gravy.

Cleanup was pretty easy. Mort had been wearing the adult diapers for two weeks after a month and a half of intense negotiations. No number of midday accidents could convince the man he needed help in the field of waste management. The deal was made only after College Boy walked around the house for two days wearing his own diaper and pretending to defile himself in the middle of conversation. That was maybe the last great laugh they'd had.

Within an hour, Mort Spell was wiped down, re-Depended, pajama-ed, bedded with a heating pad on his sore lower back, and shaking in the first bites of a BLT, one of College Boy's kitchen specialties. He was asleep by nine, which left College Boy the rest of the night to throw up, pass out, and think about calling Sheila and asking her to FedEx the rest of the Valium. Oh, right. He had changed the locks.

When College Boy came to at seven-thirty, he realized two more reasons why he had stopped drinking. The hangovers, and how difficult it was to help a seventy-six-year-old man, any seventy-six-year-old man but especially a seventy-six-year-old man with Parkinson's, to the bathroom at four o'clock in the morning with a hangover. Just as quickly, it occurred to him that there had been no bathroom run in the night. Odd . . .

And that's when College Boy heard what sounded like a moan. Or bad singing. He was right both times.

Mort was lying on the bathroom floor next to the toilet in a pose not unlike the one College Boy had struck eight hours before. He was singing "Here Comes that Rainy Day," Sinatra-style, trying to cheer himself up and distract himself from the pain in his lower back, which is where the moaning came in and fucked up his already poor pitch.

"Mort, how long have you been there?"

"Ninety choruses."

College Boy's headache, which had been ratcheted up to nuclear level by guilt, was not helped when his uncle played the good sport and told him, "Okay, you win. Best two out of three falls." Why couldn't the guy go back to being an unappreciative prick? Still, no combination of heat, ice, massage, Tylenol, or Halcion could help. He drifted in and out but woke for good early early Saturday morning, screaming.

"Bathroom, Mort?"

"No kid, hospital."

They made a bathroom stop anyway. And the hour it usually took College Boy to dress his uncle was shaved to fifty minutes when the spasms just above Mort's hip made him strangely compliant. The man must have been in agony to let himself put his arm around his nephew and be helped to the front steps. Those fucking steps. Two 12" x 30" x 12" stone landings that might as well have jutted from the side of one of the cliffs those idiots dive from in Acapulco. For the last three months, more often than not, the steps had inexplicably stopped Mort cold. He would purposefully stride out the door and get to the edge of the all-weather welcome mat, the only one in NATO airspace embossed with "Holmenkohlen 1978" (the Norwegian ski-jumping championship Mort had covered in three decades), and no further. This was the "freeze" Graham the neurologist had mentioned. The Parkinson's freeze. When the brain, even the formidable brain of Morton Martin Spell, temporarily ends its broadcast day to the arms and legs. Many restaurant reservations turned into take-out, many full-length feature films became forty-five-minute denouement, many visits to his sister Dottie's house distilled to "You're looking awfully well" over the phone because of those fucking steps.

"We'll go to Hawthorne Hospital. It's closer. We'll be there in five minutes, Mort."

"That's not enough time to thank you, kid. Good God!" He arched his back in full writhe. "Let's go to Mass General. I have a locker there."

"No, this is easier."

Within the hour, he was sound asleep. The emergency room had been empty and the doctors and nurses on duty worked on Mort like he'd come into the pits under green. The last line Mort got off was as good as anything he'd dashed since, well, at least since the Holmenkohlen.

"We're going to give you something for the pain, Mr. Spell."

"Great. I'll take all the stuff Koufax turned down."

The real trick is, of course, not letting that be your last line.

College Boy stopped by twice Saturday and midday Sunday before telling the nurses to give him a call when Mort was up and demanding. Saturday night was the first time he'd slept alone at Vinnin Estates. He thought about setting his alarm for four A.M., waking up and pissing in his pants just to give himself something to do. He didn't, but he woke up anyway and led himself to the bathroom, where it went quite well.

He was back at Hawthorne Sunday night around eight to see if Mort was retroactively verbose after almost thirty hours lolling in the arms of synthetic morphine. He found Mort. Arms outstretched to greet no one, mouth waiting for somebody to release the emergency brake, eyes looking ahead at you. Dead ahead.

"How long has he been like this?"

"A couple of hours," said one of the nurses.

The nurse mumbled something about a possible reaction to the pain medication he'd received. Mort finally fell asleep around eleven. But only for a few hours. By 2 A.M., College Boy got to witness this macabre mime from the beginning. Shaking, okay what's new, but shaking with arms outstretched, pleading for—something he couldn't say. Morton Martin Spell was at a loss for sound. His mouth now moved furiously, like a kid had a hand up his head and was working his jaw, but nothing emerged. The mouth never stopped, devouring the silence.

"Jesus, he's much worse than before," College Boy said to whoever was standing behind him.

"Yes, he is," said Mrs. Garrity.

Evelyn Garrity, the hospital administrator, the name of every 2 A.M. hospital administrator, had come by to do two things. 'Fess up to the possibility that this reaction to medication might be Hawthorne Hospital's fault, and recommend that College Boy call his mother and have her get down there immediately. He made the call at the nurses' station. It was remarkably brief and unemotional. Dottie Sussman would be right there. College Boy was grateful. Some guys just live right.

"Thanks for clearing all this up."

"My pleasure," said Mrs. Garrity.

"One more question." College Boy had several, but this was the one he really wanted to ask. "What kind of pig fuck are you running here?"

"Excuse me?"

"So far, you and your people have tossed out phrases like 'some sort of reaction' and 'neurological episode.' Could you possibly be a little more vague as you lead me on this turd hunt?"

"Ah, the doctor on call didn't realize your uncle was on Sinemet."

"Really? And how did that get by him?"

"He didn't know Mr. Spell had Parkinson's."

"FUCKING LOOK AT HIM!" Mrs. Garrity started to look back toward Mort's room.

"NOT YOU! AND NOT NOW! He doesn't look like he has Parkinson's now. Now, he just looks like an old man who's going to die."

"Well, Mr. Sussman, we don't know that yet."

"That's right, Mrs. Garrity. You just had me call my mother to come down here in the middle of the night and sign the 'no heroic measures' proxy because you thought things were going awfully well." (College Boy figured at the very least he might be able to keep Mort alive by imitating him.)

"Why don't we wait until Mrs. Sussman gets here?"

"Great. You do that, and I'll start taking depositions for the big lawsuit against Hawthorne Hospital. Can I borrow your pen?"

"Certainly."

College Boy had only one gear when he was frightened. Righteous anger. Righteous anger, boldly seasoned with self-doubt. Why hadn't they gone to Mass General? Why had he dumped Mort at Hawthorne, this intramural facility just up the street here in Salem? Was it because it was just up the street? Great. He'd saved a half hour of driving. And that was the important thing here, wasn't it? That he had been saved. Nice going, College Boy. You really dope-fiended I-93.

He should call Sheila. Let her know what was happening. And here's the beauty part. If he called now from Hawthorne Hospital, 2:30 A.M., he'd wake her and she'd be so disoriented it would take her at least a minute before she hung up on him. At least.

"Harvey, is it true? Mort had a seizure?"

"Yeah, Mom."

"I told you not to give him liverwurst."

Dottie Sussman was half-kidding. Actually, 49 percent kidding. The other 51 percent believed that food was at the root of any sudden physical tragedy. Her uncle had bled to death in the mid-fifties at the dinner table after eating a baked potato that was too hot, passing out, falling backward, and cracking his head against the floor. One of her mother's card-playing friends, Silvy Dine, had fallen face first into a bowl of bridge mix and suffocated while the others were in the kitchen getting cake. And there were a million other stories which began anything but innocently: "Well, they'd been out the night before and he'd had béarnaise sauce. . . ." The liverwurst reference was a cause of death call-back to Bob Zamcoff, a neighbor who ate a pound of the stuff during Super Bowl III and died of a heart attack a week later while watching the Pro Bowl. "The doctors said he never digested it fully," Dottie Sussman would epilogue.

"Mom, he fell, the pain got worse, I brought him here yesterday, he had some sort of reaction to the medication."

"What do the doctors say?"

"They say it was the liverwurst."

Mrs. Garrity began to hover with forms. College Boy, Mr. Sussman, said he and his mother would be looking in on Mort first, then ghoul out with her.

Mort looked like any other knocked out seventy-six-year-old in a private room. Not pretty. But still. Finally. They came back into the hall and College Boy had to describe to Dottie Sussman with zero medical syntax what her brother had been doing for the last few hours.

"Mom, he was like this . . ." College Boy leaned back next to Mort and flailed arms and mouth. Dottie Sussman snorted a laugh, the only way she knew how to respond to her son. And the one time he wasn't looking for it.

It was just after three now. Technically Monday morning. Dottie Sussman had signed the "no heroic measures" proxy and gone off to cry in a vacant room. She really let herself go—five, six minutes—and then emerged to tell her son to drive to the house in Lynn, sleep in his own bed, and come back to relieve her no earlier than noon.

"Harvey, he's my brother. You've done too much. There's not enough time to thank you." That line again.

College Boy would do his crying in the car. Really let himself go—forty, fifty seconds. He found the Buick Century station wagon in the blue darkness of March with surprising ease. It was under one of several nonworking lights in the parking lot, next to a payphone.

. . . .

. . . .

"Nnnn . . . hullo?"

"Sheila?"

"Fuck you, College Boy!"

Before things changed, then really changed, the only ritual Sheila had observed occurred around nine-thirty A.M., Monday to Friday. That was when *Live with Regis and Kathie Lee* would break for its third commercial and she would point and say, loud, "Now that. That's a whore." She would permit the show to finish its broadcast into whatever living room she was cleaning, especially the end, when Mrs. Gifford tried to cram in her last sincere syndicated good-byes, but by then it was usually drowned out by the vacuum. Which was about right, considering Sheila had already consumed her minimum daily adult requirement of irony.

There is no big story about why or how Sheila Manning retired from her lucrative part-time work in the exciting, fast-paced field of making nice-nice. No Neighborhood Watch sweep of 301 East Sixty-fifth. No twentieth anniversary retrospective of *Klute* at the Film Forum. (Sheila always thought her world was better captured in the movie *Night Shift,* where the hookers did their servicing at the New York City morgue.) No disease ribbon-worthy or penicillin-honored. One day, she was telling her client list, "The dick smoking lamp is no longer lit," the next day, she didn't have to tell anybody anything anymore. It ended when it ended and when it ended, nothing much changed, except maybe the vacuum went on after Regis and Whatshername.

That said, the changing of the locks at Mort Spell's apartment might have had something to do with it. Or at least with Sheila getting out of the College Boy business.

During that first month at Vinnin Estates, when he was mostly just a prostate surgery survivor with Parkinsonian tremors that could still be described as adorable, Mort and Sheila had talked on the phone at least twice a week. College Boy served as the emcee, but his time on the front and back ends increased with each call. Somewhere around Week Three, when Mort barked, "Get your own girl!" College Boy and Sheila realized they would have to hold their conversations elsewhere. The payphone in the parking lot of China Sails after *Jeopardy* became a popular spot. College Boy would work the "I have a collect call to Harvey Sussman from a Mr. Sirhan Sirhan, do you accept the charges?" grift on the operator, they would have their laughs and he'd be back just after eight with dinner.

The phone calls were equally divided. College Boy would lead off with a Mort Update, which was always funny, then Sheila would do her Mort Phone Call Wrap-Up, which was always funnier. Her impression of him was getting better, even if it was just her doing College Boy doing Mort. They would end with a minute or two of Mort improvisation ("Okay, Mort in *Scarface*: '*Say hello to my little friend. By the way, my little friend is looking awfully well. . . .*'") and schedule the next call.

The only time they ever talked about themselves was the week after Labor Day, when College Boy asked if she'd come up for a weekend. The tremors and the shuffling had gotten worse. It would be another month till the first Freeze, so Mort still ventured out somewhere every day. Even when he had no place to go.

"It would really cheer him up if he saw you."

"You think so?"

"Yeah. Uh, me too."

"Well then," Sheila said, "how about next Friday?"

The Wednesday before, in the China Sails parking lot, College Boy decided to prepare Sheila for exactly how excited his uncle was.

"What do you mean?"

"I mean he thinks you're coming to, you know, see him."

"I am."

"But he thinks you're coming to, you know, *see* him."

"Oh, please. Half the time on the phone I have to keep introducing myself to him."

"Yeah. His short-term memory is really going."

"Well, that's it."

"What?"

"If he tries to start anything, I'll say, 'But Mort, I just blew you ten minutes ago.'"

"Nicely done. That went awfully well."

That was the first and last segment of Mort improvisation that evening. Neither of them could ever do any better.

• • •

The weekend—Good Christ, had it been six and a half months ago—had been that rare intersection where uneventful meets memorable. Sheila, at the insistence of Mort's sister, Dottie, stayed at the Sussman home in Lynn . . . and in her son Harvey's room. She cracked herself up thinking that although she'd saved a hundred dollars on a motel room, she might have made five hundred charging College Boy for such kinkiness. Two nights sleeping alone in *his* bed? Five hundred dollars was about right. The absurdity of all this was not lost on College Boy. And if it took the littlest hiatus, Sheila would bring it back with a line like "Your poster of Vada Pinson says hello."

Dottie loved Sheila, especially Sunday morning, when she had changed the sheets and vacuumed before ten A.M. "What do I owe you, dear?" she asked. "Five hundred dollars," said Sheila. And they both laughed.

Mostly, the three of them, Mort, Sheila, and College Boy, sat quietly in front of the TV at Vinnin Estates. It hadn't dawned on anyone that spending more than a half hour in each other's company with nothing to do could be so uncomfortable. Uncomfortable as Mort letting Sheila see him try to get into a chair. Saturday afternoon, Mort had thrown two well-wadded twenties at her lap and told her to get herself a manicure and facial at "that Lancôme joint in the mall that's always empty."

"Mort, I have my own money."

"Don't make me look bad in front of the kid." Another twenty knuckled in front of her. "What the hell, get your toes Simonized, too. You never let me make a fuss over you."

College Boy told her after she left how Mort had confided to him that this was an inopportune time to have marriage pressure put on him. "I told him, 'Ah, Mort. I think she just came down for a visit. Nothing else.' And he said, 'I think I know a little more about redheads than you, kid.'"

Sheila used the money to procure a big-time North Shore clambake and they ate at the dining room table like people who do that sort of thing by design. Mort was as happy as Parkinson's allowed. He kept repeating two wishful thoughts: "Didn't the Lancôme folks do a wonderful job?" and "Isn't it too bad Sheila has to leave early tomorrow morning and this is the last we'll be seeing of her?"

They met in the China Sails parking lot at ten-thirty Sunday morning so College Boy could show her the payphone.

"I think your uncle broke it off with me."

"What did he say?"

They both blurted simultaneously—*"Good-bye, Helga."*

"You are wonderful with him," she said. "Man, could I be wrong about more people?"

He kissed her like he had just come up with the idea. She did the same thing. Neither one fell for it. And when the kiss ended, as it had to, neither one said good-bye. Not even "Good-bye, Helga." But they both thought of it.

Right around the spot where the Wilbur Cross Parkway inexplicably becomes the Merritt Parkway, Sheila Manning remembered she had a 7:30 appointment that night in front of Tower Chemists. A new guy. Marshall Something. Jesus, not a new guy. There hadn't been a new guy in over a year. Sheila was a rent-controlled building. The only openings came when someone moved or died. Jesus, not another orientation session, followed by enthusiastically feigned interest. She pulled into the next Mobil rest stop and called Marshall

Something's work number. She told his voice mail she couldn't meet him because she wouldn't be back in time and she might have Hepatitis C. Well, she might. . . .

Monday morning, she made all the other calls. The four-plus hours a week Sheila had devoted to her cottage industry were briefly reinvested in a non-profit venture, phone calls to College Boy in the China Sails parking lot. Briefly, as in eight days. The Sunday after she got back, College Boy asked if she could ship a couple of his bats up to Salem. *("How do you ship bats?"/ "In a box."/ "A bat box?"/ "Yeah."/ "And where do I get a bat box, from Bruce Fucking Wayne?")* The snow was still at least a month away and he thought he might escape to the cages on Route 1 during Mort's afternoon naps and redirect his caregiver's frustration to the pitching machine, a slightly more inanimate object than his uncle.

She called back Tuesday and said she had tried to get into Mort's apartment for two days, but her key didn't work. And neither did the one the super had. They needed Mort's approval to call a locksmith.

College Boy went cold.

"No need for the locksmith. I forgot. My fault."

"Forgot what?"

"Uh, I changed the locks before I left."

"And when did you plan to tell me that?"

"Uh, I guess now is not a good time."

"Actually," Sheila had said, "now is the perfect time." And she filled the awkward pause that followed with her first *"Fuck you, College Boy."*

There had been a few calls to Mort after the lock change exchange, where College Boy answered the phone and she tersed, almost Cajun, *"He there?"* But that got real fraught, real fast. So, she stopped calling the week before Halloween. Hey, the old guy had already dumped her, hadn't he?

As for her evenings, she stayed quit because she'd already started, hadn't she? And Sheila Manning would not let any man, any subject of that pathetic hegemony, make her restart. Just as no man had made her quit. She had closed shop eight days before she found out about the locks. Eight days. Phone company records would back this up, if it came to that. But it hadn't. Sheila Manning had received the ultimate retirement gift for a call girl. Privacy, respectfully folded and left on her dresser at home.

The last six months had been what those New Age assholes would call a "journey." Many, many more good days than bad, but the bad ones carried an aftertaste worse than pre-aspartamane Fresca. For the first two weeks, she ate a lot of questionable food in front of a lot of bad television, then reversed the process the next two weeks—bad food, questionable television.

The Monday after Thanksgiving (And don't believe that bullshit about one box of Stove Top stuffing feeding six people. That's a single serving, Jim.), Sheila walked to the north end of Roosevelt Island and up three flights of stairs to Serious Fitness, Inc. As she caught her breath and adjusted her eyes to that daytime dusty indoor sunlight, she was able to make out four masses of black men, each one bigger than the next, each one somehow laughably contained in the screaming thread count of their tank tops, their mammoth necks and arms emerging through loopholes in the laws of physics. Weights rang. Rap music throbbed. No one looked up.

That's it, Sheila thought. I went through the wrong door and now I'm in the prison yard.

Through the dustiest light, a man her size appeared. Her height anyway. Twice as wide up top, then narrowing violently into an enviable waist. And half her age. The owner's kid.

"Welcome to Serious Fitness. My name's Ray. I'm the owner."

"No shit. Sheila Manning."

"You here for a free workout?"

"No. I'm here for the night job."

"You're a cleaning woman?"

"Yeah."

"No shit?"

"Hey, kid. If you can own a gym, I can be a cleaning woman." He laughed. If you call a kid "kid" and they laugh, always a good sign. "How much?"

"It's easy work. Clean the bathroom. Vacuum. Garbage. We have a laundry service for the towels. It's like an hour a night."

"It's two hours."

"Yeah, I guess so. Now I'm embarrassed about the money."

"Well, hold your breath and tell me."

"Five nights. A hundred dollars."

"You can get someone. Just not me."

"I guess so."

"Why don't you do it after you close and save the money?"

"I've got evening clients in Manhattan." Sheila tried to catch herself from nodding. Too late. "And I take classes two nights a week."

"Very admirable."

"Oh, I'm admirable."

"Where are you from?"

"L. A."

"You didn't answer my question."

"The Philippines."

"You know, I'd do it for two hundred, but I'd never ask you for that."

"What if I give you the hundred dollars and train you twice a week for an hour?"

"What?"

"I charge fifty dollars an hour for a workout. That's a hundred dollars. Plus, you get to use the cardio machines—the bike, the stair-master, the treadmill—for free anytime."

"Anytime? Like after I finish disinfecting the toilet?"

"Sure."

"Now why would I take a deal like that?"

"Because you've never had a personal trainer before. And because you like it here. . . . Come on, you like it here."

Fucking mindreader.

Shelves are glutted with books that barf on incessantly about the merits of exercise and the need to increase flexibility, stamina, and muscle tone. And those are all damn important. But not nearly as important as having a place to go. And that, above all, is what Serious Fitness, Inc., became for Sheila. A place to go. More to the point, a place to go Tuesday and Friday mornings to collect on her two free weekly training sessions. And even more to the point, a place to go at night.

Ray Quintano, "Q-Dog," as the brothers working the weights called him, was not half Sheila's age. He was twenty-three, which was still too damn close. His family had fled to California when he was three, just after all the martial fun began with Ferdinand Marcos and his shopaholic wife, Neiman Marcos. By eight, Ray was bench pressing twice his weight. He won every junior bodybuilding title available before his career effectively ended at eighteen when he just said no to steroids. He spent two more years in L. A. learning the Zen patience required to be a personal trainer, then moved his parents and older brother to Astoria and built a Manhattan-based clientele before taking the big-time debt plunge and opening Serious Fitness, Inc.

Sheila walked in as Q-Dog was celebrating his eight-week anniversary. The place was doing okay. The housewives and self-employed who loved his riveting care and his default setting—extreme encouragement—had little problem taking the tram to Roosevelt Island, even if they didn't buy Ray saying it was "just like the one at Disney World." The others he'd see at night at Crunch or the Vertical Club or the NYHRC, and they'd have to pay the additional fifteen-dollar Visiting Trainer Fee. Mostly, the dusty-lit walk-up was a haven for Ray's former colleagues, those slabs of mankind still in the gravity of competitive bodybuilding. Men who every other weekend greased up in a high school auditorium and vied for titles like "Mr. Atlantic Corridor" or "Mr. Iroquois Region" and trophies slightly less vague. Who needed no encouragement or attention, just a brooding, stark space to hold their intensity. A serious fitness place, inc. A place to go.

Ray's older brother, Joey, helped with the renovation and trained any stray women who were more interested in the, ahem, social, nonworking component of working out. His father, a former officer in the Philippine army, was a marksmanship instructor at the police academy in Manhattan. His mother was the laundry service for the towels.

Sheila would meet all of them in the first week. She would only immediately understand Joey, whose opening line to her went something like, "Are you still modeling? Man, they were crazy to let you go." Good one, Joey. The old man repaired the plug on the vacuum her first night and bowed when he was finished. Seriously. He bowed. Sheila's second night, she helped the mother gather up the towels and asked, "What do you want me to call you? Mrs. Quintano? Mrs. Q.?" "Oh no," she said. "I'm Mom." That would take a while.

As compelling as the others were, the kid, Ray, was the star of the show. He was one of those guys who remembered everything you ever said to him and would then bring it up a few days later as if it was part of your long storied history together. *"Remember the time you said you hated the leg extension machine?"/ "You mean Tuesday? Three days ago?"* Like that. Second, he was one of those guys who remembered everything you ever said to him and would use it as ammunition to tease you, or preferably, himself. One time, once, one time, the radio was on in the gym and the song "Vehicle" by the Ides of March came on. Sheila said, "Ray, you were two when this song came out." From then on, whenever Sheila needed a break to combat her tentativeness before the next machine, Ray would cup his ear, whether or not there was music playing, and say, "Was I born when this song came out?"

Those were the easy, disarming moves that kept things lively. And that was the point with Ray. Get your work in, be serious, keep moving, keep the body guessing, but fill the moments in between with playful shit before the next challenge. *"Give me fifteen reps, one second hold, three sets, ten seconds in between."/ "You do three sets of fifteen reps, you sadist."* Like that. Sheila, who had given God the job of keeping her in shape the first forty-two years—and the Big Fella had done fine work—knew nothing about exercise and fitness other than it was a smashing idea for the rest of the world. She knew a little more about health clubs, having walked by more than a few and seen various women on treadmills and thinking, every time, "That's all I need. To officially be running nowhere." And she had an idea about personal trainers, that they paid rapt attention to most of these same women and their bodies for an hour or two a week in exchange for money. Hmm. Sheila never judged the motives or sincerity of the personal trainer. Professional courtesy.

Had she been wrong about everything! Everything, including how long it took to clean the headquarters of Serious Fitness, Inc. Maybe an hour and a half. Closer to an hour than two. She'd finish the bathroom and the vacuuming and tie the garbage up, then hop on the treadmill for forty-five minutes. Nobody there. No music. No TV. The only outside stimuli the motorized hum of time passing. At ten minutes, the first buds of sweat. At twenty-five, the endorphins, whatever they were. At thirty-five, the smell, whatever that smell was. Ah yes, triumph. So, take that great line about "officially running nowhere" and shove it up your untoned ass.

Tuesday and Friday mornings, after berating Kathie Lee in the comfort of her own living room, she found herself beating Ray Quintano to his own gym and letting herself in with her key. A key that fucking worked, too. . . . Fifty dollars an hour, which Sheila didn't have to pay, and all the self-esteem she could swallow. She would be warming up on the treadmill when Ray came in, 5–10 minutes later, and they'd have their full hour of *"Good job!"* and *"Remember the time?" "Have any pizza?"* and *"You do it, you sadist."* Ray, Q-Dog, usually came up with a nickname for each client within the first month. Free of charge. It took him six weeks with Sheila. One Tuesday or Friday morning, he walked in and asked her, "How long have you been here?" A half hour. "You're like a delinquent," Ray told her, and she laughed so helplessly he started calling her "JD," which was shortened by the middle of the session to "D." Four months, and she hadn't missed a workout. Not one. He canceled twice because of some family emergency shit, but not her. Not D.

The greatest gift from Serious Fitness, Inc., was that Sheila was never asked about her singleness. Not by Ray, Joey, nor the brothers who couldn't abide looking at someone else's body. Thank God, there was nothing to talk about. Sheila Manning's world had gotten very simple the last six months. Her apartment, 301 East Sixty-fifth, the gym. That was it. This pie had only three slices.

Oh yeah, and the two minutes when she'd been a lesbian.

A few days after Mort moved to Salem, still unaware of the lock change, Sheila was in the lobby of 301 East Sixty-fifth, telling Benny the doorman she was now available Tuesday afternoons. Before she could add the line "first come, first serve," a young woman who was clearly moving out said, "I'll give you two hundred dollars to help me unpack tomorrow." Which was Tuesday. "I'm moving down to the Landmark on Fifty-ninth and Second. Seven blocks."

"Okay."

"And how much every Tuesday after that?"

"Seventy-five dollars." Sheila had authorized herself a 33 percent raise.

"Nah. Let's just do the unpacking."

"Fine."

"Nice try," whispered Benny the doorman.

Janet Grasso was the President and CEO of Janet Grasso Associates, a publicity firm which in the past five years had grown from a one-bedroom apartment to two bedrooms and a terrace overlooking the Fifty-ninth Street Bridge. Janet Grasso couldn't do anything to make you better looking, funnier, or more in tune, but that wasn't her job. Her job was to get you mentioned, and if things started happening for you, her job was to hang on tight and start charging two thousand dollars a month. She now had three two-thousand-dollar-a-month clients: an a cappella singing group, a soap opera actor turned bad stand-up comic, and Al Goldstein.

Janet Grasso's success coincided with a major softening of her appearance and approach. Sociologists have a term for this: less dykey. The transition was so impressive—not just the longer hair, the twenty-pound weight loss, the makeup, and the skirts, but the smiling!—that Sheila did not recognize this suddenly friendly, attractive former tenant as the dour bowling ball with the Chrissie Hynde T-shirt she used to avoid in the laundry room.

"I have to tell you," Sheila had to tell her the next day at the Landmark. "I don't know what you did, but you look sensational. After we talked in the lobby yesterday, I kept saying, 'That's Janet Grasso? Wow.'"

Janet blushed, another recent addition to her 50 percent more femme repertoire. "I'm glad you won't be coming here every week, Sheila."

"Why. Can't take compliments?"

"No, because the next time you walked through that door, I would have jumped you."

"Oh."

As Sheila put away the last of the kitchen supplies, Janet handed her four fifties and apologized for the unexpected spike in mutual sexual unsettlement. Briefly. Then she was back on the job. "If you ever have 8 by 10s done, please send me some. You could get commercial work."

"I don't think so."

"Well then, just send me a Polaroid to have around." She kissed Sheila on the cheek as the new Janet Grasso kissed people. "You know where to find me."

Three weeks ago, President's Day, Sheila was riding the elevator to the thirty-sixth floor of the Landmark. 36H. Janet Grasso Associates. She had called the night before. She didn't know why. Maybe because she knew the gym was closed Monday and Ray had ordered her to take the day off. Maybe. "Janet, Sheila. I have that Polaroid" was all she said.

At 7:05, wearing the black leather trenchcoat, she knocked on the door just hard enough to find out it was already open. There must have been seventy-eight candles working. Sheila would have counted had she been there longer than the two minutes.

"Be right out."

At 7:06:40, Janet Grasso emerged. It was neither the new or the old Janet Grasso. It was the Janet Grasso who wore an open Japanese silk bathrobe and pantingly rubbed Lubriderm *(Lubriderm?)*

over her naked breasts and whatever else. That Janet Grasso. Sheila made out two words on her way out: "Ready, baby?"

So, other than that, her world had gotten very simple.

This morning had been the first time she'd heard his voice in five months. Woke her out of a sound sleep. But Sheila Manning was right there, *"Fuck you, College Boy!"* loaded up, and ready to fire, her home phone number the launch code.

She decided to call Vinnin Estates around dinnertime. It was the next right thing to do. Maybe he'd still be at the hospital with Mort and she could leave a message.

"Hello?"

Shit. "Is he dying?"

"Yeah."

"I'll be there tomorrow."

"You can stay here."

"You sure I'll be able to get in the door?"

"Fuck you, College Boy."

"Good one, Harvey."

"Ow."

She'd leave at ten. Wait. What was she, fucking nuts? She'd leave at eleven-thirty. Right after her workout.

18

The sign read: EIGHT BALLS—ONE DOLLAR.

"How many strikes do I get for a dollar?"

"Good one, College Boy," said Randy Zank. "I haven't heard that in about twelve years."

"I was probably the last guy who said it."

"Probably."

That line used to be the standard icebreaker at Route One Fun, the amusement complex at which College Boy had spent the better part of his youth. Not most of his youth. Just the better part.

"Hey Zank, what was the old guy's name who used to work in the booth for a million years when we were kids? Arnie?"

"Barney."

"Right. Remember, you'd say, 'Hey, Barney. How many strikes do I get for a quarter?' And he'd always say the same thing."

"Pig pussy."

They laughed like kids. Ages twelve and up, an old man in a token booth saying "pig pussy" is about as good as it gets. No kid can hear it once.

"He die?"

"Ten years ago. I bought him out the year before. Nineteen-eighty."

"How's business?"

"Can't complain."

It used to be eight balls for a quarter. Always. And they used to be balls, too. Baseballs. Not these mustard colored half-rubber, half-titanium orbs covered with half-centimeter dimples like they'd come from a buckshot testing range. It didn't even sound like a baseball when you made contact. It sounded like a mistake.

College Boy had not been to Route One Fun since he moved to New York. Fourteen years. Okay, it might have been six balls for a quarter the last time he was here. And Barney may not have said "pig pussy." He might have said, "Hey, dicklick. Wear a fucking helmet." But they were still baseballs, and it was still a good idea to be there.

He hadn't had a bat in his hand in almost nine months and the meager selection of house whuppin' sticks catered more to Little Leaguers and people in street shoes waiting for their tee time on the Route One Fun miniature golf course. So, not good. And the softball machine was busted so he ended up in the 60 mph baseball cage, the first time against the pills in at least ten years. And they weren't even baseballs either. That yellow shit with the dimples.

But, Christ Jesus, it felt great. The wrist and the thumb were delightfully sore, like burning the roof of your mouth on great pizza, and he sprayed four dollars worth of pitches wherever he wanted.

And then he moved next door, to the cage with the rotting VERY FAST sign. Another four dollars. Thirty-two balls, maybe twenty-two strikes. He nailed them all. Okay, maybe he fouled three straight back.

And then he was College Boy again.

"Hey, Zank. This thing is only throwing seventy-five. Can you turn it up to ninety?"

"I don't know." He came out of the token booth.

"What about if I give you ten dollars?"

"Okay. But you gotta wear a helmet."

"Here's another five for no helmet."

"Keep it. Just pay for my balls." Randy Zank quick-limped back inside the token booth and emerged seconds later with a bat. His bat. Wood.

This apparatus, one of the old Iron Mike overhand jobs, hadn't thrown ninety miles per hour since it and College Boy had been in their early twenties. It took a while for the pitching machine to find the plate, joints dizzy from the increased torque, as if Old Mike was giddy from what he was being asked to do. College Boy watched the first eight offerings sail over his head, the second eight come to him on a hard bounce—"fast-bowling," as the cricket people called it—and the third eight a variety pack of wildness.

By the fourth dollar, the machine was suddenly warm and focused. Eight pitches, six strikes. That left him and Zank to split his last five dollars. Forty pitches, forty potential strikes. Five real at bats.

"Go ahead, Zank."

"Let's see if I have anything left."

"You want a helmet?"

"Pig pussy."

Before Randy Zank left for Vietnam, he was what baseball scouts call a five-tool player. He could field, throw, hit, hit for power. And run. Run all day. Ball four, two pitches later, he'd be on third. If a ball he hit bounced twice in the infield, he was safe. If it bounced three times, he was on second. Wheels. Wheels in the late '60s, when nobody in Lynn called them wheels. Now, caged yet unshackled, down to one tool, Randy Zank whaled away for a glorious, decade-backpedaling two minutes. Twenty-four pitches, twenty strikes, twenty-four hurried destinations. All hits. All clean.

"I think you've done this before," said College Boy.

"Never before closing."

"Can I try the wood?"

"Sure."

Two bucks left. College Boy still had twelve good, quick swings in him. He sent nine balls into the deepest corner of the netting that enveloped the cages. Each time he connected, it almost, almost sounded like he was hitting baseballs. The other three belt-high strikes he lashed on a furious line back at their originator. The last one put a half-dollar-sized dent in the top crook of the metal arm of the pitching machine. So endeth the comeback of Iron Mike.

"That's enough. I'm good."

"Yeah."

"Do I owe you anything for repairs? I can come back with money tomorrow."

"Forget it."

"Are you sure? It seems a little slow here."

"Can't complain."

College Boy's only reward for putting on the batting exhibition that disabled Route One Fun's second-hardest working employee was a remarkably smooth reentry onto the highway. He negotiated the Everett rotary unconfused and headed north on U.S. 1, back to Salem.

No one but Zank had seen him rip at ninety miles per hour. This again. How come whenever it mattered at all, College Boy worked in virtual silence, with backs turned? And did it really matter now, at thirty-six, grabbing a couple of March hours to take his mind off where it refused to be in the first place? No. The career that he never had was over and the only trade he'd learned, how to care for a relative with Parkinson's, was about to be phased out by Personnel. No, not Personnel. Human Resources. Perfect.

Mort Spell had arranged the tryout in May, 1978. College Boy's senior year. Despite three outstanding seasons at Lynn South and full scholarship offers to six schools, Suss Sussman had been passed over in the 1974 Major League Baseball amateur draft. Good player. A little small. Not enough upside, they said. Upside. Was that even a word? Maybe when Fred Sanford told Lamont where he was going to smack him, *upside yo head*, but not to describe someone's baseball ability. Or not describe it. Some scout had made it up. Some guy in plaid and stains with a stopwatch and a car full of Whopper wrappers whose life had, well, not enough upside.

Scouts. They were always there to see someone else. Usually a tall blonde or black guy with black guy wheels. They knew College Boy enough to wave and move on, like meeting your date's girlfriend. Occasionally, they even said something to him. But it was always, "Suss, nice game. Can you get *Chad* (or *Reggie*) to come over here?"

Mort had stopped by that April on his way to Buffalo. He was researching two pieces for the *New Yorker*. A long hockey profile on the Buffalo Sabres high-scoring "French Connection Line," Gilbert Perreault *(Peh-ROW)*, Rene Robert *(Ro-BEAR)*, and Rick Martin

(Mar-TEHN), and a casual anthropological study of the evolution and impact of the Buffalo Wing. (That would be Buffalo Wing, the food. Not Buffalo wing, the position played by *Ro-bear* and *Mar-tehn* on either side of *Peh-row.*) Mort Spell had not seen his nephew play since Little League, and bundled in the bleachers with a dozen others (No scouts: Too cold, no blondes, no blacks.), he watched this sudden man do everything right in a 10–2 win over Cortland State.

"Where do they have you going in June, kid?"

"Who?"

"Whatever team you signed with."

"I'm with nobody."

"Rubbish. Have they seen you?"

"Yeah."

"What did they say?"

"Can you get Chad to come over here?"

"Well, that's bilge."

"Yeah, I don't get it."

"They must think you're going somewhere."

"I'm with nobody."

"No, going somewhere, like business school. Somewhere else."

He wanted to laugh out loud and say, "Good one, Uncle Mort." Instead he tried for the only time, out loud, to explain what he could not. "It's like they look at me and don't know what to do."

"By the way," said Mort, "welcome to the club, kid."

Lenny Merullo, head of the Major League Baseball East Coast Scouting Bureau, promised Mort he would swing by before the end of the season and take a look at his nephew. As a rule Lenny Merullo never ventured too far off the East Coast, and Upstate New York qualified as the Outback. But there was this big righty at Cornell, Kutzer, who one of the plaid guys thought had something. He was pitching in the first game of a Saturday doubleheader with Harvard. So, Lenny Merullo figured two hours for Kutzer, then another hour for the fifty-mile drive to Binghamton, on his way home, where this nephew would be playing the second game of his doubleheader. What's his name. Harvey Sussman. Whew, bad name.

Kutzer only lasted three innings, which was a bit unfortunate, but he was only a sophomore and Lenny Merullo would be back. Lot of upside. More unfortunate, much more, the three innings he lasted were the first three innings of the second game. Lenny Merullo would be very late.

College Boy, still Suss that day, had heard from Mort that Lenny Merullo might try to make it before the end of the season. He stopped waiting after a couple of games. Too distracting. Like waiting for the end of something that may have already ended. So, to his credit, Suss Sussman just enjoyed the last licks of his baseball life. Purely. It was a state of mind he would never perfectly duplicate thereafter, although thirteen years as a softball ringer in New York proved a facsimile that could have and did fool everyone but the boys in forensics. And himself.

Binghamton was the last stop, and the second game of the doubleheader the snack bar inside the terminal. He had gone 3-for-4 in the opener, a 6–1 win, and was 2-for-2 with a triple and a triple-robbing lunging catch through five innings of the nightcap. College doubleheaders are seven innings long. Binghamton led, 4–2, and was batting in the bottom sixth when Lenny Merullo showed up. The triple-robbing lunging catch had been in the bottom of fifth, but you probably knew that.

Lenny Merullo had the sincere sensation of watching Harvey Sussman—whew, bad name—haul in a routine fly ball for the second out. And, if that wasn't enough, in the top of the seventh, with two out and a man on second, Binghamton walked him intentionally and Lenny Merullo watched the bat never leave his shoulder. But wait, there's more! For two glorious seconds, he watched him run hard halfway to second on a 3–2 pitch before the ump wheezed *"hy-eeeeeeeek"* to end the game.

"Harvey?"

"Suss, that guy wants you."

"Hi."

"I'm Lenny Merullo."

"Mr. Merullo."

"Sorry I got here so late."

"How late?"

"Bottom six. I heard about the catch, and the two hits."

"Well, thanks for stopping by. I know you were doing a favor for my uncle."

"Look," said Lenny Merullo, "do you want to do this now?"

"What?"

"I can run you now. Or you can come to the open tryout at Fenway June twenty-second. But that's a month away. I know you're not playing on the Cape this summer. That's a long time to be idle."

"You'd do that? Here?"

"Sure."

"How long will it take?"

"Ten minutes."

"Oh, so not that long."

"Actually, it takes five minutes, but I figure you need five minutes to get a pitcher and catcher. And I'll need two bats and three balls."

College Boy grabbed Daniels, his catcher, and Fagan, Binghamton's best pitcher, a highly sought-after junior who was playing on the Cape this summer. They warmed up as he walked to the outfield with the bats, balls, his glove, and Mr. Merullo.

"Go ahead and stretch, kid. This will take a minute. Give me the bats."

Lenny Merullo dropped one bat anywhere, then took out the world's oldest tape measure and pinned the business end underneath it. He half jogged exactly sixty yards, the distance between any two bases, and dropped the other bat. The stopwatch came out of his jacket pocket. Checked jacket pocket. Not plaid, checked. Huge difference.

"Okay. When you're ready. Go hard."

You have to cover sixty yards in under seven seconds or the tryout is over. College Boy, after playing two games and running around for five hours, broke ragged but clocked in at 6.6. In the catalogue of foot speed, a 6.6 sixty is listed under "Quick white guy."

"Okay. Grab your glove and those balls and meet me over here."

Over here was twenty feet in front of the fence in straightaway center.

"What's the catcher's name?"

"Daniels. Ah, Tim."

"Daniels! Heads up! Okay, throw home."

Three hundred eighty feet away. Lenny Merullo tossed the first ball in the air, just ahead of College Boy. He ran three steps beyond after catching it, and by the time he let the thing go, home plate was a concept 370 feet away. The first throw caught the back of the pitcher's mound and skidded left. The last two sailed to the front of the mound and made it to Daniels on four bounces. Key word: sailed. Lenny Merullo was looking for a guy who could hit the catcher on a three-foot-high line from 370 feet, no bounces, no sailing. What the scouts called a "big league cannon." There were about six players in The Show who could do that. Six hundred twenty-five big leaguers, six big-league cannons. That's why Lenny Merullo kept looking.

"Okay, let's hit."

College Boy grabbed both bats and jogged in, smiling at the notion that if he walked he might stretch the tryout into its sixth or seventh minute. Fagan was warmed up.

"Okay, Harvey. Ten swings." No chance. Lenny Merullo still had the stopwatch going.

Fagan helped him out, but not too much. Lenny Merullo was watching him, too. He threw seven fastballs, which College Boy redeemed for three hits, three fouls, one fly. Then three curveballs. Two weak groundballs and one hit, a screaming double that one-hopped the fence in center, ironically close to where he had attempted his throws two and a half minutes ago.

"Okay, thanks, guys." Lenny Merullo pulled out his current ratty notebook and made three notations. "Okay, Harvey, you're on file with the scouting bureau."

"Thanks."

"Sorry I was late. Tell Mort I made it, though."

"I will."

"Okay."

"Mr. Merullo, what does that mean, to be on file with the bureau?"

"Fuck if I know."

Lenny Merullo then laughed like a guy anxious to get into his car and drive home without stopping to piss. Which he was.

"Parking lot's over there?"

"Yeah."

"Okay then."

So endeth the tryout.

"Harvey, what was the pitcher's name? Fagan?"

"Yeah."

"Fagan. Okay then."

"They look at me and don't know what to do."

"Welcome to the club, kid."

• • •

On his way home from the cages, College Boy stopped at the cash machine outside the Bay Bank in the Vinnin Square strip mall. It was Mort's ATM card (PIN: kinglear, if you must know), another thing about which he'd been incredibly responsible, appropriate, and judicious. Who was this guy anyway? He would take out a hundred dollars, always a hundred dollars, then leave the money on the dining room table and loudly let Mort know how much he was taking and what for. There wasn't even a Hiding Place A at Vinnin Estates. Seriously, who was this guy?

People will go on and on about the convenience of cash machines and they will never get to what College Boy liked best. Here it was: No tellers. No, not no tellers to transact with. No tellers to ask out.

College Boy grabbed the five crisp twenties, leaning back briefly to see if she was working inside today. Yeah. Window 4. S. Torres. Whew.

How close had he been to that grab bag of distraction? Close, but just close. But he hadn't. He had stayed on point. He was here taking care of his uncle. He was *"Oh hello, Mr. Sussman. What can I do for you?"* Every time he stopped at the ATM machine, at least three times a week, he would glimpse her on his way out. If she caught him, he'd probably wave. But he always kept walking. And when he was safely away from S. Torres, just before he started the engine in the Buick Century station wagon, he would always smile into the rearview mirror and ask himself, "What have you done with College Boy?"

He turned off the engine in the Buick wagon. He grabbed the basket of laundry he'd done that morning, before he'd headed for Route One Fun.

"Hey, what have you done with College Boy?"

A car door shut that wasn't his. He hadn't seen her when he pulled in. He hadn't noticed. She was early. No, he was late. Shit.

"Sheila. Shit. I'm sorry."

"Did we say three?"

"Yeah." Three-forty. Shit.

"Laundry, huh?"

"Laundry and, ah, batting cages."

"So, College Boy lives. Good, I was worried."

"Why are you waiting out here? Why didn't you let yourself in?"

"The key under the mat? Didn't work."

Christ Jesus, did she look great. Holding up the laundry with one hand he fumbled through his pocket. He worked out a key. The one to Vinnin Estates.

"Ahh. Unbelievable. I left you the key—"

"—to Mort's apartment?"

"Yeah." College Boy lives. He handed Sheila his key. She walked ahead of him up the flagstones. "Can I tell you you look, ah, incredible?"

She held the door open. "You look like shit."

He dropped the laundry basket on the front hall floor. "So, you ready to go to the hospital and see him?"

"Not right now." She squeezed his neck and saw the reflection of her tears in his. "You ready to stay here and make a huge mistake?"

"Not right now."

"Me neither."

"How about we just lay down for a while?"

"Take a nap?"

"Yeah."

She smiled and wanted to say, *"What have you done with College Boy?"*

"Good idea," she said.

19

Just after her workout and just before she left New York, Sheila phoned Meyer Levitz, Mort's psychiatrist. The call lasted thirteen minutes. Or minus the time she was on hold, forty-six seconds.

"Dr. Levitz, this is Sheila Manning. I'm calling on behalf of Morton Spell."

"Are you an attorney?"

"No."

"Okay, go on."

"Mort is dying. He fell and was taken to a hospital in Boston. Whatever they gave him for the pain might have interacted with the Parkinson's medication he's on. He had a serious neurological reaction. Is there anything we can do?"

"You're the attorney. I think you got a hell of a case."

"I'M NOT AN ATTORNEY!"

"Don't shout at me, young lady, or you'll meet my attorney. I haven't seen Mort Spell in nine months. I didn't even know he had Parkinson's. Bad break."

"But you diagnosed it!"

"Is that the kind of basement intimidation they taught you in law school?"

"I'M NOT A FUCKING LAWYER!"

"And I'm not the Reverend Al Fucking Sharpton. What's your point?"

"What's my point?"

"You don't know either? Look, my next twisto is waiting out there. I'm hanging up. Call back and tell Bernice to pencil me in for shiva."

No Parkinson's patient is the same after a fall, let alone a fall and whatever the medication had put Mort through. That said, Mort was as much of the way back as you could be. But for Sheila, who hadn't seen him in six months, this was a man who was more than diminished. Even asleep, which was how she had viewed him Tuesday night and twice Wednesday, this was not Mort Spell. This was a container for Mort Spell, and this was unacceptable.

Dr. Craig Coulter had returned from his first vacation in eighteen months Thursday morning. He was brought up to speed on Mort Spell's case and the malpractice bullet Hawthorne Hospital had dodged. He had called Dottie Sussman around eight to remind her that her brother was being released and to ask if she might want to chat when she came by. Dottie Sussman told him she was late for tennis and to talk to her son. College Boy and Sheila were there by nine-thirty.

Despite how many times you've been told to sit and wait, a physician really isn't allowed the choice of avoiding people with whom he has to talk. There are exceptions, most notably when the people with whom he has to talk don't want to talk with him. One look from College Boy, the look that came after, "Excuse me. Harvey, is it?" was all Craig Coulter needed to know it might be good to move on. In this case, move on to the woman who lingered behind after College Boy ducked into Mort's room to help him get dressed. "Can I speak with you?" Sheila said. "I'm Sheila."

"Sheila Sussman?"

"Good one."

"What's your relationship to Mr. Spell?"

"I took care of him for seventeen years."

"You were his nurse?"

"No, cleaning woman."

At that point, College Boy ducked back out. "Sheila, don't come in yet. He forgot you'd be here." He looked at Dr. Coulter. "Yeah. Talk to him. Good idea."

Sheila had wanted to talk with someone, anyone, since 11:43 A.M. Tuesday. Someone, anyone other than College Boy. Preferably a doctor. Preferably a real one.

"Look, Dr. Coulter."

"Craig."

"Right."

"Let me start. Mr. Spell has to have his medication reevaluated immediately. By a geriatric pharmacologist. This is urgent. I'm not saying we didn't screw up here—"

"He's alive, which I understand was not necessarily the case a few days ago. I'm glad you brought up the reevaluation thing. I need to talk to you about something."

And Sheila told Dr. Coulter, Craig, about the phone call she had made to Levitz Tuesday morning. She left out the Al Sharpton/twisto/Bernice/shiva section of the conversation. Too distracting. If there was one thing she'd learned in her years of cleaning apartments for Jews, it was to keep the word *shiva* out of the reach of gentiles.

"That's some story. And this Dr. Levitz really acted like he had no knowledge of Mr. Spell's Parkinson's?"

"Yes."

"Are you sure?"

"No, I'm lying," Sheila said. "I know how turned on you guys get when a woman tells you another doctor fucked up." Dr. Coulter blushed. Between him and College Boy and the waft of hospital disinfectant, Sheila was feeling quite desirable.

"Well, then," shuffled Dr. Coulter, "we really have to get on this. There's a wonderful doctor at Mass General. Ross Copely. I'll set up something for tomorrow."

"Great."

"Let me go make that call. You better tell Harvey."

"Who? Oh, Harvey."

There is nothing funnier than a man desperately trying to act like he's not jealous. Okay, maybe a man trying to act like he's not jealous when all he is actually jealous of is the fact that you don't need any help taking a shit. So, being among both types must be downright hysterical. Sheila had inherited this jackpot just by showing up at Hawthorne Hospital that morning.

College Boy had not witnessed Mort from the luxury boxes of

time and distance. His uncle looked maybe 11 percent worse. He was uncharacteristically quiet, but Sheila had that effect on a lot of guys. Not on the young doctor who couldn't stop talking to her, but a lot of guys. Before he jogged off, Sheila had intently hush-toned with this white lab coat and matching teeth display, and any time College Boy had walked over to let her know Mort's release was almost being processed or actually being processed, she gave him the smile and the index finger in the air. *You next.*

College Boy would let it pass. She had come here to help with Mort. This guy was a doctor. They were talking in a hospital. There was no need for a steward's inquiry.

"So, who's the greaseball?"

"Craig? Dr. Coulter?"

"Please," said College Boy, "call him Craig."

"Hey, College Boy, Dr. Coulter is going to help us out."

"I, ah, figured that. Mort's about to be processed out."

"Good."

"I'll be over there."

"You can stay here."

"Nah, that's okay. You're already here."

Dr. Coulter returned with his hair and teeth and athletic gait in a much too attentively short amount of time. College Boy, using the window on the door of Mort's room as a mirror, saw him touch Sheila's shoulder, and then saw Sheila grab his well-starched elbow and disappear with him around some corner. Wait a minute. The elbow grab. She'd done that with *him* at Mount Sinai. That was part of her act, like an opening number. "Come Fly With Me." Very cute. Very cozy. Where had she and Lance Lancer, Doctor On Call, or whatever the fuck his name was, ducked away? Into some supply closet perhaps?

Ah, no. Seconds later, she emerged in College Boy's window mirror.

"Hey!" Loud. Scared the shit out of him.

"What?"

"What was the name of the one doctor Mort liked at Mount Sinai?"

"Uh, Dr. Blair. No, Dr. Cahill. Dr. Blair Cahill. I think. Let me ask Mort."

"No! That's right. Thanks." And then back out of sight. Okay, false alarm. Everybody calm down. A minute later, when the window reflected Dr. Coulter walking back down the hall, away and alone, College Boy, his rampant mind now cooling as his projection ran the last few feet of its leader, was okay with it all. Saw it all for what it was. Two people united in concern over his uncle. The only point of contention was, well, who was prettier? Amazing how pettiness just disappears when you let go. College Boy was grateful.

"Where'd Chad go? Sale at J. Crew?"

"I gave Craig the phone number at Mort's place. He said he'd call before the end of the day."

If this 6'-3" haircut hadn't played soccer or lacrosse at Brown or some other faggot Ivy League burgh, then College Boy's powers to stereotype had shorted. Well, good for him. Good for Chad, er, Craig. And good for him to help us out. Good for him to look past this gorgeous woman tilting her magnificent strawberry head his way and focus on his sworn fealty as a healer. College Boy was grateful.

"I hope he calls, Sheila."

"Yeah."

"Do you think he'll call?"

"What?"

"Because I don't want to sit by the phone all day and wind up being hurt. I'm very vulnerable now."

College Boy was ready to apologize for that last remark if he had to. But he didn't. Sheila laughed, touched his shoulder, and whispered, "I think he'll call."

It took a while to get Mort out of the wheelchair into the Century station wagon. His tremors were now so clear-air turbulent the best anyone could do was pretend he was just anxious to get home. But he was no longer dying at the moment, and evidently, that meant he was well enough for Hawthorne Hospital to release.

Sheila waited until after they were back at Vinnin Estates and Mort was safely shitted and sleeping before telling College Boy about her call to Dr. Levitz and the call they were awaiting from Dr. Coulter. Until then, she had thought it wiser to deal with College Boy as she dealt with any man, on a need-to-know basis. Dr. Coulter wanted Mort's medication to be reevaluated immediately. Unfortunately, Ross Copely at Mass General was out of the country, and the one other geriatric psychopharmacologist he trusted in Boston was unavailable until Tuesday. That's when Sheila grabbed his elbow, led him around the corner and said, "It's Craig, right? This is bullshit, Craig. Get us somebody to see in New York tomorrow, Craig." Mort's home number and Blair Cahill's name came moments later.

"Did you really say it like that? With all those 'Craigs'?" College Boy asked.

Dr. Coulter called at four. College Boy answered "Oh hello, Craig," and got a tremendously disapproving leer from Sheila before handing her the phone. Good news. Dr. Blair Cahill had come through. Dr. Michael Zing would just play nine and see Mort at New York Hospital tomorrow morning at eleven.

"Okay, boys," she announced after hanging up, "we're going to New York. We got three hours."

Terrific. Except the way Sheila had said good-bye to Dr. Coulter, with all that giggling. Like ol' Doc Craiggers had verbally prescribed some of that trademark Ivy League fag wit of his.

He definitely had some things he wanted to ask Sheila. Maybe later. Maybe after they'd been on their way for a while. And Mort, though calmer, had to have some questions. Questions other than "By the way, do you think I'll ever take an unchaperoned crap?" Questions like, "I left the hospital eight hours ago. What am I doing in a strange car driving to New York?" and "Why is Sheila running things all of sudden?" and "If Sheila is running things, can she talk to someone, perhaps when we get to New York, about why I'm not capable of taking an unchaperoned crap?"

College Boy called the Yale Club and managed to get the last available room with a private bath at the weekend rate. Sheila went to China Sails and came back with all the stuff she hadn't eaten in six months. They let Mort sleep while they napped on the living room floor. Everyone was packed and fed and ready to go by seven.

They left at 7:35. Mort wanted to watch *Jeopardy*, then see what Vanna was wearing. It didn't go well. *Jeopardy* had those annoying teens and every question seemed to be about some event that had taken place while Mort had been unconscious. And then Vanna came out in slacks. This was what those bastards had revived him for? He was silent until College Boy wheeled him out to Sheila's car, a light blue Hyundai or Honda. "Kid, I hope you've plotted out every men's room built for two along the way," he said.

"Hey, Mort, we're going to New York for the weekend. What could be bad?" Bad question. He lifted his uncle into the foreign—foreign, like strange—car. Sheila pulled the chair out of the way.

"See if you could ask Sheila to get my cane." She was standing right there, and left on cue. College Boy began to fold up the wheelchair. Mort meant to tap his wrist once, but the tremors made that impossible, like getting a stopwatch flush at 1.00. College Boy leaned in.

"Yeah?"

"I can't take a crap on my own, fine. But I will not let myself be wheeled into the Yale Club like Tyler Rothchild, class of '06." His eyes filled. "You have to go along with your uncle on this one, kid. Be a nephew."

It was the first time he had used the n-word. "No problem," said College Boy. "And Mort, don't think of me as your nephew. Think of me as your designated shitter."

College Boy ran the wheelchair back up the flagstones to the house, crossing Sheila, who wasn't expecting him. "Yale Club," he mumbled. She waited for him to lock up and when they got back to the light blue Hyundai or Honda, Morton Martin Spell was shaking his head. Voluntarily. And smiling. His eyes were still wet, but trying to clear. Partly cloudy. "Nicely done," he said. "Designated shitter. Pretty damn good."

Mort was sound asleep before they'd reached the Salem town

limits and climbed onto Route 128 headed for the Mass Pike. Maybe it was a good time to ask Sheila about the giggling, or if she'd really talked to him the way she said she had. Or about the elbow grab. Or the "I'll definitely keep you posted." Nah. No need. Silly. Who was sitting next to her in her car, the light blue Hyundai or Honda? That's right, College Boy. Who was driving with her to New York? Right again. Who had won?

"Hey, College Boy. Remind me to pick up a gift for Craig when we get to the city."

"Who?"

"Craig."

"Oh, Dr. Cutler. Dynamite."

She giggled. "You're too easy."

Connecticut. He'd wait until they were in Connecticut.

In the last seven months, breakfast alone was the closest thing College Boy had experienced to a vacation. Mort Spell could still be good company, but his tremors turned any dining surface into a Jackson Pollock. He had been helped in the last few weeks by something Dottie Sussman had sent away for. A weighted spoon with a grippable handle, which steadied his motion enough to make eating a higher percentage game. "Kid, get the on-deck bat," Mort would say.

The heavy spoon took care of most solid food. Mort resisted the use of a straw unless absolutely necessary, which meant all drinks that weren't coffee or vodka. "What will the girls say if they see me sucking a martini?" he asked, even though it had been months since he'd dined anywhere other than Vinnin Estates or his sister's house. And God knows how long since "the girls" had existed.

There had been one eating excursion on the drive to New York. Mort's one (!) urine-related stop had been on I-84 just before the Massachusetts-Connecticut border at the Red-Art Mobil station. Functional, but not pretty. There's a term in auto racing for a brief pit stop where the crew just tops off the gas tank. Splash and go. That term would apply here.

An hour later, his pants dry from a nap, Mort woke up again in the back seat. "Are we near Vernon Center?"

"Yeah. Next exit. That's amazing. You gotta go?"

"No. We're getting ice cream at the Howard Johnson's."

"Mort," said Sheila, "do you really think that's such a good idea?"

"No," he said. "Friendly's is a good idea. Howard Johnson's is the cotton gin."

Morton Martin Spell, writer/author/intellectual, loved ice cream like someone who wasn't a writer/author/intellectual. There had been more than a few nights just after *Jeopardy* when College Boy would have this exchange with his uncle:

"Mort, what do you want to do for dinner?"

"I've decided to give you the night off."

"Are you sure?"

"I'm quite sure."

"Okay, go nuts."

"Go nuts" meant an entire pint of Haägen-Dazs coffee for supper rather than a scant half-pint for dessert. College Boy would serve it packed and stacked out of a rocks glass and wrap a napkin around the glass to give Mort's hands a little traction. It worked consistently as no mood elevator could. Or any sleeping aid. The effort required to lap up the remnants inside of the glass usually left Mort exhausted and barely able to stay awake during the mandatory face cleaning that followed. By nine, he was down for the night.

Haägen-Dazs coffee was damn good, but Howard Johnson's had a god named mocha that demanded Mort Spell's worship and drew him nigh. Nigh being Vernon Center.

This was no splash and go. The whole sticky business took forty-five minutes. They sat at the counter because Mort liked its press box feel. College Boy bought a rocks glass from the bar next door for five dollars and walked the HoJo counterboy through the packing-stacking process. "Damn good job, kid," Mort told the boy. "We're bringing you up to the varsity next week for the Brown game."

Two seats down, Sheila had a cup of coffee and watched this otherwise tragically refined man go to work on his Mocha Lisa. Near the very end, when the tremors seemed to work in his favor and help make the intra-tumbler tonguing more thorough, she nudged College Boy. "See this?" she muttered. "This is why I had to get out of the business. The competition."

That was the unquestioned height of conversation between College Boy and Sheila on the drive to New York. She went through her schedule for the next twelve hours a few times (Sheila would drop them off, drive to Roosevelt Island, clean the gym, do forty-five on the treadmill, wake up early, move her morning workout with Q-Dog to five P.M., clean her Friday and Thursday apartments at 301 East Sixty-fifth and meet him at Dr. Zing's by noon.) or until College Boy stopped saying "That's too much, Sheila." She played the polite host behind the wheel and as soon as the signal was strong enough, tuned the radio to the all-sports station, WFAN, even though he hadn't asked.

"Are you sure you want to listen to this?"

"Yeah. I love the idiots who call. Do you know Doris from Rego Park, with the cough? *Hello (ech) Jody, why aren't the Mets (ech, ech) not hitting (ech) behind (ech) the run(ech!)ner.*"

"Ah, no."

"I'm very disappointed, College Boy."

On second thought, that may have been the height of conversation. Mostly, College Boy was quiet. Especially after Vernon Center, when he began to feel exactly like what he was. A passenger. A mere passenger. The view in any direction was scary. He could look to his right and ask himself, "Where am I now?" Or look to his left and ask this woman, handling things much too well for his own good, "Where are you taking me?" Or look behind at his sleeping uncle and not know. That left straight ahead, where all the questions collided, or in his lap, where Thursday's *New York Post* lay open to page five.

"You're very quiet."

"Well, if you were me, what would you talk about?"

"Well, who are you?"

"What?"

"Well, if I'm you, who are you, me?"

"No, I'm me."

"Me me, or me you?"

"All right, Sheila. I'll ask you one question. Why are you handling this so well and I'm not?"

"I can't answer that."

"Great. Let's turn up the radio." Three minutes later . . . *"Okay, Doris from Rego Park, you're on The Fan. . . ."*

• • •

It was certainly not the intention of the Yale Club to create lodging that was best suited for the recent graduate who needed a relatively inexpensive place to pass out in Midtown Manhattan and wasn't especially picky about the quality of bedding on which he landed face-first. That's just how things turned out. The privilege of attending Yale was rewarded by the greater privilege of recreating your undergraduate housing. The rest of the place—the tap room, the restaurant, the library, the squash courts, the pool, the game room—had the smug coziness, varnished oak elitism, and extra-dry martini precision of a private club, which it was. The rooms were, well, rooms. Their starkness implied what was already known: Yale men, if they're smart, and by God they are, need not have to cough up real hotel money.

The bathroom was the problem. It was designed to hold one hygienically self-sufficient man. College Boy and Mort had not foreseen the difficulties in suddenly making their lifestyle a traveling circus. Somebody, okay Sheila, had said "We've got to go to New York," and bags were packed with no space for consequences. And this bathroom was a consequence. All of College Boy's installations that had transformed shitting and showering at Vinnin Estates from debilitating possibilities to exhausting realities—the raised cushioned seat and supporting bars around the toilet, the walker *and* chair in the shower—they were still at Vinnin Estates. The Yale Club had no handicapped toilets in its rooms (A Yale man handicapped? Maybe if he forgot his corkscrew, but that's it.), and the spacious facilities they had been blessed with made a 747 lavatory seem like Xanadu.

So, it was just Morton Martin Spell '37, his cane, and the strong neck of his nephew. They rigged a system where Mort would stand in front of the toilet and lean on his cane while dropping his pants. College Boy would then wedge himself in the eleven inches of floor space between Mort's feet and the shower. He would bow his head and Mort would let go of his cane and grab around his neck. "Bend your knees and hang on, Mort." Slowly, he would lower his uncle onto the seat, his compass due south, his vantage point a seventy-six-year-old post-operative penis. Once Mort had touched down safely and released, College Boy held him down by the shoulders so his tremors would not pitch him off the pot. Once he was finished, the process was reversed, except while Mort was back up and leaning on his cane, College Boy had additional honors of wiping and repanting.

You can bet they both had remarks to make, but during this procedure, there was no room, literally, for laughter. When they were finally out of the bathroom after the first run-through, Mort, while catching his breath, wheezed, "Ladies and gentlemen, the Aristocrats." That line kept College Boy punchy until one-thirty, then four-thirty, when Mort woke up and they were on again.

It was now five A.M. and Mort was good until nature's wake-up call at eight. College Boy was not going back to sleep. He pulled Thursday's *New York Post* off the foot of his bed and again stared at the good-sized article on page five in whatever light came through the corners of the bathroom door. He had been done reading the thing since ten P.M., after he bought the *Post* on the way out of Vernon Center. Now he just stared.

• • •

Monday Burial for Dirt King?

Hold on to your shovels.

The verdict in the trial of former Parks Department employee Ernest "The Dirt King" Giovia, scheduled for this morning, has been postponed until Monday morning at 9:00 A.M. after four jurors, including the foreman, contracted food poisoning at the hotel where they had been sequestered the last week.

Giovia, indicted last September on two counts of racketeering, four counts of extortion, and four counts of embezzlement of city funds, was fired from his job with the Parks Department eleven years ago. In five days of withering testimony, the prosecution paraded a steady stream of witnesses who testified that Giovia, once off the city payroll, nonetheless kept his office and unofficial position as "The Dirt King" through an elaborate system of kickbacks, threats, and physical harm.

Giovia's conviction has virtually never been in doubt. The jury deliberated less than a hour before court adjourned Wednesday, and now the only question confronting the jurors seems to be what caused the food poisoning rather than if they will find Giovia guilty on all counts.

Lawyers for Giovia, who served a year in jail in the early seventies for unarmed robbery, have unsuccessfully tried to cut a deal since his arraignment, and their client refused to take the stand during his trial. He did not remain silent, however, several times mumbling "This f—ing guy . . ." as each state's witness was called.

District Attorney Robert Morgenthau's office is expected to recommend a minimum sentence of ten years in prison. With parole and time served, The Dirt King may be released in six years.

• • •

It was the first time College Boy had seen a *Post* since August. He began to flip to the back and see what numbers made up the ninth race triple at the Big A. He stopped just after he realized he didn't do that anymore. *What have you done with College Boy?*

He was not going back to sleep. And Mort was good till eight o'clock. Quarter past five Friday morning in March, Manhattan dark as the future, but yet somehow, College Boy had a place to go. He showered and dressed as fast as any fourth-grader and before the Yale Club Pinkertons could bust him for walking through the lobby without a tie, he was heading west toward the park with the darkness at his back.

The security guard at WLLS-102 recognized him. The guy, Clyde or Willis—one of the old Knicks—trumpeted, "Your attention, please, College Boy returns!" and pencil-whipped him past the new receptionist on the studio floor. This girl ignored him out of necessity, already fielding calls from fans whose encyclopedic allegiance to Dan Drake had somehow turned an offhand remark he'd made six years ago (*"You know, the show is much better if you call the station and listen to all four hours while you're on hold."*) into a kind of Studio 54 phone bank. College Boy slipped easily through the halls, past the same three large retired cops ("Hey, look who decided to come in. . . ."), and into the studio, where Dan Drake sat alone, head down, hard at work on a Hershey bar. He took a full beat, the beat only five guys have ever been funny enough to take, grabbed the nearest memo pad and never looked up.

"Ah, while you were out . . . Luca Brazzi called to confirm lunch."

He threw an unopened Hershey bar, hard, which College Boy backhanded. It was Dan Drake's last Hershey bar. That's how happy he was to see College Boy.

"Can you hang out?"

"Yeah, a little while."

"That's all we can do today anyway." Dan Drake called down to the front security desk and told Clyde to let him know when Carl or Dr. Blob came in. "So, how about your buddy The Dirt King heading for the old Graybar Hotel?"

"It's funny—"

"How are you now, good? Dynamite. Do you have any idea what's going on here? Would it kill you to stop thinking about yourself for a second?"

As it happened, College Boy had a second. Dan Drake, twenty minutes away from becoming Dan Drake, spoke in a voice too soft for broadcasting. And too choppy. The softness was hurt. The choppiness was betrayal. Three weeks ago, Carl and Dr. Blob had signed a deal to do their own morning show at another station, WCRK, Crack-105. They had wanted to start immediately, and Dan Drake, who kept waiting for them to tell him of their plans, was more than willing for them to get the fuck out. Unfortunately, the station manager at WLLS wouldn't let them out of their contract, which ran through July 1 and would force them to have their big Crack-105 debut in the Arbitron drive-time wasteland of summer. Sound thinking, except rather than pay to keep Carl and Dr. Blob off the air, he required them to come to work until the end of the deal. After threatening to give himself a disease that needed four months of repeat broadcasts to cure, Dan Drake eventually got the station manager to agree to keep them out of the studio after May 15.

That was still six weeks away, and although Dan Drake drove through success with the self-pity pedal perpetually jammed to the floor, this time, he was justified. Carl and Dr. Blob now came to work, when they came to work, with the energy and passion of Eastern bloc factory workers. These days, if Carl or Dr. Blob added anything to the broadcast it was by accident, and if it turned out to be funny, well, as Dan Drake would say, send this back to the lab for further tests.

Early last week, he thought he had stumbled onto something which would at least guarantee some flow of dialogue in the studio. Blob made some remark about trying to pick up women in Bosnia . . . with a bulldozer, off the charts for bad taste, and Dan Drake held back his wince and asked, "Is this the kind of cutting edge comedy we can expect on the new show?" For the next two hours, then the next four days, he devoted almost all of *The Dan Drake Show* to Carl and Dr. Blob's new venture. There were calls to the promotions department at Crack-105 to find out how the ad campaign was coming (there was none) and a clause-by-clause reading of their old WLLS contract looking for a loophole to get them out and on their way earlier. All under the dripping earnestness of "Just wanting to make sure the tri-state region is fully prepared for the onset of audio entertainment history. Carl and Dr. Blob are stepping out." Dan Drake knew radio and he knew psychological torture. And he knew there was no better radio than steady psychological torture.

For two hours and four days, it was great. And then Carl and Dr. Blob figured out that maybe Dan Drake was making fun of them. So, they shut down again, this time aggressively. Two days ago, in the middle of a broadcast effort the host termed "A Salute to Dead Air," Dan Drake let himself sound as exasperated as he was. "You two," he said, "are just as blank as farts. Godspeed to Crack-105." The next sound you heard was two chairs being pushed back clumsily across the carpet. That was Wednesday. Thursday, Carl and Dr. Blob called in sick.

"They'll be in today. They have to pick up their checks."

"I'm sorry, Danny. That sucks."

"Fuck 'em. You know what the worst part of this whole thing is? The absolute worst? I'm doing a lot of time now with the news guy, Jason."

"I thought his name was Larry." Which was the name Dan Drake always used on the air when he couldn't be bothered with information.

"Bite me."

"Sorry," said College Boy. "You know, I remember Jason being a bit of a—"

"Load?"

"I was going to say stiff, but load is good."

"Actually, it's not terrible. He kind of gets it. Gets what we're trying to do. That this is, for want of a better word, show business.

He's not dyeing his hair and buying a Corvette, but he knows when I ask him something the idea is to answer quickly."

"That sounds okay."

"Sure, but during the breaks it's just God-awful. He's either compiling his little news update—And by the way, do you think anyone who listens to me cares about the news?—or sitting with his mouth open trying to make sixty-seven four-letter words out of 'spina bifida.'"

"That's tough"

"Fuck yeah."

"All I can think of is 'spin.'"

"Aaaaaahh!" That was Dan Drake's surprise laugh. The "Hey, somebody else in the room said something funny" laugh. "See, I don't have this anymore. At least with Carl and Dr. Blob, lazy shitbags that they might be, there was some social component. You see each other every day for thirteen years, you work up an exchange during the breaks. What did you eat last night? Did you see the Ranger game? What was that God-awful movie with Paul LeMat and the girl in the car? How's your pecker? That sort of thing. Well, that's gone because they've somehow decided that I'm responsible for them still being here."

College Boy took a stab. *"Aloha Bobby and Rose?"*

"YES!"

Clyde the security guy buzzed Dan. Carl was across the street, waiting for the light to change.

"Shit, you gotta go. See, I'd love to tell them that—*Aloha Bobby and Rose,* good Christ—but that's over. You should go before they see you. I'd rather avoid that particular brand of ungainliness today."

"Sure."

"You know I still feel like shit about you getting worked over by those thugs."

"Yeah Danny, well—"

"Hey, you gotta get out of here. How long you here for?"

"Weekend, Monday."

"Well, make sure you stop by before you leave."

"I'll try."

"Would it kill you? Would it fucking kill you to think of somebody else for once in your life, College Boy?"

One of the retired cops unlocked the door to the backstairs, Dan Drake's exclusive egress, and College Boy avoided running into Carl by a good twelve to thirteen seconds. He was back on the street at 6:02 and skirted behind Dr. Blob, who was thoroughly transfixed by his impending purchase of two bowties from the coffee cart on the near corner.

He walked the six blocks north and three blocks east and almost let himself be sucked into the Medea Restaurant as if by some Greek coffee shop undertow. The Medea had been his regular breakfast and Romanian tenderloin joint, when not just breakfast, but every meal alone had been his birthright. He was not up for *"Hey, hey, my friend! Where you been, my friend? Hey my friend, how 'bout a dlink?"*, well-meaning as the reception may have been. College Boy stopped just short of Central Park South and realized what he had done. Walked out of the studio and away from the Yale Club. Toward the park. Toward Heckscher Fields.

Somewhere in the mid-40s, between Fifth and Sixth Avenues, College Boy slipped into a diner he'd never noticed before—the New Delos. Did they have any idea how great that name was? He had bacon and eggs and potatoes and toast all at once for the first time in about a year. He raced through his breakfast, his breakfast alone, as if Mort was an oven he'd left on, and made it back to the Yale Club just before seven o'clock. He grabbed Friday's *Post* in the lobby and threw a dollar at the guy in exchange for no shit about his not wearing a tie.

Mort was still asleep. The door did not wake him when it closed, nor the rustling of the *Post,* which College Boy read backward from sports to page seven, which he devoured until 8:05.

• • •

Dirt King to Lawyers: I don't dig you no more

Former Parks Deparment employee Ernest "The Dirt King" Giovia fired both his attorneys yesterday and will represent himself when his trial concludes Monday.

Giovia, whose conviction on ten counts of racketeering, embezzlement and extortion of city funds is a virtual certainty, did not take the stand during his trial but will undoubtedly use his new position as *pro se* counsel to make a post-verdict statement before the court.

Thursday was not the best of days for Giovia's former attorneys, Salvatore Messina and Seth Axelrod. Shortly after they were scooped and tossed by The Dirt King, they were questioned by New York City police in connection with the mysterious food poisoning epidemic that struck four sequestered Giovia trial jurors Wednesday night and delayed the verdict until Monday.

• • •

"Kid, where am I now?"

"Yale Club, Mort."

"Where are you taking me?"

"The bathroom, then the doctor. And breakfast somewhere in between. I assume you'd rather eat up here than the grill room."

"Yes I would."

"Good."

"How come you're handling things so well?"

"I can't answer you, Mort."

"Fair enough. Get the on-deck bat."

"Uh, I forgot to pack it. Fuck!"

"Shhh. They'll think there's somebody from Dartmouth in here."

College Boy choked out a soft "sorry."

"Now before we head for the john, run by me again where I am."

21

Dr. Michael Zing was the best kind of bald man. The kind that laughed and pointed to his head and said, "You think you have problems? Yesterday I had hair!" He walked into his waiting room only fifteen minutes late Friday morning, a blazer weakly trying to conceal the ensemble he'd been wearing when he hustled off the ninth green to the parking lot.

"Okay, who's the sick one?"

"I love this guy," whispered Sheila.

"Don't tell me. I'll be with you in a minute."

Sheila had to run back to 301 East Sixty-fifth before Mort and College Boy got in to see Dr. Zing. When he came back out and saw she was gone, he said, "Damn. I was going to guess her."

That was the end of shtick from Michael Zing, geriatric psychopharmacologist. He had more, but he'd had better audiences than Mort and College Boy. He looked in Mort's eyes, which might have been blank with fear had they not been frozen in a particularly heartbreaking Parkinsonian symptom known as "The Mask." Then he asked College Boy for a list of his uncle's medications, which College Boy furnished along with Mort's pillbox, a four-tiered plastic file that looked like a miniature set from *Hollywood Squares*. For however long, ten minutes short of eternity, Dr. Zing poked through the list, the box, and two or three huge books, stopping only to pinch the bridge of his nose and clamp his eyes shut.

"Mr. Spell, any history of epilepsy?"

"Of what?"

"I don't think so," said College Boy. "Mort, you're not epileptic, are you?"

"No, Pierson."

"That was his college at Yale."

"Tell me about it," mumbled Dr. Zing. "They used to kill us in touch football. I'm sorry, I didn't get your name."

"Sussman." College Boy stood up to make it official. "Uh, ah, C. B. Sussman. C. B. Sussman."

"Mr. Sussman, your uncle ever have seizures?"

"Well, something happened to him in the hospital in Boston. Was that a seizure?"

"No. Epileptic seizures."

"No. Not that I'm aware of."

"Well, how long has he been on Depakote?"

"Since August."

"Eight months ago August?"

"Yes. It was one of the medications he was put on after he left Mount Sinai. By his psychiatrist, Dr. Levitz."

Dr. Zing pinched the bridge of his nose. He couldn't look up, and he knew Mort wouldn't know if he did. "Congratulations, Mr. Spell," he moaned, "I think you've been part of a field project."

Morton Martin Spell had not been a participant in the conversation since he'd uttered "Pierson." Mask hardened by room temperature, fight gone, chased by the conviction that his nephew (Had the kid made up some alias?) had now enlisted this 12-handicapper to put him away for good, Mort faded to blank. Shaking into the woodwork, he never heard Dr. Zing's sardonic congratulations, nor the long exchange that followed.

College Boy gasped for accuracy as he told Zing about Mort coming off Levitz's prescribed Valium while in Mount Sinai and the two biting incidents following his prostate operation. Once he was out, he went back to Levitz, who'd had put him on four new medications: Prozac, Wellbutrin, Halcion, and Depakote. The Halcion was for those nights he had trouble sleeping. College Boy, like the rest of the supply side economic world, had heard of Prozac. Mort told him Levitz had said the other two, Wellbutrin and Depakote, "helped the Prozac along," but, he added, "Levitz never said which one was the vermouth and which one was the olive."

Three weeks after that, Mort saw Graham the neurologist, who concurred with Levitz's Parkinson's diagnosis and added medication Number Five, Sinemet. For a while after the move, the tremors were manageable and Mort seemed less erratic. Might have been a month, might have been a day. Then life descended. At one point, College Boy called Graham, who explained the progression of Parkinson's Disease in patients over seventy tended to be more rapid and any further evaluation of Mort before six months would be a waste of everyone's time. So, they went along. It had been six months at the end of January, but by then, Mort was no longer interested in being carted to New York to see Graham. When College Boy suggested they might find a neurologist close by, Mort told his nephew, "Let's revisit this when you come to me for a raise in the spring." All prescriptions kept getting called in and refilled, and no doctors were sought until Mort's fall last Friday. Last Friday? Christ, had it been only a week?

Dr. Zing tried not to nod too much while the nephew, this earnest man, C. B. Sussman, filled him in. The phrase "brought him up to speed" is not applicable here. Once Dr. Zing saw "Depakote" and heard "last August," he parked himself two laps ahead of College Boy and waited for him to finish.

If you don't like to be wrong, don't become a psychopharmacologist. Michael Zing, who during his senior year at Yale (when he'd had hair) hit .378 as the starting shortstop for the Elis, had chosen a profession with an initial success percentage only slightly higher. It was a branch of medical science that aspired to imprecision. But after being raised in the shadow of his father's manic depression and the barbarism with which it was treated and untreated, it was the only path that emerged. Ironically, that was the last time in Michael Zing's life the guesswork had been removed. The second-to-last time had been in 1974, nine days short of his old man's fifty-third birthday, when he stood outside of Central Synagogue and refused to let his father's psychiatrist in to the funeral.

"Let me tell you everything I know, Mr. Sussman."

Sheila was right. You had to like this guy. What doctor ever said, "Let me tell you everything I know," even if he didn't? And what doctor could do that while casually, stunningly casually, siphoning five vials of blood from a seventy-six-year-old man?

What Dr. Zing should have said was "Let me tell you everything I'm sure of," but he opted for comfort over semantics. The reason he'd asked about epilepsy was because, since its introduction in the United States in 1983, Depakote had been marketed exclusively to treat epileptics. Only recently had the possibility been raised that the drug could be effective in combating bipolar depression or mania. There were side effects—whoo boy were there side effects—but so many of them, including tremors, were shared by many antidepression medications.

"What are you saying?"

"I'd rather not come to a conclusion before I look at the bloodwork," said Dr. Zing. "But until then, let's drop his Depakote from 1,500 milligrams down to two pills, 500 milligrams, for the next few days. This medication business is unfortunately a lot of trial and error. You ever play baseball, C. B.?"

"Huh? Baseball? Yeah, a bit."

"I knew it. You fail seven out of ten times for fifteen years in the big leagues, where do you end up?"

"Cooperstown."

"Right. I'll see you and your uncle Monday afternoon at two. We'll know a little more then."

As he helped them out, Michael Zing put his arm around College Boy and asked him if, in lieu of his fee, he might sell him some hair. Mort, in a blaze of perfect timing, jumped in softly. "You'll have to go through me, doctor."

They staggered to a cab back to the Yale Club, College Boy only slightly better than his uncle, and collapsed dead asleep until Sheila woke them with a phone call just after six to ask how it had gone in the room with Dr. Zing.

"It's four less pills and we have to see him Monday."

"And?"

"That's all I know."

"Well, it sounds like he has some idea."

"I was hoping you'd tell me how I should feel."

"I'd be scared and hopeful."

"Okay."

"Okay?"

"You be scared and hopeful. I'll be over here."

They spent the rest of Friday, most of Saturday, and all of Sunday bunkered in the room. When the chambermaid poked her head in to make the daily towel exchange, it probably looked like a plainclothes cop guarding an informant before the big trial. When they weren't eating, watching television, or appearing in the bathroom as "The Aristocrats," you could find Mort asleep, which was a nice break from his ping-ponging disorientation and despair.

College Boy was stretched out on the other bed, rewriting the same three pages of Yale Club stationery. Both sides. He planned to bust out for an hour early Monday morning and air his work out on the radio. *("And now it's time for a brand-new feature here on* The Dan Drake Show: *'Closing Arguments from The Dirt King . . .'")* The agonizing slowness of writing, or trying to write, or whatever the fuck he thought he was doing, was a glorious distraction from the notion of this old man he was obviously overmatched to care for, this name and persona he had outgrown to tatters (*C. B.? C. B. Sussman? Is that really what we're going with from now on?*), this woman who was never a minute too early nor a second too late, who he was obviously overmatched to care for—Shit! He already used that analogy on the old man! Some fucking writer.

Sheila came by Saturday and Sunday afternoons. She sat in the hard-backed chair at the desk and restrained herself from straightening the place up or making any locker-room smell remarks. When Mort would drift off, she and College Boy headed into the refreshingly musty hallway, cracked the door, and walked the corridor trying not to get to know each other.

"Can I ask you a question, Sheila?"

"I don't know."

"You don't know if I can ask you a question?"

"No. That's my answer to your question."

"Okay."

"Fine."

"What do you think is going to happen?"

"Ah—"

"If you had to guess. . . ."

"I—"

". . . because I won't hold you to it."

"Don't—"

"Yes?"

" . . . know."

"I should apologize."

"For what?"

"I haven't had to talk to too many people in the last few months, so I'm pretty incapable of conversation."

"Well, this is as close as I come to glib."

"So, you don't mind this awkwardness between us?"

"Actually, I'd like a little more. I can't remember the last time I was this uncomfortable."

"You're uncomfortable too?"

"Yes."

"Great! Let's see what else we have in common. What's your favorite book?"

"*Magister Ludi*. No, no. *The Microbe Hunters*. No, wait. *Henderson the Rain King*. Hang on. *The Easter Parade*. No, fuck it. Anything by Lovecraft."

"Let's go back to awkward."

"Okay."

"Can I ask you a question?"

"Sure."

"I said awkward."

"Sorry," she said. "Ah, I don't know."

Saturday night, the two of them roused Mort to where he was willing to be dressed and taken to the Oyster Bar in Grand Central Station. They made it out of the Yale Club, across Vanderbilt Avenue to the top landing on that east-facing marble staircase just inside the entrance off the cab stand. A staircase built for overblown entrances. Saturday evening, seven P.M. Grand Central off-peak and humane. Yet Mort froze. And fast. The only thing moving were his tears. It had taken four minutes to get to the landing. It took almost thirty to get Mort back to the room, half of that Sheila calming him down to where College Boy could pick him up and carry him back across Vanderbilt with no threat of crumbling. Man, he'd gotten thin.

College Boy set him down across Forty-third Street, far enough from the entrance to the Yale Club where, if anyone had been there, no one would have paid attention. Sheila ensured the focus would be off Mort getting his sea legs back by walking way ahead of them, slowly, her chocolate suede trenchcoat opened to distraction. A move she had picked up from Barbara Bain, she would later tell College Boy.

During a time when everything was lost on Mort, the gestures made by these two to enable him to walk into the Yale Club unaided and unnoticed were not. They were still planning to leave him there to die, and now they'd enlisted a doctor, that sand trap Bedouin, Fing or Wing or whatever his changed name was. Of that he was still sure. But to be back in his bed, in his Chipp robe, waiting for room service, as if the world thought he'd gone out to pick up the *New York Review of Books* and a roll of pep-o-mint Life Savers and sauntered back, well, they were owed.

Sheila showed up Sunday afternoon around three o'clock. She brought the Hyundai or Honda in from Roosevelt Island and thought Mort might like to drive around Manhattan for an hour or so. Mort was not interested. But he thought it was a smashing idea for the two of them and began to push thusward. College Boy and Sheila took turns telling him no until five, when he said he wanted to watch the rest of the Doral Open alone and nap and they would be doing him a great favor if they would be so kind and get the hell out of his room until supper time. At five-fifteen, they withdrew their final protest.

"I'll be honest, the last thing I want to do is go somewhere else and sit. Even if we're moving."

"Fine."

"I feel like I haven't stopped sitting since October."

"You wearing sneakers?"

"Yeah."

"Come with me, C. B."

"Why did you call me that?"

"I can't call you College Boy anymore. Can't find him."

"Okay."

"Come on."

She lied. They did get in the car, but it only took fifteen minutes to get over the Fifty-ninth Street Bridge and out to the end of Roosevelt Island and Serious Fitness, Inc.

They walked into the tiny gym. Five-thirty in March and already pitch black, as if they'd traveled two times zones rather than one borough. Sheila flicked the light over the two treadmills and tossed College Boy a shirt, shorts, and socks from the laundry she'd done for Q-Dog yesterday. "You can change in the incredibly dark room next to the shower."

"Where are you going to change?"

"Already there." Sheila opened her shirt and peeled it back with both hands to reveal the top of a leotard, reached inside her pants to yank up the elastic waistband of what could only be gym shorts, then lifted her pant leg just enough to show a heavy white athletic sock. It was all done with great fake furtiveness, like some mild-mannered cleaning woman unveiling her true identity—calisthenic superhero.

College Boy emerged and saw Sheila adroitly stretching her quads and felt the rare mixture of arousal and sickness. The arousal was Sheila grabbing one of those legs, puffing that magnificent chest. He was 36. He wasn't made of stone. The sickness was the realization that *he* would have to stretch.

Maybe he was made of stone. It had been a long time. So long, it might as well have been never. Even when stretching had been an agonizingly regular part of his life, when life for College Boy had turned into what happens between stretching, it was a sentence. A customized Dantean ring at the foot of Purgatory—inflexibility.

He tried the hamstrings first. *"Jesus God."* After three separate attempts, he mumbled, *"We'll get back to those."* He tried the quad stretch, which used to be the least of his problems. *"Good Christ."* He hung in, fueled by a growl that sounded like the last words of a Mr. Coffee machine *("Arrurghppppp . . .")*. Sheila had finished with her calves and was in the middle of a long toe touch, trying not to laugh. But she wasn't made of stone.

"Hey, Nick Nolte . . ." She knew.

And then College Boy began his lunges. The growl turned to a spitting Tourette-like skein of half-expletives *("Fu . . . bas . . . pri . . . shi-fu . . . fuuuuu . . .")*, then to a soft plaintive wail, then finally to the high-pitched helpless titter of distress. *"Why are you doing this? That's enough. Enough. Somebody stop. Please. Please. Enough."* All of which wasn't helped (Well sure, hence the word "helpless") a few minutes later, when Sheila, fresh from fifty crunches, pulled up alongside him and growled, spat, cursed, and tittered in highlight reel fashion. With that, College Boy's suspect infrastructure gave way.

"Let me know," he puffed, "when it's all too overwhelming for you."

Sheila rolled over and laughed for a while. A while. *Enough. Please. Somebody stop.* Finally, she bounced up and started the treadmill. College Boy struggled to his knees. If I can do twenty push-ups, he thought, I'll keep going.

Who knows why, but he breezed past twenty—don't question the Universe—and kept his pace and form steady until fifty, when he stopped, surprisingly refreshed, nothing left to prove. Sheila caught it all in the mirror on the wall facing the treadmills. Some second wind. She watched him bound up and walk around in a small circle, hands on his head, each inhale inflating a smile. So, this was College Boy.

They both did forty-five minutes on the treadmills, although only thirty-six at the same time. The reflection of each other's company and its stirring silence was broken occasionally—"How's it going?" "What incline are you at?" "What should I do here?"—but neither of them wanted interruption. And it was crowded enough since they had been joined by the endorphins.

College Boy waited until Sheila was out of sight to crank his machine up to eight, then nine miles per hour and do a pre-cooldown two-minute sprint. None of that "Ooh, such a big strong man" nonsense. And he rather she find him dead of a heart attack, slumped over the machine, treadmill belt still churning, than have to witness the actual coronary. And besides, she'd already had her laughs for the day watching him stretch.

Q-Dog's T-shirt was completely soaked through, and the shorts had the requisite crescent puddle below the waistband. Great, he thought, where am I going to find a laundry tonight? I'm not letting her touch this stuff.

College Boy slipped off his sneakers and wandered in Q-Dog's damp socks towards the sound of the shower in the darkest part of the gym. Suddenly, the water stopped running. Maybe somebody needed a towel. He danced into the changing room and turned left. No one. And then, his back got colder, damper, the way it can only get from another cold, sweaty shirt pressed against it.

Sheila was leaning against the post that separated the two changing rooms. Bare feet, no shorts, arms only recently pulled through the shoulder loops of her leotard. Face flushed, the beginning of a spectrum of red that arced from her ample mouth to her cheeks and tumbled in three more shades down to the still wet darker ends of that great hair. She had fully intended to shower. Maybe he'd be there at the end with a towel. But when she sat in the changing room and heard him running, she changed her mind. And when she heard him stop, that's when she wanted to run. To him. Nah. That would have scared him. So, Sheila kept the shower going, stayed hidden in the dark, then switched it off and let sweat find sweat.

There aren't too many better places to have sex than an empty gym. The mats. The benches that you can adjust. The benches you can't. Bars of varying heights. All those towels. And if the College

Boy and Sheila had thought about it, they might have really utilized the facilities. Given an alternate meaning to "circuit training," "reps," "squats," "pumping iron," and any other workout-inspired double entendre of your choice.

But they didn't think about where they were. Serious Fitness, Inc., Gym/Personal Training/Carnal Playground. They never made it out of the changing room. Hell, they never made it past the post against which Sheila was leaning. All of which made perverted sense. From Day One and since, for all their maneuvering, College Boy and Sheila had never gotten past each other.

They took turns peeling off their last layers of sogginess, then bathed their faces in one another. Their clothes lay in a dank heap on the floor, all turned inside out. Eventually, they would be in the adjoining pile. When each had shuddered their last, they stared with gasping smiles for what felt like the first or millionth time.

"All right," panted Sheila. "No funny stuff in the shower."

They made out in the car like kids until she pushed him out in front of the entrance to the Yale Club. (How long had it been since that had happened?) It was almost eight. She'd be back to get the two of them at one tomorrow.

College Boy had hoped to return to the room and find Mort asleep, or better, awake but slightly disoriented. Ah, no. He got off the elevator and saw Willie, their favorite room service waiter, heading back down the hall with a full tray.

"Is that from us, Willie?"

"Sí."

"Wait here."

Morton Martin Spell was on the toilet, singing "I Get Jealous." He had been there a while.

"Mort, how did you get there?"

"I knew somebody in admissions, you little shit. Now help me up so I can be left to die in bed the way you planned things."

If such a thing is possible, Mort was surly and abusive in the best way. Somehow, he had ordered dinner for himself. Somehow, he had made it to the toilet without a trail. Okay, so his timing was off. The food got there and he couldn't get up. The nephew got there and he hadn't planned his escape. But he had done two things with nobody's help. Two things on the way to everything else. Morton Martin Spell, respected journalist and author, would not give himself the right to be proud. But he would let himself be nice and angry.

After dinner and until he dropped off during "George Michael's Sports Machine," there was a lot of "Don't think you'll get away with this." And maybe College Boy was looking at it all through a lens ground in postcoital optimism, but it was all good. Anger was strength. Paranoia bred energy. Combat looked like hope. All good.

And forgive College Boy if he suddenly tacked hopeward, but during their four o'clock sojourn to the bathroom that morning, he could have sworn Mort was 10 percent steadier. Ten percent. Just enough to notice.

He walked into the studio at 5:35. Dan Drake did not look up, even after he dropped six Hershey bars in front of him.

"How long can you hang out?"

"Eight?"

"We go till ten here."

"I know. But I have to get back to the Yale Club before my uncle wakes up. And I wrote something, Dirt King stuff, if you're interested."

"I'm not interested, but we'll do it anyway."

Dan Drake glanced through the three pages of Yale Club stationery and in two minutes made the thing 50 percent better. Fifty percent. Just enough to notice.

"Closing Arguments from The Dirt King" aired after the 7:35 local news break. During the first ninety minutes of the show, College Boy had resumed his former role of in-studio laugher. He even chuckled at a couple of remarks from Jason, the news reader. Jason seemed to possess that custom blend of absolute focus and utter cluelessness to Dan Drake, who kept luring him into what he thought might finally be a serious discussion of the news and what always ended with some question like, "Did they serve pie at the state dinner? Check that out for us."

Dan Drake gave a long, flawless introduction to "Closing Arguments from The Dirt King" that ended abruptly, on purpose, a favorite disarming tactic of his. It took College Boy a few lines to get his impression in stride and a few more to slow down. But there were a couple of real FM morning moments *("I have no affiliation with organized crime. The only ting I ever whacked was the weeds in Sheep Meadow. And myself when I did time upstate. . . . I never put a rake up anybody's ass. That was a creation of the media. And besides, it is physically impossible to put a rake up somebody's ass. Except your sistah . . .")*, and Dan Drake loaned a cup of credibility with three or four high-pitched tee-hees and two "Good Lords!" Twenty minutes later, after an extended fake heated phone exchange with Charles Grodin *("What the hell happened to your career? You can't even do a movie with a good-looking dog.")*, before throwing to the eight o'clock national news break, Dan Drake gave his only acknowledgment to College Boy's presence, a combination compliment and guilt shot as College Boy moved for the door. "Folks, while we break for news, I'm going to find out if we hired a new audio guy. Because a few times this morning, it has actually sounded like we're doing a radio show. This must be a mistake."

College Boy gave a titular look for a cab, then planted his right foot hard, cut, and busted it crosstown. He knew his body well. It would take twenty-four hours for the horrific soreness from yesterday's cardiovaginal romp to check in and trash every muscle, tendon, and insertion. He still had ten hours, eleven with adrenaline. So, he ran. Loose. Free. No sweat. Plenty of wind. Good wheels. Happy wheels.

College Boy walked in on Mort at 8:15, who was trying to pretend he'd been up much longer than five or ten minutes.

There had been a few times in the last three days when Mort was sure the trip to New York had been nothing less than a dump job. Thrice, *thrice!* he had awakened alone in some room (right, the Yale Club), the note from his nephew too far away and scary to ponder. Now, here was the kid, upon him suddenly, ready with some pre-smother-with-the-pillow bromide like, "You slept good, Mort."

"You slept good, Mort."

"Sorry if I disappointed you by waking."

"Huh?"

"What's your story?"

"Uh, I was out getting you a paper."

"Well, where is it?"

"No luck. Why didn't you tell me the *Herald-Trib* folded?"

"Go climb a gum tree . . . and smile on your own time."

Mort's dump job scenario was reignited twice more during the morning. First, when College Boy received a phone call just after ten, stayed on for twenty minutes, never said more than "What can I tell you?" and "Okay, I'll try," and made no mention of it afterward, although he was clearly happy. The second time came two hours later, as they were starting to get ready to leave for Dr. Zing.

"We have plenty of time. Sheila will be here at one and the appointment is at two."

Sheila. The redhead. She was in on it, too. "What appointment?"

"Dr. Zing."

"Who?"

"The doctor we saw Friday."

"I remember somebody with a dish of ballmarkers from Century Country Club on his desk."

"That's the guy."

"He should remind people they aren't mints."

"Yeah, he should."

"What's after the doctor?"

"I don't know."

"Shall I be going home?"

"Hopefully."

"Check that word."

"Ideally."

"How are we getting back to Salem?"

"Can't help you with that right now, Mort. Haven't gotten that far."

You bet the kid hadn't gotten that far. He was still a shovel and a bag of lime short. Maybe that's what the redhead was out buying.

Or whoever it was he'd been talking with on the phone. *What can I tell you? . . . I'll try.* Try what? To bury your seventy-six-year-old uncle with Parkinson's in the woods off the dogleg No. 5 at Century C.C. and use his money to restart the *Herald-Tribune*?

Well, the kid had been pretty damn good to him.

That was the problem and blessing to this particular spate of Mort Spell paranoia toward his nephew. Gratitude kept loosening his grip. So, he went along. He would be pleasant and distant and hope the kid had a change of heart. Maybe that's what all the smiling was about.

Mort didn't smile until he walked into Dr. Zing's office and saw a familiar face. For the last however many years, the only indelible people to Morton Martin Spell were handsome men in their midforties. The faces of his prime.

"Mr. Spell, I hope you remember me. I'm Dr. Blair Cahill."

"I certainly do. You're the last man I got along with before I was shipped overseas."

"How have you felt the last three days, Mr. Spell?" Dr. Zing asked.

Mort continued to talk to Dr. Cahill. "I think a bit better. It's hard to tell. But we forgot the weighted bat and I seem to be managing without it."

"The heavy spoon," College Boy muttered. Dr. Cahill smiled.

Dr. Zing tried again. "Do you feel depressed?"

Mort turned. "What did you shoot the other day?"

"Thirty-nine. My best nine ever."

"It's great to play by yourself, isn't it?"

College Boy and Sheila dropped their heads snorting. Dr. Zing picked up a pad and pretended to write while mouthing "not depressed."

"Mort," coughed Cahill, "how would you characterize where you are now?"

"Well, I don't walk as well as I'd like, I'm still shaking, I'm not able to swallow when I need to, and I need bullpen help when I go to the john. On the other hand, I never thought I'd get back to New

York. Although"—he turned toward College Boy and Sheila—"I'd prefer not to be left here."

"I'm not sure what that means, but you can go back to Boston today. You've been getting some bad advice for a long time, my friend."

"Well, we can't all have your barber. By the way, you're looking awfully well today." Mort Spell hadn't said that in months. He shook hands with Dr. Cahill and hung on while he lowered himself into the nearest chair.

Dr. Zing took College Boy and Sheila out to the waiting room. "I'm taking your uncle off the Depakote entirely. And forget the Halcion. If he has trouble sleeping, and I don't think he will, give him a Benadryl. We won't cut back on the Wellbutrin for a while, maybe a month. You can call me anytime, but I'm not planning on seeing Mort for six weeks. Until then, I'll set you up with a neurologist at Mass General. You'll see him in a month. After the next visit here, Mort will have his own geriatric psychopharmocologist in Boston. I just want to see him one more time, and I need six weeks to come up with a response for that crack about me playing alone."

Now College Boy and Sheila were looking for a place to sit.

"So," said College Boy weakly, "Depakote was the problem?"

"Certain antidepressant, anticonvulsant medications can create Parkinsonian-like symptoms. Like tremors. Your uncle had all of them. Up and down the block. By the time Dr. Levitz had him see the neurologist, there was no other diagnosis."

"So," Sheila blurted, "he doesn't have Parkinson's?"

"Only a neurologist can say that for sure. After all this, he may still have PD, which is why I kept him on the Sinemet. But we'll know more soon, and by the time he sees someone at Mass General, we'll know almost everything. Either way, the Depakote does not help."

"Why the fuck would you give it to him in the first place?"

"I can't answer that. I'm not Meyer Levitz. You can ask him, but I'm sure you know what that's like. I suspect he found out about Mort's behavior at Mount Sinai—you know, the biting—and thought he'd try this combination."

"That prick."

"Mr. Sussman. C. B., isn't it?"

"Yeah."

"Who told you?" said Sheila.

"He did."

"Oh."

"C. B., feel good about this. I do. If Mort is not better in two weeks, markedly better, bring him back down here. But you won't have to."

Laughter came from inside Dr. Zing's office. They went back in, where Dr. Cahill and Mort were examining a three-foot-long plastic shoehorn inscribed: CENTURY C.C.—1989 FALL FROLIC. FIFTH CLOSEST TO PIN.

"Mike, Mort and I want to know why this thing isn't locked in a trophy case somewhere," said Cahill.

"Well, sometimes I have trouble getting my shoes on."

"I think he's had enough of us." Mort put his hand out for Dr. Zing to shake and used the leverage to get himself to his feet. Much better than asking for help. "I'm sure it was a hell of a shot. Thanks for putting up with me."

The two doctors worked like a dance team. Zing grabbed the opportunity to tell Mort all about the shoehorn-winning shot, while Cahill took Sheila and College Boy off to the side.

"Nice to meet you both finally. We'll try for better circumstances next time. There's one more thing. I told your uncle if he wants to get better, he needs someone in the house during the day. A professional. Someone who can cook him meals, bathe him, keep the house clean, and make sure he takes his medication." He stopped and looked at College Boy. "You've done yeoman's work, but you can't be expected to know what a professional caregiver knows. The responsibility cannot rest solely with you. Not when he can afford it. And besides, with two people there, you'll outnumber him."

College Boy smiled like he knew better. "He won't go for it."

"I think he will. I shamed him into it. I said, 'Mort, you retire to a big house and the two of you don't have a full-time housekeeper? I'm shocked. You can forget about me visiting.'"

"What did he say?"

"He asked me if I knew anybody. I guess the key word was 'housekeeper.'" Sheila squeezed College Boy's arm. "I told him I'd give you a list of agencies. I lied about that. Hawthorne Hospital should be able to hook you up."

College Boy had long ago run out of space within him to take all this in. His gravy boat overfloweth. Who knew today's doctor's appointment had been for him? Who knew this whole trip had been for him? Who knew anything? Okay, he knew Sheila squeezing his arm felt good. That he knew. Now College Boy, in the uncharted depths of good fortune, somehow thought better than to flail. Maybe it was Sheila squeezing his arm. So, he bobbed. That felt good, too.

Dr. Zing helped Mort on with his coat in the waiting room. "How are you getting back to Boston?"

"You better ask the doctor."

"He means me," College Boy said. "Ah, ah, we're . . ."

Sheila interrupted. "They're taking my car."

He looked at her and thought about flailing. She winked. "He's promised to bring it back soon. Two weeks tops."

Mort and Sheila waited in the Hyundai or Honda outside the Yale Club while College Boy packed. She promised Mort she would come by Vinnin Estates periodically to check on his new full-time housekeeper. Mort confided he was tired of Chinese food.

She kissed Mort good-bye, but not College Boy. "You have to come back for yours." He brushed the back of his hand against her shoulder and told her he'd call that night from the China Sails parking lot. She didn't have the heart to tell him Mort was tired of Chinese food. Instead, she looked at the wrong wrist and said she had to go.

Sheila was a good two blocks away when the Yale Club bellman came running out carrying a bright orange box.

"Are you C. B. Sussman?"

"Ah, yeah."

"They forgot to give this to you at the front desk."

The bright orange box was from Lobel's, the big time Madison

Avenue butcher shop. Six shrink-wrapped frozen rib-eye steaks and two Freeze-paks to keep them that way. And a note. "Mondays, 5:30 A.M., 102 FM. Would it kill you? Dan."

He tossed the box in the back seat, next to Mort.

"What's in the box?"

"Frozen steaks."

"Frozen? Christ, now we'll have to get a girl to come in."

College Boy pulled out onto Vanderbilt Avenue and stopped short when he misjudged the brake pedal. Too high. He'd have to get used to that.

If it hadn't been for Mort's diligent bladder, they might have made it back to Vinnin Estates in under four hours. As it happened, they did roll in with plenty of time to spare for *Jeopardy*. Unfortunately, it was Celebrity Week and the questions were beneath both of them.

"I'll take Bad Career Moves for a thousand dollars, Alex," said College Boy to no one, co-opting a line he'd heard Letterman do a year ago, during the last Celebrity Week on *Jeopardy*.

"What was that?"

"Nothing."

"Sounded like something."

"I just said, 'I'll take Bad Career Moves for a thousand dollars, Alex.'"

"Damn funny, kid."

Mort viewed Celebrity Week as any learned man would, the second sign of the end of civilization (The first, of course, was the photograph of Adlai Stevenson with the hole in his shoe.). Instead, he had College Boy turn off the television and put a Ray Noble album on his turntable, a $259 Lex and Forty-second bargain in 1974.

Every old record sounds the same. The hissing, the thumping, the popping. All before the melody, which seems to strain as if from under some war surplus blanket. No one under fifty should be expected to crack this scratchy, distant code to fill in the distracting din with the toothsome memory of how it must have sounded the first time. So, College Boy didn't bother. But he knew that Ray Noble did not find its way onto Morton Martin Spell's stereo just because he had nothing to watch on TV. That would have been a job for Goodman, Ellington, Basie. Ray Noble and His Orchestra signified something else. The ten-thousand-word magazine piece that made it in under deadline and was too good to cut, so they pushed John McPhee or Calvin Trillin back to the next issue. Ray Noble meant victory.

Don't kid yourself. She had been in on the dump job. The redhead. Mort was sure. Well, he had been sure, but now that she'd loaned them her car to go back to Vinnin Estates, maybe she wasn't in on it. Maybe there was nothing to be in on. And he had made it back. And since last night, he couldn't wipe the smile off the kid's face with a Zamboni. So even though he was incapable of taking a sure step, even though he was forever being handled by only the occasional person who looked familiar, even though this torturous life of the past nine months had now slowed to where sadness and confusion squeezed into every free seat, even though it was goddamn Celebrity Week on *Jeopardy*, Morton Martin Spell had made it back. It had not been a dump job. So, cue up Ray Noble.

"That's a little loud, kid."

No it wasn't. College Boy turned up the volume even more.

"How's that, Mort?"

"Just fine."

22

I'll stay twenty minutes, she decided. Fifteen minutes. Ten minutes, and then I am so gone.

She didn't know anybody, and there must have been two hundred people crammed into the second floor viewing area at Campbell's. The Frank E. Campbell Funeral Chapel. At least two hundred people. She didn't even know the guy who had called her.

Ten minutes, one lap around the room, and gone. Gone, out of the heels, back into the New Balance and quick-stepping, dead ahead, straight ahead, down Madison Avenue sixteen blocks, four turns with the lights, and into 301 East Sixty-fifth, where she'd change out of the black knit dress at the Goldschmidts and back into her work clothes.

At least two hundred people, at eleven in the morning, and she didn't know a soul. Not a soul. How could that be? How had the guy who called her Wednesday night gotten her number? She'd have to ask him, but how could she? She didn't know what the fuck he looked like, and though Sheila had done many ballsy things in her life, she was not going to start tapping strange, teary-eyed people on the shoulder and asking where she might find Fifth Step Johnny.

And where was College Boy? He should have been here. Was it too much to expect that he might fucking show up? At least he would have known somebody. She knew nobody. Not a fucking soul. Except the guy in the nice box with better makeup.

And then Sheila softened. She sniffled and smiled and understood why College Boy wasn't there. Why he couldn't be there. She hadn't told him.

"Sheila?"

"Yes?"

"Hi, I'm John Duffy."

"Hi."

"Fifth Step Johnny."

"Oh, hi. How did you recognize me?"

"Picture in the apartment."

"Oh."

"And you were the only one standing by yourself. We all know each other."

Sheila knew the photograph. Had to be fourteen years ago. Her on the couch at Uncle Kevin's house in Astoria, laughing under the weight of two mixed-breed puppies, half setter, half IRA. She never let people take her picture, and people asked—a lot—but this one had slipped in under the tent flaps. Can't believe he still had it. Still had it out. Son of a bitch.

"I should apologize," Fifth Step Johnny went on. "I just called everyone in Jerry's book that had his last name to let them know what happened and leave this address. It wasn't until after I left the message on your machine that I realized, 'Oh, that's Sheila.'"

"He mentioned me?"

"By name? Just once."

"Fifth step?"

Fifth Step Johnny laughed. "When else?"

Admitted to God, ourselves, and to another human being the exact nature of our wrongs. Forty-two years old, and a million years removed from the gravitational pull of Al-Anon, Sheila still knew Step Five cold.

"So, what happened? Heart?"

"Yeah." And then Fifth Step Johnny gave Sheila the account that didn't deserve to be heard on an answering machine.

Jerry Manning and his fiancée, Chelle, had been walking uptown after a morning meeting at the Mustard Seed. She had stopped at the deli to pick up another coffee and when she came out, he was slumped on the sidewalk, head propped up by a hydrant. Big kidder, Jerry M. Always loved to pretend he was back on the street, so proud he wasn't anymore. Well, just for today. And just for today for a little over two years now. He was forty-three.

Twenty-seven months clean and sober. Five years slipping and sliding—ninety-two days back, eighty-four days back, thirty-nine days back, four days back—until the hand of God squeezed his shoulder as he tried to walk out of a lunch-time meeting and whispered, "You want a new life or do you want to keep trying to fix the old one?" The hand of God attached for that moment to Fifth Step Johnny. Jerry M. stayed. That had been twenty-seven months ago.

"Wow."

"Come on, I want you to meet some people."

Fifth Step Johnny took Sheila by the hand and introduced her to a couple dozen men and women in the second-floor viewing room. All anxious to tell her stories about her ex-husband. About how his struggle, his insanity, and the honesty that flowed from both, had helped them. All filling loss with humility at another one of their own who had died sober.

"Do you know the elevator story?" a woman asked.

"No."

"Let me tell it!"

"No, let me tell it!"

"I do it great."

"No, I'm telling it," the woman said. "Jerry would tell this story about how just before one of his bottoms, he was in such bad shape, drinking so much, he had no control over his bowels. But his denial was so great, he thought because he lived on the twentieth floor of a doorman building, he didn't have a problem. Everything was fine. So, one morning, after he's been out all night, he staggers onto the elevator, his pants full of shit. Full of shit for God knows how long. He presses 20. Just before the doors close, a good-looking woman, a babe, gets on and presses 15. The whole ride up, the babe keeps staring at him. And as Jerry says, 'My denial was so great, all I could think was, 'She digs me. . . .'"

No one likes to be shushed, but you can understand why the good folks at the Frank E. Campbell Funeral Chapel would try not to encourage raucous laughter. Sheila wiped her eyes for the eighteenth time and was almost composed when she heard a voice nearby say, "Somebody must have told the elevator story. . . ." That set her off again. She hugged the woman who told the story, her left hand clenched tight around various slips of paper with strange phone numbers from the other women she'd met. She hugged Fifth Step Johnny, who was clearly skilled at all things hugging.

"Going?"

"Yeah," said Sheila. It had been almost a half hour. Wow, indeed. "Have to."

"Feel like saying good-bye?"

Sheila looked back at the coffin. "Nah," she said. "Old life." Fifth Step Johnny nodded. "You can point me toward the fiancée, though. Chelle?"

"Yes, Chelle. Over there, with the short blond hair."

Sheila borrowed his pen and ripped one of the slips of paper in half. She walked over to Chelle. How pretty. How could sadness have such radiance?

"Chelle, I'm Sheila Manning. Jerry's ex-wife. I'm so sorry. I have to leave. But here's my number. You call me."

Chelle smiled. "I didn't recognize you without the puppies." *Puppies? Right, the photo.* She looked at the paper and tried not to cry. "Another gift."

Sheila changed into her New Balance, cinched the belt on the chocolate brown suede trenchcoat, and prepared to turn her collar up against the gray April morning of the outside world. She then did something she didn't normally do. She went over what had just happened. Getting phone numbers from strangers. Giving a stranger her phone number. Another woman, yet. Letting other people make her feel better. All in a half hour. No charge. The price was high, though. The price was showing up and asking for help. Could she afford that?

You want a new life or do you want to keep trying to fix the old one?

That's when Sheila Manning realized she already had a new life. She'd had it for a while. And who knew that this, this new life, would be the next thing that worked? Great, she thought. All of a sudden, I'm eligible. What now?

She stopped at the light and looked both ways, to make sure there would be no witnesses. She reached into the box on the corner and grabbed a Learning Annex catalogue and stuffed it into the pocket of the chocolate brown suede trenchcoat.

She was no more than a block and a half down Madison when the sun plopped out like a ceremonial first pitch on Opening Day. Another gift.

23

" . . . coming up in the next hour after the news, Bob Costas will be on the phone letting us know who he'll be cravenly sucking up to this week on *'Later.'* . . . Well, why else would they go on that show? Also, from *Murphy Brown,* Grant Shaud will be here in the studio. Is that right? Here in the studio? Grant Shaud? See, that's who we get. Who does Costas have tonight? Michael Caine? And who do we have? Grant Shaud? That's about right.

"Who is this guy anyway? He plays what? He plays the executive producer on the show? The young guy with the glasses? Oh, I like him. Maybe he'd like to stay and pretend like he's producing a radio show.

"This is actually a pretty good booking. Which means somebody here at the show made a call. More impressive, it means somebody here figured out how to get an outside line.

"Grant Shaud, now he plays Larry? Miles? Right, Miles. Well, he's the only one I like on that show. Should I wait till he's here or should I run down the *Murphy Brown* cast for you? Wait? We're running late? Okay, you got Murphy Brown her own self, Candice Bergen. Lovely woman, the daughter of Jerry Mahoney, but, as I've mentioned many times, walks like a man and confuses younger viewers. You got the guy doing Ted Baxter, you got the young guy, Larry, Miles, who I like, and not just because he's in the green room waiting to come on. You got the housepainter, Earl, it's Earl, right? Like I care. Anyway, we were supposed to have that guy here last week, but he canceled at the last minute because he went down to Atlantic City for a Floyd Patterson fight. And who else? Right, the blond. What's her name. Corky? Seriously? Wait. Am I the first person to notice you have two completely different characters on prime-time television both named 'Corky'? You have, of course, the one with Down Syndrome who can barely speak, let alone act. And you have the kid on *Life Goes On*. . . .

(Ah-HAH!)

"And now it's time for a brand-new feature here on *The Dan Drake Show,* 'The Dirt King Goes Before the Parole Board.'"

"Thang youse for see—"

"Wait. Let me set this up, College Boy. The Dirt King is a guy named Ernest Giovia, this J.V. gangster who controlled all the dirt in Central Park and used to terrorize people there even after he was fired by the Parks Department. A few weeks ago, he was convicted on ten counts of racketeering and sentenced to six years in prison. I think I speak for all New Yorkers when I say, 'Where do we now go for all our racketeering needs?'

"Anyway, we've been beating this thing to death for the last two months, but it's the only impression College Boy can do. Well, we found out that the Dirt King was recently transferred from Rikers Island to Dannemora, so that's where this hilarious bit of radio play comes from. What the kids today call 'Found Comedy.' It's 'The Dirt King Goes Before the Parole Board.' So, strap in."

"Thang youse for—"

"Was that about right, College Boy?"

"Ah, yeah."

"And I'm the parole board?"

"Yeah."

"Well, that's silly, because they're going to know it's me."

"So?"

"So, nobody's going to buy that I'm the head of the parole board."

"You're worried about people buying this?"

"It's a concern."

"Since when?"

"Well, what time is it?"

"Hah! Good one. College Boy just did a watch take. Man, would that have been funny if this show was on television. What? One minute? Hey, maybe after we come back, Grant Shaud can be the parole board."

"Maybe Grant Shaud can get us on television."

"Are you mad?'

"No."

"Don't be mad. We only see each other three days a week."

"Two."

"Would it kill you to stop by three times a week?"

"I, ah—"

"Seriously, would it kill you?"

"Danny . . ."

"Okay, let's go."

"What?"

"You know, 'Thang youse . . .'"

"Thang youse for letting me come before youse."

"Well, you threatened us, Mr. Giovia."

"Fair enutt."

"Now, your appearance before this parole board is very puzzling."

"And why perhaps is dat?"

"Well, you're not eligible for parole."

"And?"

"And you've only been in this prison for three days."

"Two days."

"Would it kill you to be in for three days?"

"*Heh* . . . Hey, what kind of balls—"

"College Boy, just go right to the end."

"What? Oh . . . well, if I can't get out, you gotta let me change my prison nickname."

"You're not The Dirt King?"

"No. Dat's another guy. Long story. You wouldn't want to know."

"That's right. So, what's your prison nickname?"

"Ah, Corky?"

"*Hah!* Okay, that's enough. Here's Larry with the news. I mean Jason."

(*June*)

The woman behind the counter told him if he wanted to, he could fill out an application and the change would be processed in about a month. But there was no guarantee he'd get all his miles transferred to the new account. Sixty-two thousand. That's a good chunk. Doesn't get you a seat on the space shuttle, but it will cop you a couple first class upgrades to anywhere.

And besides, why bother? You want to risk sixty-two thousand Delta Sky Miles on a silly first name change?

"Yeah, I do. I'm changing my billing address. I might as well change the name."

"Fine. But for today, for this flight, you're still Harvey," said the woman behind the counter. "Sorry, C. B."

College Boy had to check his luggage. A first for him on the Delta Shuttle. Bagzilla, an overstuffed WLLS, Wheels-102 shoulder tote, and an FBI-tempting amply taped carton containing a clock radio, lamp, three pairs of shoes, and the six-volume collected works of Thackeray.

The new guy, Warren, had driven him to Logan for the shuttle. Nice job, too. Like all those times growing up when Uncle Mort had come to visit the house in Lynn and it had been College Boy's job to drive him to the airport. A mostly straight shot on Route 1A. They'd get to the Eastern terminal, when it was the Eastern terminal, and Mort would jump out while the car was still rolling to a stop, turn back and say something like, "The way you negotiated that second rotary was crucial, kid." Then Morton Martin Spell would fling a wadded-up five at his nephew and dash through the revolving doors before his nephew had the chance to say "Please, you musn't." Which he never did because what kid 16 to 21 years old couldn't use five bucks and what kid 16 to 21 years old ever used the word "musn't?"

"Thanks, Warren," said College Boy. "Here's my number in New York. Call my mother or me if anything happens or he gives you any trouble."

"Relax, Mr. Sussman. Your uncle is no trouble. He's a pissah."

Warren Franks had been driving Mort around since the third week of May. An earnest man who for fifteen dollars an hour would give you fifty-dollars-an-hour loyalty, he had begun transporting the elderly six years ago after his landscaping business had become a casualty during the little-publicized Massachusetts landscaping recession. When College Boy's Delta Shuttle commute to New York to do *The Dan Drake Show* mushroomed to three times a week, Mort needed someone on call to cart him around. The fact that his father, Jake Spell, had employed a chauffeur named Warren clinched the deal. That and a recommendation from Warren's aunt, Claire Concannan, who was now in her third month as Mort's caregiver. Mort, of course, preferred to continue using the term housekeeper.

The woman in charge of in-home care at Hawthorne Hospital had described Claire Concannan to College Boy thusly: "Mr. Sussman, I'm sending you and your uncle a present." No kidding. Late fifties with a laugh in her early twenties. Heavy-set as if to anchor a featherlight spirit. Boston Irish yet anything but provincial in the kitchen. And most admirable, and inexplicable, the ability to NEVER be in Morton Martin Spell's way. "A man like your uncle, when he wants you, he'll find you," she tried to explain to College Boy. "Otherwise, he's doesn't want to find you. So, don't be they-ah."

"So, where should you be?"

"Right he-ah."

Her nephew, Warren, *that* nephew, had originally come by Vinnin Estates to move a heavy appliance or two while Claire Concannan straightened up the kitchen for the first time in eight months. He ended up driving Mort to the dentist and taking him to Howard Johnson's afterward for an ice cream. Howard Johnson's. *The cotton gin.* Where had College Boy been that day? Must have been a Monday. No, Friday.

Today was Sunday, and instead of his traditional dash to make the eight-thirty P.M. shuttle, he was facing nothing but change-ups. A one-thirty P.M. departure. Luggage. A guy driving him to Logan. A conversation with a customer service rep.

"Okay, let me just make sure of the new address one more time."

"Sure."

"301 East Sixty-fifth Street, New York, New York."

"Right."

"Okay, then."

"And you have the name?"

"E. F. Sussman."

"No! C.—"

"—B. I know C. B. Sussman. I was just teasing. Sorry."

"No, I'm sorry," said College Boy. "It was funny."

Mort had not been on the ride to Logan. It was understandable. Who has the bad taste to move back to New York during the final round of the U.S. Open? Poor planning by both of them. Ten days ago, when he had told his nephew his work here was done, their thoughts were not on the PGA Tour schedule. Not that it would have mattered. Mort would not be along for the send-off. Throughout his professional life, whenever the whiff of acclaim was heading in his direction, Morton Martin Spell ended up conspicuous by his absence. The only exception anyone could remember was the Bertram Hargan Cup, a good prostate ago. Now, at the moment of this most recent honor, winning his old life back while a new one was bestowed upon his nephew, Morton Martin Spell would not attend the award ceremony. He was where he most always was at the time of triumph. And where he wanted to be. Alone. Alone and no trouble to nobody.

Humans are prone to err less in solitude. He'd said many things after this, but that was the final point he had made to College Boy ten days ago. It's unfair to pin everything on ten days ago, especially given what they had witnessed over the last ten weeks. Once Mort was off the Depakote, his mind and body became eligible for parole. After two weeks, the improvement was daily. Sometimes twice daily.

Sure, the addition of Claire Concannan and her stealth care was giant, but she caught Mort at the beginning of his upward graph. "Your uncle's smaht," she'd tell College Boy, "he knows I'm nought fahllin' for him being any sickah than he is."

"Claire, you have no idea how he was."

And after a month, neither did College Boy. The sixteen-hour Sunday/Monday jaunts to Wheels-102 soon became Sunday/Monday, Thursday/Friday. And with that, the Delta Shuttle became a time machine. Leave Thursday night, May, 1992, return Friday noon, Mort 1989. Leave Sunday night, May, 1992, return Monday noon, Mort 1986.

They kept their sixth week appointment with Dr. Zing, who was professionally stunned by his patient. He had received promising updates from College Boy, but to actually witness this man almost jig into his office was something else. "Mort, if you're not busy this summer, we could tour medical conventions and make a fortune."

"Not if you keep telling people you're a twelve-handicap."

Zing cut his Wellbutrin in half, with instructions to taper off it completely in another six weeks if he still felt good. Between this and his Boston-based neurologist's decision to shut off his intake of Sinemet, the occupancy rate of Mort's pillbox had gone from Vegas to Laughlin.

Dr. Blair Cahill did not make the big office reunion, but he and his almost-as-handsome surgeon wife, Lesley, joined Mort and College Boy that night at Rainbow and Stars, where they sat through Michael Feinstein's early show. All of it. By his own admission, Mort hadn't done anything like this in ten years, though his critique muscle showed no signs of atrophy. "Next time," he said to College Boy as they stood with the rest of the audience, "I'd like a little more Gershwin, a little less Feinstein."

They checked out of the Yale Club the next day, Wednesday, and left after an early lunch with Sheila at the Regency Deli, just up

Second Avenue from 301 East Sixty-fifth. The guy behind the counter saw Mort and wordlessly began making a chicken sandwich on white with salt and pepper only. "That's amazing," Sheila said, "I see these guys every morning and I can't get them to *stop* putting sugar in my coffee."

"They're not dumb. They just want to see you come rushing back in," announced Mort. Sheila blushed, and after ducking behind the potato chip rack, so did College Boy.

It took almost fifteen minutes for them to walk Sheila the two blocks back to 301 East Sixty-fifth. Don't be alarmed. For the last year, Mort had been forced to suspend his favorite habit, stopping in the middle of a busy intersection or sidewalk to make a point or take in something said by the people with whom he was walking. He could neither expound nor ponder while in motion. The focus and energy that made Morton Martin Spell such a staggeringly thorough writer could rise up to rivet him at any time, but usually seconds before the light changed.

Mort spent another ten minutes talking with Miguel the doorman (*"They kept telling me you was alive, but I dinnent believe it. I say, 'Mr. Spell, he would have say good-bye to Miguel. . . .'"*), while Sheila and College Boy went up to his apartment to fetch his three-wood for the trip back to Salem.

Sheila and College Boy did not dawdle too much. Not enough time for a blast on Mort's mattress. Besides, he'd be back on the shuttle tomorrow night.

"Would it kill you to fly in three times a week?"

"Your Dan Drake impression is getting better, Sheila."

Of course it was better. Sheila had been putting in eight hours a week listening to the show. By now, she could have been fluent in Italian or halfway through the audio version of any Herman Wouk novel. Instead, she spent Monday and Friday mornings, six to ten, locked in on Wheels-102, ear cocked past the star Dan Drake for the room tone of his steady studio loyalist and occasional confidant, C. B. Sussman.

"Now, when you used to stop by and give us a hand, didn't you used to be College Boy?"

"That's right."

"So, help me out here. You're no longer College Boy?"

"You want to call me College Boy, you can. It's your yard."

"And don't you forget that."

"It's just that I'll be fifty-two next month. It's enough with College Boy."

"You're not going to be fifty-two."

"No . . . but I was hoping to set an example for Mike Love and Al Jardine."

"Good one. Excellent pop analogy. So it's now C. B.?"

"Yes."

"Does it bother you that people will associate you with an obsolete, hackneyed method of radio communication?"

"It's never bothered you."

"Ahhhh! You understand I have to cut your mike for the remainder of the show."

"Ye—"

Like every woman who listened to the show, Sheila had a stone crush on Dan Drake. She'd seen the photos and the shots on Letterman, and in the old days, the referral days, she would have never returned his call. Besides that, you really should have your emotional dukes up over someone who believes there is nothing more entertaining, nothing, than him talking on air for twenty hours a week, even if in fact there isn't. And sure, you had to respect, hell, love anyone who during a phone-in with Pat Buchanan would say, "Now, let me get this straight. You're anti-abortion and pro-death penalty. And I thought I had good timing. . . ." Sheila's crush on Dan Drake was one-note. She was infatuated with his fondness for College Boy.

"Tell the folks why you're here again."

"Because I fill in the awkward silences with genuine sycophantic laughter?"

"And?"

"And . . . I have no desire for a career in broadcasting?"

"And?"

"And . . . I'm the one person in New York who hasn't annoyed you?"

"Correct. From now on, all we'll need is that last one."

College Boy did not have to be great on the radio. Didn't have to be good. He didn't even have to be College Boy. No one was counting on him for the late-inning double down the line or the diving catch. *The Dan Drake Show* needed only one ringer. All that was required of College Boy was his presence. It was the oddest of ways to make three hundred dollars a day, but shit, Dan Drake had paid people twice that *not* to be in the studio.

That's right, three hundred dollars a day.

"Well, that's it. We've been ordered by the FCC to close down for the day. I'll be back tomorrow, along with Larry the news guy."

"Jason."

"Right, and some big-time celebrity guests. C. B., you'll be here, right?"

"No, Dan. I'm only here Monday and Friday."

"Would it kill you to stop by three times a week?"

"Dan, I-ah . . ."

"Save it. We all know about the fine charity work you do. This, of course, is not charity, but there's only enough in the budget for me to have a friend two days a week."

Dan Drake would use that line often and Sheila would well up every time. College Boy had no idea. He described the whole setup as "half-gig, half-goof, half-guilt." She was not about to set him straight, other than to say, "He's lucky to have you." Which sounded very girlfriendy, but that, like having a place to go once, then twice, then three, and now five times a week, was pretty damn good.

For all its improbability, College Boy took the gig/goof/guilt seriously. Even though he and Dan Drake had never discussed it, he always showed up with at least one scripted two-minute "Dirt King"–like piece. The Dirt King got a rest after two months, even though Dan Drake was far from tired of fucking around with a little-known demi-mobster while every other drive-time show was doing "The Gay Brady Bunch" or some even less inspired contrivance. "Give me all of that you got," he said, and from that pat came "The Dirt King at the Prison Canteen," "The Dirt King's Gardening Tips," "The Dirt King Writes a Letter to Joe Pesci," "The Dirt King Receives a Letter from Joe Pesci's Lawyer." At best, the bits were cute, short with a couple of decent jokes. At worst, Dan Drake would pretend like he was calling a messenger service to have the script sent over to the Museum of Broadcasting.

"Now, how long did it take you to write that little comedy skit?"

"Five hours."

"Seriously?"

"Yes."

"Hah! Good Lord. Well, I liked the line about Joe Valachi."

"You wrote that joke before we went on."

"So, the five hours wasn't a complete waste."

That was the other thing Sheila could have loved about Dan Drake. He encouraged, even celebrated, the possibility of failure. So, College Boy began to develop a stable of characters who were but a lame name change removed from their real identities. Julio Rentas, softball ringer/pothead/massage therapist, became Raoul Juntas. Meyer Levitz, shrink/pusher/litigant, became Myron Vantz.

The one character College Boy could never solidify was, of course, the only impression he could do flawlessly. Fielding Herbert, intellectual/man of letters/recluse, never emerged from his legal pad cocoon in any form other than cartoon. And that was unacceptable to College Boy. He thought of having him do editorials, but why? He thought of making him the Wheels-102 station manager and speaking fluent delirium. No, Fielding Herbert was best left alone. *Humans are prone to err less in solitude.* Too bad. It was a waste of a good impression. And a better story.

A month after they returned from New York, Mort, as instructed, saw Roger Stoeckler, a neurologist at Mass General to whom he'd been referred by Michael Zing. Stoeckler saw him walk in with a gait whose only tentativeness arose from deciding which chair to step around when he shook hands. And the hands? No more tremor than rightfully belonged to any seventy-six-year-old man who never married.

"He's been doing much much better, Dr. Stoeckler," said College Boy. "I wish you could have seen him five weeks ago."

"Is that true, Mr. Spell?"

"Yes it is," said Mort. "Amazing what a haircut can do."

"Let's try this. Cut the Sinemet in half for a week, then stop it altogether. I'll see you in a month."

And that was it. They shook hands. If someone had stumbled in at that moment, they would have thought it was the end of a job interview. In a week, there was no more Sinemet. No Sinemet, no Depakote, Wellbutrin in half. Less Pills and his Band of Renown, as Mort now referred to himself. Only his sister Dottie and Claire Concannan got it. Fine.

Dottie Sussman had the best perspective on Mort's recovery. After supervising the move to Vinnin Estates nine and a half months ago, she had made a point of seeing her brother every ten days. No more, no less, and always with plenty of notice. Unknowingly, it turned out to be just enough space with which to compare her last visit. In the last couple of months, it had proved invaluable to College Boy. Each time she'd leave, Dottie Sussman would have her son walk her to her car and palm him the progress he couldn't identify. *"Mort's voice is much stronger, don't you think?" "How long has he been swallowing his medication so easily?" "That check he wrote for the Ouimet Scholarship Fund? That's his old handwriting. He won awards when we were kids." "Tell him his elbow is a little cocked on his backswing—like always. . . ."*

The only change College Boy could track was at night. Mort still had to go—he was seventy-six, not dead—but the trip to the john was now strictly solo. Five days after they returned from New York the first time, "The Aristocrats" had unceremoniously disbanded. Claire Concannan stayed over the first few Sunday nights College Boy shuttled to Dan Drake, and slept undisturbed *("This sofah's so much bettah than my excuse for a bed.")*. When his gig/goof/guilt moved to twice a week, she'd get up at six o'clock, put up coffee, and head back to her house for a few hours. When she returned, Mort would always greet her with the ultimate compliment: "Thanks for abandoning me. That was damn thoughtful."

As promising and humane as things had become, neither College Boy nor Mort were prepared for their second visit with Dr. Stoeckler eleven days ago. He was neither an ironic nor a dramatic man, this

Roger Stoeckler. But you would have never known it by his first two lines.

Line one: "You're looking awfully well, Mort."

Line two: "Mr. Spell, what can I tell you? You don't have Parkinson's Disease."

There was a Line Three, which was both ironic and dramatic *("I'll see you in three months, Mr. Spell, at which time I'll take great pleasure in dismissing you as a patient. . . .")*, but, as is the way of these things, it was lost. Lost in the sight of Morton Martin Spell jumping from his chair, taking two laps around the desk, pumping Dr. Stoeckler's hand, walking out, then poking his head back in.

"Nicely done. Let's go, doctor." College Boy stood frozen until he realized, *oh, right, I'm doctor.*

The next night, Thursday, ten days ago, College Boy was back on the shuttle. Sheila would figure out what this all meant. Why was he still so furious? Sleepless, blind fury. And the most infuriating thing of all, he was the only one still furious. Forget "still," he was the only one who had ever been furious.

"Mort," he said that Thursday morning after zero sleep, before Claire Concannan arrived and during a cup of his distinctively less-than-coffee, "be honest. Aren't you furious?"

"Why?"

"That prick Levitz stole at least a year of your life."

"Kid, I don't have time to be angry. I'm too busy thinking about all the things I want to do."

One afternoon the third week of May, Warren Franks had ferried Mort over to the Willows Country Club to get his three-wood regripped. An hour later, he had a regripped wood and an honorary membership. One of the perks of winning the Bertram Hargan Cup and not dying. The following Thursday, the Thursday after Memorial Day weekend, ten days ago, around five o'clock, Morton Martin Spell hit half a small bucket of balls at the range. His nephew stood far back and swallowed hard. "I would have let you hit some," Mort said afterward, "but I think the club is still restricted."

College Boy dropped him back at Vinnin Estates before he left for Logan.

"Nice going, Mort."

"I think it's time for you to think about going back to New York."

"I'm leaving now."

"I mean going back and staying." He'd just hit the other half of the small bucket.

"But Mort, you'd be alone."

"I'm at my best alone, kid. Like Crusoe. Humans are prone to err less in solitude." Morton Martin Spell, respected journalist and author, underrated uncle, punctuated that last line with archaic flair. He sent a crumpled five-dollar bill through the passenger window of the Buick station wagon. "*Caveat rotary*, doctor."

Sheila would figure out what this all meant. And she did. Again. Funny, for the last two months, that had been their afterplay every time they had sex. College Boy sputtering out his confusion over all the good stuff and Sheila kindly telling him how he felt. Sometimes, he couldn't wait that long to be straightened out. He would cab right from the late shuttle to Serious Fitness, Inc., and help her finish cleaning the gym. He'd yak and she'd nod. Rarely say a word other than, "Well, that blows." Her mere presence was enough.

They would take the tram into Midtown and try to eat responsibly and always fail. Or go back to Sheila's apartment and order way too much from one of the three Greek coffee shops on Roosevelt Island that delivered. One night, College Boy leaned over after dessert and tried to kiss her.

"If you touch me," Sheila said, "I swear to God, I'll vomit."

"Hey, I know I'm not the most attractive guy in the world. . . ."

They'd make love and wind up with one of their heads in the other's lap. And College Boy would finish talking and Sheila would say, "It's fear, baby doll. It's all fear." Once, after Jerry's funeral, they switched roles and Sheila did all the yakking. College Boy stroked that great red hair and whispered, "It's fear, sweetie. It's all fear." He'd learned well. Now, if he could just get it above a whisper.

He'd always leave Sheila's place around midnight so they could both handle the morning. There was one time when they ate in Midtown and she stayed over at 301 East Sixty-fifth Street, but even though Mort's bed now had appropriate linen, it was just too weird. Sheila did what she could to chase the weirdness that night. She kept knocking on the headboard and saying with mock surprise, "I thought you said this was your place." So, they'd split up around midnight and he'd tram back alone. But the next day, always, College Boy would purposely leave his overnight bag behind so he could fetch it on the way to LaGuardia from the studio and spend five minutes in some fellow tenant's doorway kissing the cleaning lady goodbye. He never missed the eleven-thirty Delta shuttle back to Logan. Maybe now it would be different, now that 301 East Sixty-fifth was his address.

The one-thirty shuttle took an easy bounce on the runway, a charity hop, and taxied toward the Marine Air Terminal. Sunday, 2:25 P.M. Late June, and all the softball rosters were frozen for the regular season.

Whither College Boy? He'd come back next spring. Play for two, maybe three teams in the morning leagues at Heckscher, after the radio show. For free. The Improv and Columbus on Monday, Roy's Tuesdays. Wait. The Improv played at 10. So two teams, Columbus and Roy's. That would be enough. That would be pretty damn good.

The other passengers were taking forever to get off, which was just fine. The shuttle was the last thing he knew, the end of the familiar. His sure hands started to shake, and when he started to get frightened, he told himself it was just Mort helping him off. That worked for about two seconds, then College Boy let himself get as fearful as he was.

What now? Right, Baggage Claim. But where the hell was Baggage Claim?

What now?

He walked out of the jetway and went right past her. The chauffeur's outfit might have confused him. Or everything else he wasn't looking for.

"Hey!"

He didn't stop. She thought about yelling "College Boy!" but didn't. Instead, she ran after him and lightly tapped his shoulder.

He turned around and his eyes caught the white sign she was holding:

COME HERE, it read.

And then he looked up. Sheila. Chauffeur's cap now doffed, a torrent of red hair followed. Red. The official hair of great-looking women.

College Boy had no idea what to say, but he had learned. Learned from a master.

"You're looking awfully well today."

She laughed. And she knew how to get to Baggage Claim.

Some guys just live right.

Acknowledgments

I don't know when we'll be doing this again, so I'm going to try and get everyone in.

This book does not see the light of publishing day without Cara Stein, my friend and television agent at William Morris, who last February walked it across the hall to Jennifer Rudolph Walsh, who read it twice over the following weekend (risking expulsion from the literary agents union) and four months later, sold it in about a day and a half.

David Hirshey of HarperCollins, an old acquaintance from the Dubious Achievement Awards, bought the book (as predicted by New Jersey licensed psychic Carol DeWolfe), and subsequently introduced himself to all my friends as "The Bravest Jew in New York" (not predicted by New Jersey licensed psychic Carol DeWolfe).

The job of editing this manuscript was shared by Hirshey and Jeff Kellogg. Hirshey you've met. Let me say this about Jeff Kellogg: Scary good. Made the book infinitely better and left no fingerprints.

Barbara Gaines was the only person who read every word as this book was being written and her infectious joy was equaled only by her impatience to see the next chapter.

Peter Grunwald got me through a couple of tough spots and helped me do "the thinking you don't like to do."

Amy Williams read the first 100 pages in September, 1999, a year and a half after I had stopped writing this thing, and told me to start again.

Steve Wulf made me a columnist at *ESPN Magazine*, 20 years after I had given up such notions.

My five brothers and sisters—Tom, Andrea, Sally, Harriet, and John—who responded with such giggling glee when the book was sold, I had to check to make sure they weren't from another family.

My parents, Gitty and the original Bill Scheft, who, as the ultimate display of their love, never asked me to explain my decision to major in Latin or any of the quixotic careers that followed.

Herbert Warren Wind, who generously showed me the possibilities of the writer's life in Manhattan.

And David Letterman, who has made me a billion times funnier than I ever made him.

And the rest, for you and God knows what over the years: Larry Amoros, Dave Anderson, Tom Aronson, Randy Burns, Mike Barrie and Jim Mulholland, Peter Beilin, Jude Brennan, Bill Brink, Peter Brush, Rob Castillo, Larry David, Laurie Diamond, Maureen Dowd, Clyde Edgerton, J. P. Elder, Barbara Feldon, Garrison, Neil Genzlinger, Buzz Gray, Don Harrell, Howard Josepher, Chris Knutsen, Nathan Lane, Hart Leavitt, Harriet Lyons, Dusty Maddox, Bruce McCall, Tim McCarver, Seamus McCotter, Robert McDonald, Gerard Mulligan, John O'Brien, Steve O'Donnell, John O'Leary, Tom Perrotta, Arthur Pincus, Bob Reinhart, Adam Resnick, Stephen Sherrill, Jeff Stilson, Kevin Talty, Jeff Toobin, Ben Walker, J. J. and Marilyn Wall, Lydia Weaver, Rick Wolff, Richard Yates, Margot Zobel, and Eric Zoyd.

Lastly, the book is dedicated to my wife, Adrianne Tolsch, a singular package of beauty, brilliance, and devotion who will forever be my best quality. And if I'm ever lucky enough to do this again, the boys in production won't have to change the dedication page.

My time is up. You've been great. Enjoy Tower of Power.

Bill Scheft
New York City
November, 2001